A Summer of Second Chances

A *Summer of Second Chances*

Carol Thomas

Where heroes are like chocolate – irresistible!

Copyright © 2022 Carol Thomas

Published 2022 by Choc Lit Limited
Penrose House, Crawley Drive, Camberley, Surrey GU15 2AB, UK
www.choc-lit.com

The right of Carol Thomas to be identified as the Author of this Work
has been asserted by her in accordance with the Copyright, Designs and
Patents Act 1988

A CIP catalogue record for this book is available
from the British Library

ISBN 978-1-78189-489-7

Printed and bound in Great Britain
by Clays Ltd, Elcograf S.p.A.

In loving memory of
my wonderful mum. Xxx

For my brother, Dave, and my sisters
Karen, Pam and Angela. Thank you for always
being there. I love you lots. Xxx

Acknowledgements

During the writing of this book, which I started before my previously released novel, *Maybe Baby*, my life has changed in ways I couldn't have imagined. I wish my mum were here to see its release as she sat with me in various cafes and outside my children's schools awaiting pick-up time while I wrote whole chunks of it. For research, she came with me as I attended a local wildlife charity seminar; she loved chatting to the wildlife officers and the funny stories they shared. She read part of my manuscript, and it made her smile. I know she would have celebrated its release with me. My mum was an inspiration in so many ways; I miss her love and warmth more than words can say.

In the writing of this book, thanks must go to:

Kirsti Lelliott, who always listens to my ideas, reads drafts and offers insightful suggestions. Thank you for not minding when whole villages and characters changed name mid-creation.

Victoria Seaby, for giving advice and offering insight into living with hemophobia.

Dan Jones, who kindly treated my own, not blood related, phobia, and whose time spent chatting to me about hypnotism during several Arundel Festivals inadvertently helped in the writing of this book.

My charity shop pals at Cancer Research UK, Arundel, I love working with you all, and I hope to be back soon.

All who entered a competition on my Facebook and Twitter pages to name a puppy in this book, especially the winner Chrissy Wright. Blossom is perfect.

Author Janice Preston, for helping and pointing me in the right direction when I was getting my titles of the peerage in a twist.

Cecilia Bristow, my lovely Italian niece, who triple checked Gino's words for me. *Grazie mille!*

Wadars animal rescue charity, for their afternoon seminar at Haskins Garden Centre and the offer of further advice via email.

Julie Thomas, who brought the lovely Hubble into my life, for advice on dog mating and gestation.

My writing family – the wonderful ladies of Apricot Plots – and all at Georgian Gardens Community Primary School, especially the lovely year six team and children, who offer constant encouragement.

My husband, Mason, and our children Kirsti, Amelia, Madi and Edward for their love and support. Thank you for not minding half answered questions while my head is full of other shenanigans, although I am sure you've learnt to use me being distracted to your advantage!

And finally, but by no means least, a massive thank you to the team at Choc Lit and Ruby Fiction for all they do and the encouragement and support they offer. In a tough year, it has been appreciated more than you know. Special thanks also to my editor for her great insight and my cover designer for the fabulous cover – I want to move into Dapplebury House! I am also hugely grateful to the wonderful Tasting Panel (Liana Vera, Hilary Brown, Melanie Russell, Lisa Vasil, Amy Nordon, Monica Mac, Jenny Mitchell, Shona Nicolson, Ruth Nägele, Gill Leivers, Glynis Kenney, Fran Stevens, Carol Orpwood, Honor Gilbert, Jo Osborne and Yvonne Greene) whose lovely words about *A Summer of Second Chances* put a big smile on my face. Your kindness is hugely appreciated! xx

Chapter One

Henry stretched out his legs and pushed his hand through his too-long hair. The seemingly static view from the window belied the speed at which the miles were slipping by. Feeling a throb at his temples, he looked in the bag of well-being essentials he had been given for his in-flight comfort. Deciding there was nothing in it that would ease his headache, Henry welcomed the sight of the flight attendant, carrying a glass of whisky towards him. He sat up accepting the much-needed drink, with thanks. The tall, slender woman flashed him too much cleavage, and a smile – her cherry-red lips contrasting against her bright white teeth – as she held on to the glass longer than was necessary.

If only his father's PA hadn't insisted on booking the flight, he could have flown economy, and got a little less attention from the cabin crew, and a further ten and a half hours to be himself before the pretence began.

'The thing is Mary, this might be a charity shop, but not every donation that's brought through that front door is suitable for resale.' Ava looked again into the carrier bag she was holding, still not quite able to take in its contents. With the back of the shop so full, after it seemed the entire population of Dapplebury had donated the bounty of their post-Christmas clear-out, she was beginning to feel overwhelmed.

The wooden pens separating Gift Aid and non-Gift Aid donations were overflowing; the bric-a-brac shelf was bowing in the centre, the box of shoes was spilling onto the floor, and the children's shelves looked like a Marvel meets Disney mash-up. A stack of boxes donated while she had popped out to get milk that morning hid the books and media shelves.

'Flo means well. You know she finds it hard to say no.' Mary poured three mugs of tea. 'Perhaps it's a post-war mentality?'

'Flo's in her sixties. I don't think we can blame her inability to say no to a bag of forty-four, double-D cup bras, on the war. Do you?' Ava held up a handful of the offending items, revealing an array of bright colours and animal print material before dropping them back inside the carrier bag. She thought about her own bra collection – two black, one white and one nude for when discretion was required. 'Who even owns this many bras?'

'Ask Flo, she'll tell you.' Mary laughed and moved to dodge the zebra print bra Ava threw at her. Picking it up, Mary slipped it on, leaving it flapping over her sweatshirt. 'Hey, they're not Gift-Aided are they? You could find out who donated them and return them.'

Ava rummaged through the bag. 'As tempting as that is, I'm not sure it's ethical. I'll just have to remind Flo about our no underwear policy, *again*.' She held up an emerald green bra to her definitely-not-forty-four-double-D-cup chest and slipped it on over her clothes, as Mary had. They both looked in the mirror, tilting their heads as they assessed the inadequacy of their busts to fill the garments draped over them. 'Unless, of course, you want to remind her for me.'

'Sorry boss, discussing underwear with Flo is not in my remit.'

Ava scoffed. 'I never imagined it being in mine either! Honestly, Mary, when I took this place on, I never thought it would be so … so …'

'Glamorous?' Mary struck a pose in the mirror, flicked her bobbed, blonde hair and mock pouted as she pulled the zebra print bra tighter over her chest. It was a look that contrasted with her skinny, muddy jeans and Doc Marten boots.

'Ha, no, definitely not glamorous. I just never thought it would be quite so … consuming, I guess. I don't know. Sometimes I feel these clothes and'—Ava held up an item from the bric-a-brac shelf, unable to identify what it was she put it back—'things, have seen more of life than me.'

2

'But—'

'I'm twenty-eight years old and spend most of my time in the back of this shop, sorting through other people's cast-offs. And I know I sound bloody ungrateful because without those cast-offs I couldn't keep this shop going, but last night I dreamt I was drowning under a sea of clothes unable to call for help. It was terrifying.'

Mary snorted as she attempted to hold in a giggle. She put her arm around Ava's shoulder and gave her a squeeze. 'What are you like?'

'Overwhelmed, in need of a break and it's not like it's just here – at home I still have Mum's things to sort through, too.'

Mary looked directly at Ava's reflection in the mirror and sighed. 'You need to make Critters' Cottage your own. You know your mum would want you to. It's time. And you're right, you do spend too many hours in the back of this shop, and we are going to rectify that situation starting with you coming to The Brown Dog with me tonight—'

'You know I can't. I'm sorting the window display. I need to get this sale underway. Mum was amazing at what she did, but she never paid much attention to the fact that books still need to balance, even when you're running a charity, so—'

'It's Friday night. What kind of friend would I be if I let you spend it stressing over this place and sorting the shop window instead of coming to the pub?'

'But—'

'Besides, I told Gino we'd go. It's his 1950s night. He's even hired in a jukebox. You have to come.'

'Honestly, I can't.' Ava gestured to the donations surrounding them.

'Of course you can. You just said you need a break.'

Ava thought about the bubble bath, good book and bottle of wine type of break she had in mind and went to speak, but Mary continued.

'Come on. You can't let the life these clothes and other

things have seen get you down. Let them get you inspired. You can be the belle of the ball.' Mary held out the skirt of a pre-used prom dress from the rail, before dropping it and grabbing a pair of binoculars still in their tan leather case. 'You can go on adventures. You can own a'—Mary picked up the same item Ava had held from the bric-a-brac shelf—'well I think this is a butter cutter and nobody needs to own one of those.' She tossed the white plastic implement into the bin. 'But you know what I mean. Live your best life, Ava. Your mum would want you to.'

As Mary pulled Ava into a hug, Ava's eyes fell to the stack of framed paintings on the floor. She knew Mary was right, but there were only so many hours in the day.

'So that's why I haven't got my tea, is it? You two are playing dress-ups and up to goodness knows what out here.'

Catching sight of Flo staring at them, hands on her hips and eyebrows raised, Mary and Ava pulled back from their embrace. Whipping off the bras they had forgotten they were wearing, they burst into giggles.

Ignoring their laughter, Flo pointed at the discarded bras. 'They're all new, donated from that posh one that owns the lingerie shop up the hill. She says she's moving away, following her son and his family, clearing out the last of her stock, today.'

'Oh.' The mirth gone from the room, with the mention of another shop closing in the village, Ava stuffed the bras back into the bag, before holding it up to Flo. 'The thing is, you know we can't take them, Flo. Underwear is a no-no, even if it is new.' Ava reeled at the sound of her own curt voice. Shooting the messenger was not her usual style.

'Well, I know that. That's why they're not for the shop. Not yet, anyway.' Flo took the bag. 'They haven't sold in Lady Muck's shop, so they'd be no good to us for resale would they? So, I thought I'd put them to a new purpose.'

The bell rang, announcing that a customer had entered. Flo

took her tea from the side and headed back out to the shop floor.

Ava called after her, 'Sorry Flo, I didn't mean …'

Flo grunted and disappeared back into the shop.

Looking at the door, as it swung shut, Ava wondered what purpose Flo could mean and realised she shouldn't have jumped to conclusions. Flo was a regular volunteer and a good, reliable worker. She was the kind of person Ava needed to hold on to, not fall out with. All Critters Great and Small was a wildlife charity. The rescue and rehabilitation centre, known locally as Critters' Lodge, and the related charity shop that supported it, relied on the kindness of volunteers, as much as it did on bequests and donations to keep it going, and Ava knew it.

Unsure if the ache she could feel in her chest was caused by the mention of another shop closure, or because she'd inadvertently upset Flo, Ava turned to Mary and let out a long breath. 'OK, you're right. I do need a night out. It might even be fun. But I'll need to sort the shop a bit first.'

'I'll stay and help you.'

'No, I'll be fine. I've got an idea for the window in mind and then once the sale is underway I might need your help to sort some of this stock mountain. I can't take up all of your time.'

'You know I don't mind.'

'But I mind – I can't take advantage of you.' Ava was ever grateful for the time her friend spent helping her in the shop, but she knew her role within the charity was demanding enough. Being an animal rescue officer, Mary was frequently called out at random hours of the day and night.

Mary looked at her watch. 'I suppose I could get a few hours in at the centre before heading home to get ready. We're trying to get a few repairs and bits done while we're not so busy, and I'd like to check in on Quill.'

'Quill?' Ava raised an eyebrow.

'Quill Smith, he's enjoying being warm and safe, but I'll feel better when he gains a bit more weight.'

'The hedgehog! You've called him Quill Smith?' Ava giggled.

'Yes. He's got a big personality, so the name fitted. You should come and meet him … when you get a chance.'

'I will.' Ava managed to say the words with conviction despite the fact she knew she wouldn't. She looked at her watch. 'You should go. I'll be fine, and I'll see you later.'

'Are you sure?'

'Of course. I can shut up a bit early, and if you give me until, say, eight o'clock and meet me here, I'll make sure I'm ready.'

Mary drank her tea and picked up her bag. 'You remember Gino said it's a 1950s dress code, right?'

'Of course.' Ava cringed inside. She hadn't paid attention to that fact. Going out was one thing, dressing up and going out required a whole lot more of an effort. *What have I let myself in for?*

Chapter Two

Ava looked around the shop, pleased with what she had achieved. For a moment, while her creativity had been flowing, as she had been selecting colours, outfits and accessories, she had become completely immersed in what she was doing. She realised for the first time in a long time that the tension had gone from her shoulders. Drawing on her creativity to turn something ordinary into something extraordinary relaxed her and gave her a sense of satisfaction, she hadn't felt for too long.

Using coloured umbrellas, painting a different letter on each to spell out the word "sale" had come to her as she lay awake the previous night. Putting the idea into practice had been trickier than she imagined. The shape of the umbrellas proved challenging when it came to keeping the letters straight, but taking in the sight of the result, she felt the effort had been worth it. Now that each umbrella was teamed with colour-matching accessories, hanging from an invisible thread, it gave the effect of a rainbow in the window. She hoped it would look bright and attractive; a contrast to the grey January days they had been experiencing and a way to draw the attention of passers-by. Inside the shop, she had carried the theme on with clothes hanging in blocks of colour on the rails. She'd also put a striking single coloured outfit on each of the two dressmaker style mannequins. She hoped her vibrant revamp might encourage sales.

'Wow! You've done a great job.' Mary blustered in through the door, breaking the silence as she put her own sodden umbrella in the bucket by the door and shrugged off her coat, revealing a navy swing dress with needlepoint, pale pink, polka dots. Her bobbed blonde hair had been curled and sprayed into place in the style of Marilyn Monroe.

Taking in the sight of Mary, Ava realised working on the

displays must have taken longer than she thought. She had said she would be ready by the time Mary arrived but she hadn't even got her 1950s outfit ready.

'Oh sod it. I'm so sorry, Mary. I forgot the time, and I haven't even sorted an outfit yet.' Ava gathered up the rejected accessories, scissors, bits of thread and other items she had strewn across the floor as she worked.

Mary bent to help. 'I expected nothing less. That's why I'm half an hour early. I'm here to get you sorted.' She passed the bits she picked up from the floor into Ava's hands. 'Now you go and get cleaned up, and I'll find you something to wear.'

'Really?' Ava smiled and didn't wait for a reply as she hurried through to the back of the shop trying to ignore everything else calling out for her attention. The display was done; even with that job sorted, one of many she knew she still had to do, Ava felt keener to go out than she had earlier in the day.

With the image of Mary, looking stunning in mind, Ava felt that a quick wash, retouching her make-up and attempting to tame her hair was a bit of a poor effort. Looking at her dishevelled self in the mirror, she wished she had at least spent a bit of time sourcing what she was going to wear. Running a charity shop meant there was a host of clothes from across the decades at her disposal, but it also meant there was no guarantee as to precisely what those clothes might be or look like at any given time. As she began to wonder what on earth she might be heading to the pub in, Mary tapped on the toilet door. Taking in the sight of the outfit in Mary's hands, Ava smiled.

'Blimey, you're good!'

'I know!' Mary giggled. 'Now get those on and let's get you out of here.'

Less than thirty minutes later, Ava was dressed, had scraped her hair into a high ponytail and curled her fringe under using her brush and the hand drier in the toilet. Despite being restricted by their outfits, she and Mary did their best to run across the cobbled street and round the corner to The Brown Dog, avoiding puddles as they went. Before entering, Ava turned to Mary. 'You look amazing by the way, and I love the shoes.'

Mary lifted her foot, smiling at her polka dot patterned, four-and-a-half-inch high-heeled sandals. 'The shoe industry's gain today – is your shop's gain, tomorrow. They're already killing me!' Mary winked.

Ava laughed as she swung open the door to the pub.

Considering it was a small local pub that relied on the tourist trade in the summer and the revenue from the locals in the winter it was unusually busy. In contrast to the damp evening outside, the low, beamed ceiling, moderate lighting and large stone fireplace gave it a warm, welcoming feel. The ale-and-smoke-from-the-open-fire smell, which usually permeated the air was masked by the heady mix of perfume, aftershave and hair products worn by the 1950s clad clientele. Except for the hardy regulars at the bar, the men had colourful shirts and Brylcreemed hair, while most of the women wore flared skirts teamed with tight blouses, scarves and ankle socks.

Ava and Mary made their way across the flagstone floor to the bar. Ava spotted Gino at the other end in conversation and laughing with the woman he was serving. He was in his element behind the busy bar, utilising his good looks and Italian charm on all comers. Looking at him from behind Ava could tell that his black denim jeans, turned up as a homage to the 1950s, and capped-sleeve-torso-hugging T-shirt, revealed every flex of his toned muscles as he moved. Pushing away the thought that perhaps Mary was right when she had repeatedly told her that a night with Gino might be just what she needed, Ava reminded herself that taking things further with him would be a mistake. He wasn't the type that she usually went for, and they had already moved into the friend zone. Negotiating their relationship out of it for a night of naked abandonment made no sense. *Did it*?

Mary nudged Ava out of her Gino evoked daydream as Pauline, the barmaid, approached.

'Seen something you fancy, ladies?' Pauline, known locally as The Oracle, smiled and lifted an eyebrow.

Ava hoped the flush she could feel spreading across her cheeks wasn't as obvious as it felt. Pauline would undoubtedly read too much into it and share her thoughts and erroneous opinions around the village. 'Umm, I—'

Mary giggled. 'I'll get the drinks in. Why don't you nab us that table?' Mary gestured towards a table between the bar and fireplace. It offered a good view of the room without being so near the jukebox they wouldn't be able to hear each other.

Ava settled herself at the table. The heavy curtain that normally separated the extra dining spaces from the bar had been tied back. The mismatched tables and chairs had been moved, and a makeshift dance floor created in their space. Gino had clearly gone to a lot of trouble to make the evening a success.

Ava watched those brave enough to take to the dance floor; some looked like they'd been jiving for years. Their movements were fast and fluid, every step in unison with their partners. It came as no surprise to her that she didn't recognise most of the faces. For the inhabitants of Dapplebury to be this good at jiving there would have to be a secret dance society meeting up regularly for covert practice, but Dapplebury didn't have secrets. It was the type of place where everybody knew everybody else and their business.

Chapter Three

Henry sat at the end of the bar, lifted his baseball cap and rubbed his hand across his forehead, trying to clear the fog from his mind. He wasn't sure if it was jet lag setting in, or the fact that he was back in Dapplebury, that was causing his head to throb. Finding himself in the middle of what seemed like a fancy dress party for people old enough to know better, wasn't helping; especially when all he wanted was a moment to be himself and a cold beer before facing his parents. He remembered The Brown Dog to be a quiet place. There was nothing quiet about it this evening. The music, the clientele and their clothes were all too loud.

Glancing around, Henry could see few people he recognised. Five years was a long time, but he thought it unlikely that so many new faces had moved into the village. He knew it wasn't the type of place that welcomed newcomers with open arms, *any more than it embraces change*. It was more likely that the event had drawn in people from out of the area. While Henry didn't appreciate the homage to the 1950s he could appreciate the initiative; the need to attract new life into the village and to make the most of the revenue that brought was apparent even before he went away.

As for those few who weren't strangers, those he knew from his past, Henry was grateful his years away, his baseball cap, collar-length hair and beard were offering him anonymity. He didn't want people to recognise him until he found his feet again. He needed time to readjust before he faced the backlash he anticipated from the community, especially his father's old stalwarts.

Henry drained his glass and began to gather himself to go, but as he turned from his barstool, his feet faltered. He couldn't be sure. It had been twelve years since he had seen her, but the red hair and the striking blue eyes sent him back to being a teenager again. She was just eight months older than him, but at sixteen Ava Flynn was a force of nature, with a mass of wild hair, unlike anyone else he knew. He remembered her scrambling through the trees in the grounds of Dapplebury House challenging him to climb higher, to skinny-dip in the lake and, on the last day they spent together, to kiss her. A heated first kiss for them both, fired by teenage hormones. He could remember how dizzy it made him feel. He could also remember the sting of the slap he got across his face when his mother caught them.

Chapter Four

Mary returned from the bar. Ava looked at the highball glasses in her hands, the opaque deep-berry liquid contrasting with the ice, the lime wedge on the rim of each glass, and the umbrella and straw adding an extra flourish.

'I'm guessing they're not cokes.'

'Bay Breezes. Gino came over, said to say hello. Apparently they're a must on a 50s night. Besides, he said these two were on the house, so I could hardly argue with that.'

Ava looked round to the bar to thank Gino. He blew her a kiss that reignited her blush, and she hastily returned her focus to the drinks. Picking hers up, she smelt it. 'Wow, that's fruity! What's in it?'

'Cranberry juice, pineapple juice, oh yeah and a whole lot of vodka.'

'Vodka? I'll be flat on my back.'

'The way you were looking at Gino, I thought that might be what you wanted.'

Ava gasped in mock indignation and swiped her hand in Mary's direction, 'Bog off, you! I was just admiring his look, very—'

'Sexy?'

'Greased Lightnin' I was going to say. So don't start.'

Mary laughed and sipped her drink. 'OK, so I'm not allowed to get you so drunk that you spend the night with Gino. How about just enough to get you dancing?'

Ava lifted her hand. 'No! No way am I dancing. I agreed to a night out, to support Gino and to keep you quiet. It's meant to be fun and making a fool of myself in front of this lot is not my idea of fun.'

'I bet you'd have a blast if you gave it a try. Look. How hard can it be?'

Ava glanced over at the energetic jivers still filling the dance floor. 'In this outfit? Very!' Besides from the fact all of the dancers seemed to know exactly what they were doing, Ava didn't fancy attempting to jive in the black figure-hugging pencil skirt, slightly-too-fitted blouse teamed with a wide belt and kitten heels that Mary had picked out for her. Content with watching from afar, Ava lifted her Bay Breeze. Wondering if it would taste as good as it smelt, she removed the umbrella before taking her first sip. The tang of the fruit hit the back of her mouth, while the alcohol warmed her throat. 'Wow. That slips down easily.' She grinned, removing the straw to take a proper swig.

When the bell rang for last orders, Ava slumped back on her chair, attempting to regain her equilibrium. Several Bay Breeze cocktails and a bit of persuasion from the Jive to Thrive dancers, as she learnt they were called, had eventually seen her slipping off her shoes, hitching up her skirt and, along with Mary, giving it her all on the dance floor. Her cheeks were flushed, and ringlets of her hair were escaping her ponytail. As they had stepped out of the charity shop, mere hours before, Ava had felt demure. While Mary's outfit gave a shout-out to Marilyn Monroe, she had felt her own gave a subtle nod to Audrey Hepburn. Now a sweaty mess at the side of the dance floor, she felt far removed from the iconic film star and in much need of a glass, maybe even a jug, of water. *Oh, Audrey, I've truly let you down!*

Ava dabbed her forehead and called out to Mary – who was still giving her all on the dance floor, 'I'm going to grab some water, do you want anything?'

Mary shook her head and winked as she twirled into the arms of her very proficient dance partner.

Slipping her shoes on, Ava attempted to tidy her hair and made her way to the bar; avoiding Pauline she decided to seek Gino out, instead. As he passed her a glass of ice-cold water, Ava gulped it down.

'Blimey, I needed that.'

'You never told me you were such a good dancer.'

'I'm not sure you can call what I was doing dancing, but I've had a lot of fun. Thank you.'

'Well, you've certainly got some moves. You've drawn a fair bit of interest tonight.' Gino nodded, directing Ava's attention along the bar.

She followed his gaze, but the stools he gestured towards were empty. Ava shrugged. 'Glad to have provided some entertainment.' She smiled at Gino and drank down the rest of her water before placing the glass back on the bar. 'It's been a great night.'

'You're not going, are you? I'll be closing up soon. Thought we could catch up.'

For the briefest of moments, Ava thought how nice it would be to catch up with Gino. He had proved a good listener after her mum's death, a trait he insisted came from being a bartender since leaving school. And then she remembered the shop, the need to get the sale underway and the bags and boxes she still needed to sort through. She would have to be up early in the morning. 'I'm sorry, I've got heaps to do tomorrow.'

'Dashing off before the clock strikes midnight?'

'Something like that.' Ava smiled. 'But really, thanks for tonight. You must be so pleased it's gone well.' Ava knew The Brown Dog, like every business in the village, was under pressure to draw in more revenue. With the health of the current Lord Bramlington in question and so many residential lettings owned by the estate, everybody feared looming changes to the status quo of the village.

'Hmm, I'll let you know when I've crunched the numbers, but on the face of it, it's been a good night.'

'I'd say so. I think you're going to have to chase this lot off the dance floor.' Ava turned to see Mary being lifted, her legs being flung first to the left and then the right of her dance partner. She had being single down to an art form. Ava knew Mary wouldn't be wondering if she should take things further, or what the consequences might be if she did. She prided herself on being an independent spirit who lived in the moment.

'Are you going to lend a hand, or do I have to do everything around here?' Pauline interrupted the conversation and Ava's thoughts.

Gino pulled a face. 'You'd never guess I'm the one in charge, would you? Landlord duties call. I'd best get to it.'

'Of course.'

As Ava turned to leave, Gino called after her, 'But we'll catch up soon, right? Maybe breakfast.'

'Breakfast … sure.' Ava's cheeks flushed as her thoughts ran amuck with the implications of having breakfast with Gino.

'It's easier to escape earlier in the day.'

'Of course.' Ava turned a darker shade of red. *Ava Flynn, a few drinks and your mind is in the gutter*!

Chapter Five

With his body feeling the effects of a ten and a half hour flight and a restless night in a bed that no longer felt like his own, Henry zipped up his fleece and pulled on his hood. He had forgotten how the damn cold had a knack of seeping into your clothes in England. The temperature, while similar to that he had left behind, felt much colder. England in January was a grey, damp place – a stark contrast to the blue skies and beaches of Los Angeles. He stretched; his muscles felt heavy and uncooperative. Despite the cold, he needed the exercise and knew he would soon warm up once he started running. After a whole night of being inside the confines of Dapplebury House, he was ready to escape. He looked out along the gravel driveway flanked by a trimmed edge of lawn, the wispier more unkempt grass of the parklands beyond, and the woods he had explored as a child, all stretched out before him.

Returning home after dark the night before meant he had been met by a view of Dapplebury House lit up against the backdrop of the night sky. It was, without doubt, an impressive sight, albeit that it caused a tightening in his chest and increased the throbbing at his temples. The irony was never lost on him that he'd been brought up in a grand stately home that never truly felt like home to him. Outside at least, he felt less like he was being suffocated and the view, in daylight, was stunning. How had he forgotten that? How had he not realised how much he missed it until he was back?

Crouching to pull the laces of his trainers tighter, Henry was surprised to see Granger, one of his parents' retired gun dogs, lumber out from around the side of the house. Henry had been touched by the genuine warmth of the greeting Granger had given him the previous evening. He found the dog's enthusiasm about his return more honest than that of his mother. Pushing away an image of his father looking frailer than he had imagined, Henry beckoned the chocolate Labrador, who wagged his tail and walked towards him. Henry had known Granger since he was a puppy. Having bred the pedigree gun dogs for generations, chocolate Labradors were synonymous with his family. The irony that both he and Granger were the product of years of selective breeding wasn't lost on Henry. He put his arms around the dog, welcoming the contact and his warmth.

'You and me, Granger, are more similar than you know.' Henry sighed and stood up. 'What do you say, want to join me?'

Granger stood still and huffed a silent bark that rose into the early morning air as a puff of smoke.

The exercise, the low mist that shrouded the land, the cold air on his face, and the freedom of being outside, was exhilarating. Henry knew the grounds well as if he had an internal map for them. As a child, when he wanted to disappear, he could do so for hours, much to his mother's frustration. He knew all the best places to hide and only ever got caught that once, the last time with Ava.

The earth felt boggy beneath his feet; nettles covered the path and brambles threatened to entangle him. Five years was a long time. The plants had grown in his absence, reclaiming whole stretches of land. When he was a boy, Henry would have hacked them back with a scythe he snuck from the gardener's shed; now he attempted to step over, move or dodge them, while Granger seemed to have no trouble in finding his own path.

Henry pressed on, turning at the old oak tree that still bore the scars of having once been struck by lightning. It was his favourite path to take to the lake. He once encountered the largest of the stags from the deer herd on that very path. The stag had stared at him, his round eyes fixed on him intently, his nostrils moving rhythmically, as he assessed the man before him. In that moment Henry felt keenly that he and the stag had a mutual respect, both treading the paths of their ancestors and trying to live up to their positions in life; both happy to be left alone. Henry knew once he was through the woods, he would be back onto grassland with the lake and the village beyond, in view.

Nearing the edge of the woods, Granger darted forwards. Wondering what had caught the dog's attention, Henry went to follow, stopping in his tracks when he saw a woman walking a dog in the distance. The winter sun offered little warmth, but its low position in the sky meant it was glaring in his face. She was some distance off, but the red hair, tied up as it had been at the pub the night before, and the fact she was trespassing, as she always had, convinced him it was … 'Ava.' The word came out as a whisper.

Not wanting her to see him, hot from his run, caught off guard and after a night in which she had filled most of his thoughts, he slipped back under cover of the trees. The shade shielded him from the glare and made it easier for him to see as Granger ran up to her, wagging his tail. She crouched to greet him before standing. Granger sat as she gave him something, he seemed to expect, from her pocket. Her dog, a smallish spaniel, welcomed Granger happily. The two dogs sniffed each other, wagging their tails wildly, play-bowing and enticing one another to give chase as they ran in circles while Ava laughed. Henry watched feeling like the trespasser, as the three walked on towards the lake.

Having been away, Henry had no idea how long Ava had been coming back to the grounds of Dapplebury House. He remembered the last time he had seen her there, the heat, the briefest touch of her smooth skin as they swam in the lake, and their kiss. He remembered too his mother's anger, the sting of her slap and his regret that he never saw Ava again. At the end of that summer, he was sent to boarding school. After that, holidays, and walks in the grounds felt empty without her, and his resentment at his parents' control over his life grew.

While Ava, Granger and the spaniel were walking parallel to the trees, Henry followed, being sure to stay out of sight. He knew the lake would cause them to come nearer, and the dogs might give his whereabouts away but, at that moment, he was willing to take the risk to get a closer glimpse of Ava. When he'd seen her in the pub, on the previous night, she had looked different from how he remembered her. Of course, she had grown up, so had he, but there was more. As a young girl, she had freckles on her skin and colour in her cheeks from the hours they spent outside. When he had seen her at the pub, she looked pale. Her hair was in a ponytail, which he felt suited her less than the unkempt curls he remembered and her clothes, he was pretty sure, weren't her own. While he appreciated the fact her black skirt and shirt showed all too clearly that the boyish figure she once had, had changed to feminine curves, they didn't reflect the Ava he felt he knew.

Hearing Granger bark, Henry jumped from his thoughts and paused, his heart thudding.

Ava stood still, not far from the line of trees, appearing to listen.

Henry knew he should show himself. So what if he was hot and sweaty? So what if he was in an old tracksuit? As the words, *she's right there,* echoed through his mind, his legs felt uncooperative. *You'll look an idiot if Ava Flynn finds you skulking here*. Henry attempted to steady his breathing.

Granger barked again, this time facing Henry's direction. Aware his cover was blown, Henry went to move, but as he did so, Ava started to jog away, calling back as she went, 'Thanks for the heads-up, Granger. You're a star. Come on Myrtle, before the wicked witch finds us.'

Henry stared after them, amused at the reference to what he could only presume was his mother, and cursed. For twelve years he had waited to see Ava Flynn again. Now he had seen her twice in twenty-four hours and yet he'd hidden from view like a fool on each occasion. The last time he had seen her run away from the grounds at Dapplebury House, he had regretted not following, so why did he just let it happen again? 'You're a bloody idiot!'

Granger, having walked back into the woods, stood in front of Henry and whined.

'Not you. I think you might be the only sensible one in this place.'

As they turned to head back to the house, Henry thought about his conversation with the landlord of The Brown Dog the night before. After seeing the way he had been looking in Ava's direction, Henry had spoken to him, to sound him out, and discover if he and Ava were an item. Learning they weren't, was small comfort when picturing the blush on Ava's cheeks as she had stood at the bar talking to the man, as he had gone to leave the pub.

Henry picked up his pace. 'Come on, Granger.' He thought about the things the landlord had said. Amongst the who's who in the bar that night, he'd mentioned that Ava Flynn ran the local charity shop. Henry had no idea why. She was a talented artist and full of ambition when he had known her. She wanted more from life than the limits Dapplebury could offer, and yet there she still was, not looking like herself and running a charity shop of all things. Giving herself to good causes was her mum's mission, not Ava's.

Henry glanced down at Granger as the pair ran side by side. 'Dapplebury House is a big place. We must have something to donate to a charity shop, don't you think?'

Chapter Six

'A full English and the company of my two favourite ladies, what a way to start the day!' Gino smiled, picking up his knife and fork from the blue-gingham tablecloth.

'Flatterer!' Mary reached for the maple syrup and poured it over her icing sugar topped waffles.

Ava thanked the waitress who was still placing mugs of coffee down in front of them and buttered her toast before turning her attention to Gino. 'What a treat, thank you.'

When she'd got his text about meeting up for breakfast, Ava knew she ought to say no. The sale had been underway for just over a week in the shop, and she was beginning to make some headway into the piles of bags and boxes for sorting out the back, but there was still plenty left to do. Having a sign on the door saying they wouldn't be accepting donations until further notice, she knew she had to crack on. The last thing she wanted was people taking their donations and their loyalty elsewhere.

'Toast is not much of a treat is it. You could have ordered a proper breakfast.' Gino gestured to the mound of food on his plate.

'Honestly, it's good. I had cereal at half six this morning.'

Mary paused, her cutlery hovering over her waffles. 'Half six? Why were you up at half six? Flo's opening up the shop for you, you could have had a lie-in!'

'It wasn't my fault this time. Myrtle needed to go out.'

Mary sliced the corner off a waffle. 'And that's why you should never have pets.' She popped it in her mouth decisively.

Gino shook his head. 'But that makes no sense. You work with animals all day. You go out at all hours to rescue them, and when you get time off, you spend it checking on them.'

'But that's different. They're wild animals trying to fend for themselves and live freely in a world where the odds are increasingly stacked against them. They don't seek human company, and I do my best to ensure they can keep their independence and return to their natural habitat.'

Mary's words and passion made Ava think of her mum. Not wanting to get emotional, she changed the subject.

'Myrtle's just used to our routine. So am I, to be honest. I love to have breakfast early, shower and be out in time to watch the sun come up. The orange glow of first light spreading across the land and—'

'Oh, God, she's off.' Mary put her knife and fork down.

'Oi!' Ava hit her playfully on the arm.

'I'm teasing. You know I love the way you see the world in pictures to be painted, and for the record, I love Myrtle – she's the coolest pet I know.'

'Well, she loves you too.' Ava smiled. 'And, honestly, the sunrise over the grounds of Dapplebury House is beautiful. You should come and see it sometime.'

Mary picked up her cutlery, returning her attention to her breakfast as she spoke. 'Getting out of bed to see the sunrise on a day when I'm not on call sounds like torture. But Gino might be a taker. Fancy seeing the sun come up with Ava, Gino?'

Ava kicked Mary under the table and hoped Gino wouldn't notice the flush she could feel spreading across her cheeks as she said, 'The sunrise is stunning. Worth a look if you're ever up at that time.'

Gino glanced up from his plate. 'Sure, though I'm more of a late-night than an early morning type, me.'

'Sunset then?' Mary raised an eyebrow at Ava who decided to change the subject.

'Talking of late nights, now you've had plenty of time to reflect on it, how did the 50s night go? It seemed a real hit from where I was sitting. I know Mary did quite well out of it. Didn't you say you learnt some new moves from your dance partner?' Ava giggled.

Mary poked her tongue out. 'Well if you must know the night culminated in a very satisfying threesome.'

Gino choked on a piece of bacon and reached for his coffee.

Mary patted him on the back and giggled. 'Just me and my good pals Ben and Jerry,' she clarified.

Ava laughed. 'How about you, Gino? Was it a success for The Brown Dog?'

Gino put his knife and fork down and took a quick swig of his coffee. 'It was good. Not quite the money-spinner I'd hoped for, but good.'

'Really? But you'd drawn in a crowd. We couldn't believe how busy it was when we got there.'

'Yeah, but busy dancing and busy drinking are two different things. What I need is to come up with a plan that gets bums in seats, and people eating and drinking. That would be a winning combination in terms of money in the till.'

'And we all need more of that,' Ava put in.

'OK, so … like what? Come on, start by running your ideas by us. Together, we might be able to come up with something. Ava's creative.' Mary shifted in her seat, keen to hear Gino's ideas.

'I'm not sure my largely unused degree in Fine Art is going to help.' Ava bit into her toast.

'You know what I mean.' Mary tutted, turning her attention back to Gino.

'Well, the theme seemed to go down well. I just didn't pick the right concept.'

'So a theme you can connect with a meal? Eighties night, cheese and pineapple or prawn cocktails to start?' Ava offered.

'No not decades. I think no matter which I pick, the evening will be about the music rather than the food and drink if we go down that route.' Gino pushed his plate back and folded his arms on the table.

'So a theme, where the music is secondary to the food and drink?' Mary wiped the last piece of waffle around her plate, mopping up the remaining maple syrup, before putting it in her mouth.

'Yeah. So ...' Gino looked at her expectantly as she finished chewing and swallowed.

'So ... I don't know. Sorry.' Mary slunk back in her chair and patted her stomach. 'I'm too stuffed to think.'

Gino screwed up his napkin and threw it at her. 'Well, that's a great help!'

'Maybe there's a way of us working together?' Ava was thinking on her feet as ideas popped into her head.

'You want to work in the bar? We can't take anyone else on at the—'

'No, not like that. With a theme.'

'What do you mean?'

Both Mary and Gino looked at Ava expectantly.

'Well if you picked a theme where people needed a costume, and I had a rail of clothes suitable for that theme, in the shop, then bingo! Everyone's a winner. I'd advertise your night and you'd advertise where people could get their outfit.'

'That's bloody genius.' Mary grinned.

'Yeah but what would work? If we pick a colour, the food could be hard to sort, and I'm not sure people would be bothered to be honest.' Gino motioned for the waitress to bring them more coffees.

'No, it's got to be smarter than that.' Ava leaned back in her seat. 'The 50s night was busy because it appealed to people out of the village. Most of those there weren't from Dapplebury. We need something that will get folks around here interested in going to their local. So from the events, you can build a steady trade, remind them their pub is still there and able to offer them a decent night out. The village is dying, and people are letting it happen. We need to build some oomph.'

'Oomph?' Gino questioned.

'Yes, oomph, back into this village.'

Mary smiled. 'Wow, Ava, I haven't seen you this fired up in a long time.'

'Wait, I've got it!'

Mary and Ava turned to Gino, who looked fit to burst.

'Countries!' He beamed.

'Countries?' Ava pondered the concept.

'Yeah, food and drink from different countries. The music would be secondary, and people could dress up if they wanted – with clothes from your shop.'

'It's a great idea. Cuisines from around the world. I like it. But, I'm not sure many people will be bothered to dress up,' Ava said, attempting to hide her disappointment.

'I could offer an incentive if they did.'

'I wouldn't want you to lose money.'

'I wouldn't if I accounted for it in my mark up. Say I offered a free dessert with their meal, for those who dressed up. They wouldn't be getting the freebie if they hadn't already had a meal. It could be a win, win.'

'What if their outfit wasn't from Ava's charity shop? They could have already had it at home, or got it from somewhere other than All Critters Great and Small?'

'Hmm, OK. So Ava gives them a voucher for a free dessert when they buy from her. What do you think?' Gino looked at Ava. 'We could start off with Italian. You know how long I've wanted Chef to add some Italian cuisine to the menu. Now he'll have to.'

Ava was still pondering the idea. She wasn't sure how well it would work when surely it would be cheaper for the people just to go and pay for their dessert than buy an outfit, but she could see how enthusiastic Gino was about it and she wanted to be supportive. And who knew, anything that might bring more money into the charity shop was worth a try.

Established in the late 1980s – off the back of her mum's passion for being there for all animals that didn't have owners to look after them in their time of crisis – the wildlife rescue centre needed as much cash coming in as Ava could generate. Surviving on the revenue from the shop, bequests, donations and the goodwill of volunteers got them so far, but more money was always needed. Ava knew her mum's mantra well. The aim was "rescue, recovery, rehabilitation and release" and that came at a price. While she was unable to go to Critters' Lodge, and take a front-line role in the rescue centre, managing the charity, and the more recently established shop that supported it, enabled her to feel she was actively helping to keep her mother's legacy alive; albeit that it required maximum dedication for a minimal wage.

'It sounds like a plan to me.' Ava smiled and lifted her coffee cup from the table. 'A toast, to "Cuisines from around the World" and may the good people of this village support our venture.'

Mary raised her mug to each of them in turn. 'May your gourmets be great and your outfits plentiful.'

Gino banged his mug back down on the table and looked at them both, eyes wide. 'I've got it! We'll call it'—he lifted his hands as if seeing the words in neon lights—'Around the World ... in Eighty Gourmets.'

Mary and Ava looked at each other and burst into a fit of giggles.

Gino looked at them, stunned by their less than enthusiastic response.

Mary managed to control her laughter long enough to speak. 'Gino, how ... how the hell are you going to come up with eighty gourmets?'

Chapter Seven

Realising there hadn't been a charity shop in the village before he went to America, Henry had no idea where it might be, or if there was more than one; he cursed himself for not doing more research. He could hardly walk in, proffering a donation, ask if Ava worked there and leave, box in hand if she didn't.

He'd spent the past week trawling Dapplebury House for an appropriate item but finding anything that wasn't classed as a family heirloom had proven problematic in a home that had passed through generations for more than two centuries. Eventually, opting for the easier criteria of something his mother wouldn't miss expedited the task. He didn't want to delay reconnecting with Ava any longer. *Carpe diem!*

The wise words of his Latin professor, lost on Henry as a child, had grown in pertinence since seeing how rapidly his father's health and faculties had become cruelly compromised as a result of his brain tumour. His father's illness had seen him send for him and pass on the estate long before either of them had ever imagined; for Henry it was a wake-up call.

Having walked into the village, Henry found himself wandering along the cobbled street, carrying the box awkwardly, as he searched for the shop. It had been a long time since he had walked through the centre of the village. There were more coffee shops than he remembered, a couple of bookshops, an art gallery and too many antique shops – seemingly closed by virtue of it being, what ... *a Monday? Before noon?* He didn't know what the answer was but sighed. *No wonder the village is on its arse.* Seeing two empty shops, Henry groaned. The state of the village, and the fact he still hadn't found Ava's charity shop was doing nothing to improve his mood. Deciding to give up, he strode across the road.

Pushing his hair out of his face, Henry glanced at the final run of shops and spotted a sign that said "All Critters Great and Small". He recognised the shop name as the same as that of Ava's mum's charity, as he said it aloud. He hadn't seen it as he'd walked up the street, due to the fact the road forked around a central arc of buildings, housing a further two coffee shops, the butchers and a sweet shop, before stretching into the main high street. At least knowing the shop's name provided some explanation as to why Ava worked there. Her mum was known as a woman with a mission, but Henry also knew it was a mission that generally left her daughter to roam the village and the land of Dapplebury House while she gave her time elsewhere.

He cleared his throat and picked up his pace. Glancing at himself in the shop windows as he went, Henry wondered if he should have got his hair cut. He had been home just over a week, but still hadn't done anything about his collar-length hair, much to his mother's frustration. Trimming his beard, taking a shower and putting on clean jeans and a T-shirt, now hidden under his coat and scarf, suddenly didn't seem enough with the prospect of seeing Ava, just moments away. As he reached the door, he paused. Having spotted a sign saying "No donations until further notice" he muttered a curse. Now so close, he wanted to see it through. *What kind of charity shop doesn't want donations?* Shifting his grip on the box, he decided to go in anyway.

A bell rang as the door, lighter than it appeared, clattered into the shelves of bric-a-brac behind it.

'Oh, bugger. I mean, sorry.' Henry shut the door apologetically and flicked his hair from his eyes.

The lone customer looked up before returning her attention to an array of pink T-shirts, while the elderly lady at the counter met his gaze and smiled. 'Not to worry, it happens all the time.'

Henry realised he was staring, disappointment at her

not being Ava hitting him with the realisation that this was another turn of events he hadn't contemplated. To gain thinking time, he smiled and began browsing the shop – impressed as he took it in. The charity shop he'd seen in his university town looked cluttered; he'd imagined it musty inside, full of unwanted and outmoded clothes and artefacts.

This was orderly, more like a boutique. Women's and men's clothes were in separate sections, and neatly arranged in blocks of colour on wooden hangers all facing the same direction. The shop wasn't big, but there was an array of clothes, five shelves of completely random ornaments and cookware, as well as a CD and DVD area, and a children's section. It smelt much better than he had imagined, with the scent of sweet apples emanating from a diffuser tucked in the corner of a top shelf, reminding him of warm apple crumble – a welcome smell on a chilly day. The shop was a treasure trove hidden amongst the coffee shops and antique places in the village. He wondered how well known it was and how busy it ever got.

Unfortunately, the men's section of clothes was the smallest of all the displays. Balancing the box in one arm, Henry held up a couple of shirts and looked thoughtfully at the shoes – none of which were his size. With limited reason to stay in the shop, he risked looking like someone loitering with intent – which he was, but he didn't want the woman at the counter to think that.

'Looking for something specific?' The elderly woman was perched on a stool, looking at him expectantly as she awaited his response.

For Ava to walk through that door was his instant thought but he didn't want to answer questions about what he wanted her for, or how he knew her. So far his return to the village had remained discreet. He hoped to keep it that way. If too many people knew he was back and that his father was passing over the responsibility of Dapplebury House and the land that went with it, it would lead to speculation about the prospect of change. As Henry was sure change was listed as something to entice fear, dread and anxiety in the local dictionary, he didn't want that happening. He needed time. His mind had been in turmoil since he had been back. Discussions had over the telephone and decisions made in theory, became more complex when faced with the realities of their consequences.

'Umm.'

'Only, if you tell me, we might have what you're after out the back.'

Out the back. Henry held on to the words. Perhaps the very thing he had come into the shop looking for was out the back. 'Umm.'

'There's as much out there, as what you see in here. Just not enough time in the day to sort it all.'

Henry began thinking on his feet. 'So that's the reason for the sign is it?'

The woman looked puzzled.

'No donations. Too much stuff, not enough time?'

'Oh that. Yes, exactly that. Mind you I've been taking a few bits in. Can't bear to send folks away when they are offering donations. You never know what you might be turning away.'

Deciding it might be easier than he thought to take a look out the back of the shop, Henry placed the box on the counter. 'In that case, I'll confess to this being a donation. I wasn't going to leave it, but if you're happy to take it, then it would save me taking it home again.'

The woman gave a cheeky smile. 'Worth having is it?' she asked, with a glint in her eye.

Henry smiled as he thought about the antique, gold photo frames he'd found, wrapped in yellowing tissue paper, stashed away in his father's office. His mission to find something to donate had been inspired by his desire to see Ava; he hadn't thought about actually helping the charity. But on reflection, that was precisely what those unwanted but no doubt valuable items would do. The realisation appeased his guilt about taking them, somewhat. 'Photo frames mostly, but valuable ... I'd imagine.'

'Well, at the risk of getting in trouble, such is the story of my life.' The woman winked. 'I'll take them.'

'That's great, thank you. But the box is heavy, shall I put it out the back for you?' Henry flashed her a smile. He liked her cheeky style and decided to play along. The few older women he'd met in Los Angeles had stiff, expressionless faces. Those he knew from his own circles – his mother, aunts on her side and those he met at functions – tended to be stiff in other ways – serious, stuffy sorts. This woman had lived, and it showed. She reminded him of Mrs Perkins, who had been the housekeeper at Dapplebury House when he was younger. He liked her.

'You're not going to steal from us while you're out there are you?'

Henry let out a deep laugh. 'No. I promise.' He held up his hands.

'Good, you didn't look the sort, and I'm usually a good judge.'

As Henry lifted the box from the counter, pretending it was heavier than it was, the woman grabbed his arm. 'Wait, I'm meant to ask you if you'll Gift-Aid your donation, sir.' The mocking tone in her voice suggested she had been told this many times.

Hmm, details. Henry didn't want to give details.

'Do you pay tax? Oh, bother, I'm not meant to say that. I mean ... ah hum.' The woman reached under the counter and read from a piece of paper she had to hold at arm's length despite her glasses. 'We get twenty-five per cent extra, from the government at no cost to you, you just need to pay tax within the UK to be eligible.'

Henry softened at the thought of his donation raising more money for the charity. 'Sure, why not?' Taking the form, he wrote down the details of Ted, the elderly, but still on payroll, resident gardener at Dapplebury House.

The woman looked at the form and peered over her glasses. 'Well Ted, I don't know what you've been taking these past months, but my goodness, you've aged well since I saw you last.' She raised her eyebrows expectantly, causing her glasses to slip a little further down her nose.

'Ha!' Henry swallowed. 'You must know my … uncle. I'm … staying with him for a bit. Sorting a few things from his cottage,' he lied.

The woman's expression softened. 'He's never mentioned you. But I'm pleased he's got someone looking out for him – family, such a treasure to have. Tell your uncle, Flo said hello.' With that, she winked again.

Henry wondered if Ted had any family looking out for him. They had spent many long afternoons together when Henry was younger, and an enjoyable few hours wandering the grounds of Dapplebury House since his return, but Henry realised, he knew little of his personal life.

Flo stuck a Gift-Aid sticker on Henry's box of donations and continued, 'I've missed Ted this past year. My herbaceous border's not been the same since he stopped calling. He had the best hardy perennials for miles your uncle.'

Henry coughed and picked up the box once more. 'I'll, um, just pop this through shall—'

'Can I try these on?' The customer who had now chosen two pink T-shirts from the rail interrupted.

'Of course.'

As the woman disappeared into the changing cubicle, Flo leaned over the counter and whispered, 'At that size, you either go for baggy and have no shape, or go for fitted and show your shape. Neither's ideal, but my money's on the latter with that one.'

Feeling embarrassed for the woman, who Henry was quite sure could hear every word of Flo's not so hushed whisper, from behind the curtain, Henry didn't respond but motioned to the box instead. 'So shall I?'

Her full attention returning to their conversation, Flo smiled. 'Where were we? Oh yes, back in the day—'

As the door to the shop opened, and a young woman holding hands with a toddler came in, Henry couldn't help but think he'd had a lucky escape regarding whatever "back in the day" memory Flo had been about to share. He seized the opportunity to head through the door that was marked private at the back of the shop.

If the front of the shop was a treasure trove, the back was an Aladdin's cave, packed with all manner of things waiting, yet to be discovered. Henry called out hello, but the silence made it clear nobody was there. Not knowing which of the overflowing sorting pens he should put it in, he placed the box on the floor next to a large sorting table – surrounded by an array of price stickers, hangers and size cubes. Disappointment welling inside, Henry turned to leave, but as he did so, he spotted the noticeboard. A newspaper clipping with a picture of Ava and her mum stood out, alongside it was a tribute to "The Founder and Much Missed Champion of All Critters Great and Small". It spoke of Lily Flynn's passion for the charity and her untimely death from natural causes. Henry was shocked, his thoughts instantly with Ava. She and her mum had had a tumultuous relationship; Ava often feeling second best to the animals her mum cared for. He looked again at the article and then at his surroundings. Would guilt have made Ava give up on her own hopes and dreams? Henry didn't know, but he intended to find out. Leaving the box under the table littered with piles of clothes that were presumably part of the "too much stuff" to sort, he left.

As he headed back through the shop, Flo gave him a wave from the counter and held up the slim-fitting pink T-shirt of the now crimson-faced customer with a wink.

Chapter Eight

With Mary kindly offering to take over from Flo to ensure cover at the shop, Ava decided to head straight home and take Myrtle out for a walk. Discovering the dog had been sick and didn't seem her usual tail-wagging self, made her reconsider. Myrtle was rarely ill, no matter what she ate or rolled in on their walks. Ava looked into her large, doleful eyes, and promptly decided that an afternoon in, snuggled up in front of an open fire, might do them both good.

Once she was satisfied that Myrtle was comfortable, Ava made herself a coffee and decided to get her sketchbook and materials out. Working on the display at the charity shop had reminded her how long it had been since she had done anything creative. It was no wonder she had been feeling so tense; she had long known drawing was good for her mind, and spirit.

The dozy dog, in her cosy surroundings, provided the perfect muse. Blocking in Myrtle's basic shape and features was made easy by the fact she didn't stir. Using a light touch, Ava began to sketch in a few details. It was satisfying, calming even. With Myrtle sound asleep Ava didn't have to focus on getting her eyes straight; practice over the years meant she'd improved at this, but still it was always the part she found most difficult when putting pencil to paper. Next, she started drawing in the details, and the portrait began to take shape. She confidently added faint lines to gesture at Myrtle's folds of skin and ruffles of fur.

Ava knew the trick was not to overthink but to let the ideas and the pencil flow as one. Working from dark to light, Ava added in shading to demarcate the shadows, and the picture began to have greater depth. Even asleep, Myrtle's gentle, loving personality was evident, and Ava could feel how blessed she was to have her in her life.

Picking up her coffee and taking a swig, Ava winced at the fact it was now cold. She decided to make herself another before beginning to remove her guidelines and starting to add definition and final touches. She enjoyed working methodically. Ava knew one of the things she found hard about working in the charity shop was the unpredictability of what would come in. She had no control over the quantity, quality, or size of donations they received, sometimes making it a matter of doing what she could to organise the chaos.

A knock at the door interrupted her thoughts. Myrtle lifted her head and barked, but didn't move from her cosy spot by the fire. Few people called at Ava's house. Generally, Mary would be her first thought, but she usually let herself in the back door and, besides, Ava knew she was at the shop.

Ava pushed her fingers through her hair and then noticed the pencil smudges on her hands and wiped them on her jeans. She went to check she hadn't put any black marks on her face, but the knock came again. Ava tutted and muttered about the lack of patience of some people as she went straight to the door. Opening it, she did a double take as she took in the sight of the unexpected visitor.

'Gino! What are you doing here?' Ava tucked a stray curl behind her ear, aware that she must look a mess, having rubbed her hand through her hair as she contemplated her drawing.

Gino was leaning against the wooden porch, his legs crossed at the ankles, the sun causing a glint in his dark eyes. 'Mary told me to come, so here I am.'

Ava stared at him, discombobulated. 'Why? I mean …'

'She said you needed a hand.' Gino stood up straight as if readying himself to enter the cottage.

'A hand? No. Perhaps she meant at the shop. I can't think—'

'In the bedroom.'

Gino stated the words matter-of-factly, and yet it took Ava a beat to absorb what he said.

'What?' Heat rose to her cheeks.

'Pauline wanted to swap shifts, so I've got a few hours to spare. I went to the shop to talk through our idea a bit more, but Mary said I should come here to help you as you were having difficulty in the bedroom.' He spoke slowly, making his accent more pronounced.

'Wh—?' Ava could scarcely believe what she was hearing. 'I don't … I mean, it's been a while, but—'

'With your mum's things,' Gino explained, attempting to curtail the grin that mischievously tugged at his lips. 'Mary said you needed a hand to shift a few boxes and sort a few of your mum's things.'

Ava stood, heat spreading across her neck at the thought of what she had almost said, attempting to make sense of Gino's words.

'She said she would help you herself, but she doesn't do sentimental, or family. So, here I am.' Gino shrugged as if his words explained everything.

Ava stared at him.

'I don't do sentimental either really, but family … family I get. Being part Italian, how could I not? And'—he held up a bottle Ava hadn't realised he was holding—'I've brought wine! Also, Mary's suggestion.'

Ava looked at the bottle. She couldn't think of anything worse than going through her mum's things with Gino. *What was Mary thinking?* Wasn't it the type of thing people had to do in their own good time? Ava thought about all the time that had passed since her mum's death and the room upstairs, still crammed with her possessions. She knew she was a hypocrite; she regularly encouraged people to have a sort out and donate to the charity shop. Yet she'd been unable to let go of her mum's things, leaving them idle when she knew her mum would rather they went to a good cause. 'OK.' Still thinking it was a crazy idea, Ava found herself standing back and inviting Gino in.

Mary had obviously sent Gino to give her a kick in the right direction, which direction Mary exactly intended that to be, Ava wasn't sure. But she knew she'd be foolish to turn the offer of help down. As Gino passed her the wine and stepped inside, Ava shook her head. 'But you don't know what you've let yourself in for.'

Chapter Nine

Having opened the wine and poured herself and Gino a glass, Ava realised she couldn't keep putting the inevitable off. Gino had come round, as a friend, to help her. Not sorting a single box would mean she had wasted his afternoon off. It would also mean she would have to suffer the wrath of Mary. Leading Gino up the narrow twisting staircase, Ava felt tension wrap itself around her chest like a thick rubber band. *You can do this.* What she hadn't confessed to Mary was that she had tried to sort her mum's things a few times. But whenever she tried she felt engulfed by waves of sadness and fear at having to face her feelings. Putting it off seemed the logical solution. Before opening the door, Ava turned to Gino. 'Are you sure you're up for this?'

'Of course, I'm here to help and—'

Ava pushed open the bedroom door.

'Wow!' Gino's eyes boggled at the site of the boxes, stacks of paper and clothes in the room.

'Bit of a hoarder was she?' He shook his head.

Ava giggled, releasing some of the tension in her chest as she exhaled. 'No. This is my fault. I put everything in here, like this. It was … easier.'

'A kind of open the door and throw it in strategy?'

'Something like that.' Ava looked at Gino, embarrassed at her only strategy having been denial. 'You really don't have to … I mean … this, it's my fault.' Ava gestured to the room and the chaos within it, but as she spoke the last word, her voice wobbled. She felt tears well in her eyes and feared she was going to cry – *in front of Gino, for goodness' sake*.

Holding her gaze, Gino offered a reassuring smile. 'I know I don't have to. But I want to help. Mary sent me because she wants to help. But you're right. This is too much.'

'I'm sorry, I—'

'Ogni viaggio inizia con un singolo passo.'

Ava stared at Gino. She had no idea what he'd said, but she always appreciated the way in which he could switch easily from English to Italian formed with a perfect accent, at least to her ear.

'Every journey starts with a single step. My nonna used to say that to me.' Gino flicked his long dark fringe from his eyes.

'That's lovely.' Ava thought how lucky Gino was to have the support of his large family around him as he was growing up. Though his mum was English and his family had lived in England for many years, his dad had ensured they retained and respected elements of his Italian roots.

'Hmm, she said it when she wanted me to go and do something – get something from the shops, clean my room, collect my sister from school. She had a way of making things sound grander than they were.'

'Oh.'

'But in this instance her words make sense. There's too much to tackle here all at once. You should face it a box at a time.'

'I suppose.' Ava looked at the room and felt unexpectedly grateful that Gino was there.

'How about if I bring a box downstairs and you start with that? While you see what's inside, I'll stack the other boxes to one side and make piles of the clothes and other bits. When you can get in the room properly you'll find it easier to face.'

'I can't leave you to sort all—'

'I won't be sorting through it as such. I'll just be making it more manageable, putting it in piles ready for you.'

'Are you sure?' Ava knew it made sense. For Gino to sort the items into manageable piles would be akin to what she did at the shop; it was just a process. He had no emotional attachment, either negative or positive, to the things in the room. For her almost every item held a memory.

'Of course.'

'OK. But I can't expect you to carry boxes up and down stairs. I'll sort them in my room. It will be easier that way.'

'I am more than capable of carrying boxes up and down the stairs.'

'I know you are.' Ava's eyes flicked to Gino's biceps and her cheeks flushed for fear that he had seen her.

The twitch at the corner of his mouth suggested he was very aware of her checking out his muscles.

Ava coughed. 'Right, well, I'll get my room ready.' As she walked into her bedroom she wondered why she had made such a crazy suggestion. *Bring the boxes in here, Gino. Come into my room. See my cute-woodland-animal-print duvet cover! Oh my goodness, I've got my cute-woodland-animal-print duvet cover on my bed!* Ava cringed. All of her duvet covers were animal related, purchased by her mum back before she had a choice. *Why have I not thought to change them?* She hurriedly threw a blanket over her bed, and looked around the room. It really wasn't befitting a woman beyond her mid-twenties. Ava grabbed an armful of soft toys from the chair in the corner and threw them into her wardrobe. As she scanned the room, for what else she might need to move, Gino knocked on the door.

'So here's the first box.'

Catching sight of the ears of Raspberry Rabbit – a favourite teddy when she was little – sticking out of her wardrobe door, Ava decided she couldn't face having Gino in her bedroom, and met him at the door. 'If it's OK with you, downstairs might be more appropriate.'

'Not a problem!' Gino turned and led the way downstairs.

Ava picked up her wine that she'd brought up with her, shut her bedroom door and followed. At her suggestion, Gino placed the box on the large oak kitchen table. He placed his hand on her shoulder, checking she was OK before leaving her to it. Ava took a drink, welcoming the alcohol as it spread through her, numbing her nerves.

Opening the box she saw and remembered its contents: evidence of her mum's success stories; polaroid photographs of animals she'd saved and released, newspaper clippings and scribbled notes. Ava remembered that this is what kept her mum going on the tough days – the days when the rescue was a challenge or the rehabilitation impossible.

On the outside Ava's mum had appeared a pragmatic woman, someone who took everything in her stride, driven by her mission. But, looking at it all now, Ava remembered moments, albeit that they were fleeting, when her mum had revealed her vulnerable side; the part of herself that she couldn't and wouldn't let get in the way of her achieving her goals.

Flicking through the images and clippings, Ava wondered what she should do with them all. She took a breath. *Think objectively.*

When Gino appeared with the next box, Ava looked at him apologetically, having not emptied or made any decisions about the contents of the box she was sorting.

'Woah. Your mum was a legend.' Gino gestured to the newspaper clippings.

'She was. But what do I do with it all now?'

'Does the charity have a website, or social media pages?'

'They have a web page, just a contact page really.'

'A lot of that looks like it was reported back when news was shared on paper rather than the Internet. So why not upload it? Spread the word about the work of All Critters Great and Small beyond Dapplebury.'

Ava looked at the box. There was a wealth of information within its depths. Perhaps ordering and cataloguing it all online would make sense. 'It would be good PR that's for sure.'

'There could be publicity to gain from launching a new website and social media presence, and if nothing else it would provide a record for prosperity for … your children.'

My children? Ava wondered if she would ever have children. There was no man on the scene she could imagine spending the rest of her life with, so children seemed an unlikely prospect. Should she have them though then their grandmother's work, All Critters Great and Small and all that it stood for, was their heritage – *no grand estate like the Bramlington's for the Flynns.* 'I like that idea. Thanks Gino.' Ava smiled.

'That's why I'm here.'

Marking the box so she'd know its contents, Ava put it to one side; it's purpose clear in her mind. She would take it to Critters' Lodge and speak to the volunteers to see if anybody had a technical background they could put to use. While it was a long shot, experience had taught her that volunteers came from all walks of life and had a wealth of skills that they were generally only too happy to put to good use.

Having discovered several wildlife figurines in the next box, Ava marked it to be valued. The shop next door to the charity shop was an antique dealership; the elderly gentleman that ran it frequently valued items for her she couldn't assess via Ebay and other online avenues.

'Difficult to buy for was she?' Gino gestured to the box of ornaments.

'I guess. She was never really into possessions.'

'So people went with what they knew. My cousin made the mistake of telling my Mama he likes Marmite. Birthday, Christmas, any excuse she gets him a Marmite gift.'

'At least he can eat it.' Ava lifted the box of animal figurines to the floor.

'No, she got him a cushion, a mug, a key ring – all in the shape of a Marmite jar. I told her if he loved it, she was going to make him hate it!'

Ava laughed, realising what type of gift Gino was referring to, and thinking of the similar items that helped fill the homeware shelf of the shop. Having Gino for company really was making the task more manageable in more ways than one and for that she was grateful. 'I'm so pleased you're here, Gino. Really. Thanks for your help.'

'Happy to.' Gino got the bottle of wine and replenished their glasses.

When he returned, Ava looked at him hopefully. 'Two boxes down. Can we stop now?'

Laughing, Gino pulled his phone from his pocket before scrolling through his messages and holding the screen up to Ava. On it was a message from Mary: *Don't let Ava give in too easily. I've seen that room!*

'Ha, what is she like?' Ava sipped her wine.

'A good friend.' Gino smiled. 'The room is looking a lot better. I've put clothes on the bed. Boxes against the wall, oh but I found an album in the bottom of the wardrobe. I think you should see it.'

'What's in it?' Ava imagined more animal rescue pictures.

'I only had a brief look but I'd say pictures of you. Unless you know some other child with freckles and wild red hair.' Gino emphasised his point by motioning wild ringlets from his head.

Ava laughed. 'Hmm, there's only one of me.'

'I'll get it.' Gino thudded up the stairs, returning just moments later with a spiral bound photo album. 'I'll leave you to look at it.' He smiled, before going back upstairs.

Ava looked at the album, recognising it as one she had looked at many times, growing up. Opening the brown cover, revealed a yellow edged page, centred on it was a picture of her as a baby, wrapped in her mum's embrace, while her dad looked at them, the love evident in his eyes. Ava smiled at the sight of the red hair and curls she had inherited. It was one of only a few pictures of her with her dad; a tragic car accident having taken him from them when she was barely a toddler.

Her hand shaking, Ava turned the pages, careful not to dislodge the photographs as the plastic sheets came away from the once self-adhesive pages. Before her, was a pictorial record of her childhood. She was a freckle-faced, beaming girl, with unruly hair, often pictured outside: at the beach, in the woods, at Critters' Lodge, and climbing trees. She looked happy – her grin mischievous and her eyes, alive and eager. Ava wondered when she had begun to carry the angst she had felt so keenly in her teenage years. As she turned to the final page, a note secreted in the back, that she had never seen before, caused tears to well in her eyes and the air to escape her, as the sentiment of her mum's words struck her.

Chapter Ten

Ava woke feeling cold, the only warmth emanating from Myrtle as she lay heavily against her legs. Black and grey embers filled the grate, where the glow of the fire had been. Ava wiped her eyes realising she had fallen asleep on the hearthrug. When Gino had left early in the evening, she had finished the wine and settled by the fire, eventually succumbing to the sobs that wanted to escape her.

Myrtle had sat by her side; concern etched in the dog's large brown eyes as she snuggled in close in an attempt to offer comfort, while Ava cried herself out. Fat tears had rolled down her face until her eyes stung, her throat hurt and her chest ached from the exertion. When she could cry no more, sleep had been a welcome release from her throbbing head.

Standing was an effort – her back was stiff and her limbs too cold. Wrapping herself in a fleece she had hanging in the hall, Ava went to the kitchen and poured herself a drink of water. It eased her dry throat but did nothing to warm her up. Realising the sun was rising, she pressed the button on the kettle. Myrtle was standing at the door, looking livelier than she had on the previous day, causing Ava to smile despite her headache. Deciding there was little point in going to bed, Ava looked at the dog. 'How about a walk in the woods?'

Myrtle spun as if she understood the words, and Ava bent to stroke the soft fur at the back of her ears.

A hot shower, some warm clothes, and a cup of tea later, Ava wrapped herself in her coat. Closing the front door, she and Myrtle made their way down the gravel path towards the village before taking their usual hedgerow detour into the grounds of Dapplebury House. Once in the woods, Ava slipped off Myrtle's lead, and the dog leapt around, bouncing on her paws as she enjoyed the freedom. Ava stretched out her limbs. The chill, early morning air was enlivening and a tonic for her lack of a comfortable night's sleep.

Following the line of trees, they walked towards the lake. Her head feeling clearer, Ava took the note she had found tucked into the back of the photograph album, from her pocket.

She read, tracing her finger across her mum's handwritten words: "I'm sorry I'm not in more of your pictures as you were growing up. I was behind the camera. All of those beautiful smiles, you were giving them to me".

Ava wiped her eyes before reading on.

"I love you, my beautiful, red-haired, strong-willed girl. Forgive the choices I made, and always remember that you were my special gift and my greatest accomplishment. Perhaps life would have been easier if we were less alike, but being feisty you get from me, and I wouldn't want you to be any other way. Never give up on your dreams and remember you are my girl, Ava Flynn. Xx".

There was so much to take in. Ava had looked at the photographs of herself growing up. She had seen the album many times before; as a teenager, she had considered the pictures of her childhood-self alone at the park, the beach, and at home, as evidence to her coming second best to her mum's cause. She had bucked against her, causing arguments where none were needed and in hindsight erroneously considering herself a greater victim than the animals her mum rescued. And while she realised a long time ago that she had been selfish in her thoughts and actions, it was only after reading her mum's words as she sat by the fire the night before, that she had seen the bigger picture.

Ava knew that since her dad died when she was two, her mum had raised her as a single parent, bringing up a strong-willed girl alone, while never giving up on fighting her own causes. She wished she could tell her she knew that now. And that she appreciated all she had done for her. While they'd established a good relationship as Ava had got older, she never truly thanked her mum for all that she had done. And now, it was too late.

Anger welling inside – at herself for the wasted years, and at the loss of her mum – Ava began to run. Feeling a surge of frustration she wanted to release, she screamed. The piercing, primal sound echoed through the silent woods, causing birds to flee from the treetops. Myrtle looked at her, her eyes wide, stunned by the unexpected noise. The confused spaniel followed in excited pursuit.

Ava felt the cold air burning in her lungs as her rapid breaths became increasingly loud and ragged. Her legs, uncooperative and heavy just an hour before, now carried her on swiftly through the dew-covered grass. The trees went by in a blur, as her heartbeat thudded through her body. Myrtle ran by her side, her head flicking between looking ahead and turning towards Ava. Fixing her eyes on the lake in the distance, Ava pushed on.

The sensation was freeing. She was running too fast for rational thought. Too fast to think about all that she would like to say to her mum; too fast to think about the weight of burden she felt at keeping All Critters Great and Small afloat; too fast to think about the never-ending mountain of donations at the shop, and – *Oh God*! – too fast to do anything to avoid the man stepping out from the line of trees just feet ahead of her. With the deft agility that came from being half a metre from the ground, and in possession of four paws, Myrtle darted out of the way, while Ava braced herself for impact. Seeing the alarm in the man's green eyes as if she were registering the situation in slow motion, Ava slammed into him, knocking him to the ground as the breath left them both.

Shocked at the abrupt stop as much as the fall, cushioned only by the fact she had landed on top of the man, it took Ava a moment to regain her faculties. Embarrassment taking over, she cursed and began scrabbling up from the horribly awkward situation. Myrtle ran around the unexpected scene in a frenzy of excitement, as Ava and the man disentangled their bodies.

Ava stood, attempting to gather herself together. 'Are you crazy? What are you thinking just stepping out like that?' she blustered.

Slowly getting to his feet, the man laughed, the unexpected response doing nothing to ease Ava's anger.

'Seriously?' Her nostrils flared. She felt the beads of sweat on her temples prickle.

'I'm sorry—' The man, still doubled over with his hands on his hips, sounded winded. 'I heard a scream … and came to see if everything was all right. I had no idea you were about to come … like a banshee, hurtling along from nowhere, on what is …'

'Private property, I know,' Ava retorted, flailing her arms in the direction of the woods.

She inhaled in readiness to continue, but as the man stood to his full height, flicking his fringe from his eyes, and offering the hint of a smile, no words came. Instead, Ava stood transfixed – recognition slowly dawning upon her.

Too much of the man's face was covered by his beard, but she was sure it was him. 'Henry?' His name slipped out as a question. It had been so long since she had seen him.

'Ava.' Henry smiled, his green eyes – the colour of the ferns on the forest floor they used to play on – meeting her gaze and causing her breath to hitch.

Ava heard the rush of blood in her ears and felt her pulse thudding throughout her body, a stark contrast to the quiet woods and the calm manner of the man standing before her.

While he didn't seem surprised by her presence, she was trying to assimilate the Henry she had explored the woods with in their youth, with the man in front of her.

'I can't believe it's … you're back, and I'm'—Ava put her hands to her face, feeling the heat in her cheeks—'Oh God!

I've got puffy eyes, and I was running. I'm a sweaty mess and my hair, it's ...' Realising she didn't need to point out her hair was a mass of wild curls from the shower, even before she started running, Ava bit her lip.

Henry attempted but failed to stifle a giggle. 'Perfect.'

Ava looked at him, confused.

'Your hair. It looks perfect.' He leaned in closer to tuck her stray curls behind her ear. 'It always looked perfect like this.'

Ava saw the movement of his Adam's apple as he swallowed.

Feeling that she might melt on the spot if her cheeks burned any brighter, Ava welcomed the distraction of the dog, jumping up in an attempt to get their attention. Feigning the need to get an excited Myrtle back under control, Ava looked away – taking longer than she needed, while her mind attempted to catch up with the unexpected turn of events.

The memory of the last time she had seen Henry, by the lake at Dapplebury House, came flooding back: the pleasure of the time they had shared, the touch of his soft lips on hers, and his mother's anger at discovering them. And now, well now he was back and all grown-up, and she had not only knocked him over, but she had been lying prone against him as he lay on the damp grass.

It was all so unexpected. Over the years, knowing he had gone to boarding school and then hearing rumours that Henry had moved to Los Angeles, Ava had tucked all thoughts of Henry Bramlington to the back of her mind. Living abroad meant he was at a safe distance, and if he returned on visits Ava knew it was unlikely that he, the heir to Dapplebury House and its estate, would be dropping things off to the local charity shop. She and Henry belonged to the past. The two of them existed in another lifetime. *And yet, here he is, all grown up, and you were pressed—*

Shaking her head, Ava reminded herself that attempting to regain her composure and decorum wasn't going to be made any easier by recalling the firm mass of muscles she could feel beneath her as she had tried to disentangle herself. In the days when they had skinny-dipped together, Henry had the lean body of an adolescent boy. His muscles were defined but not developed. Whatever he had been up to in his years away from Dapplebury, the firm body she could undoubtedly feel below her suggested it involved working out.

Having got the dog back on her lead, Ava took a breath, letting it out slowly, before turning to face Henry. 'Sorry, about ... about before. I didn't expect to see anyone, and you took me by surprise.' Pleased with the fact she sounded a whole lot more sensible, Ava smiled and pushed her hair back from her face. *That's better, keep it light, breezy and breathe.* 'Why are you here?'

Henry laughed, a deep easy laugh that was matched by a mischievous glint in his eyes. 'I live here.' He grinned.

His words cut through Ava's bravado, as she remembered where she was. 'Yes ... yes ... of course you do. I'm sorry. Silly question. I should ... I should go.' Pulling on Myrtle's lead, she took a step backwards.

'No. Don't go! I mean, please, stay. I'd like you to stay.'

Ava faltered, while her head told her she should leave, her feet seemed reluctant to receive the message.

Henry looked at her. 'There are things I need to'—he rubbed his hand through his beard—'things I should have said, and done, before now.'

Ava swallowed. Did he mean the things she hoped he would have said and done all those years ago? There was a time when she longed for him to make a stand and defend her against his mother's tirade. But now, what was the point? She pulled her coat around herself a little tighter. 'It was such a long time ago. Really it's—'

Henry reached out and placed his hand over hers as she held Myrtle's lead. It caused a sensation to ripple through her, Ava attempted to ignore.

'I know. I do. But Ava, will you just give me a bit of your time? A chance to speak to you and then, well then I'll leave you alone. If that's what you want.'

Leave me alone. There were times when Ava craved peace and solitude, times when she longed to be left alone, but she had never felt that in Henry's presence. She had never wanted him to leave her alone. She swallowed. 'All right, but I don't want to keep Myrtle out too long, she hasn't been herself the last few days.' Ava congratulated herself on thinking clearly enough to give herself an excuse to leave, should she want to.

Having pricked up her ears at the sound of her name, Myrtle barked. Henry knelt to stroke her, causing the dog's whole body to wiggle with excitement. 'What do you say? Do you fancy a walk down to the lake?' He looked up at Ava, lowering his voice. 'Would that be all right with you?'

The hint of uncertainty in his tone made it clear he too remembered the last time they had been to the lake together. Ava pushed away an image of them kissing. Something she had reimagined many times on her walks, wondering how it would have played out if Lady Bramlington hadn't discovered them.

Ava fiddled with the edge of the lead in her hand. 'I don't think I have a choice. You seem to have swayed Myrtle.' The dog, looking so animated, was doing nothing to corroborate her need not to have her out too long, but it was good to see her looking more like her old self. 'I haven't seen her this lively for days. I think you've gained a fan.'

'She can probably smell her good friend, Granger.' Henry smiled.

Alarm pricked at Ava's nerves; Henry must have registered it and held up his hands.

'I haven't been stalking you or anything, honestly.'

Ava swallowed. The blush across his cheeks, and his words refuting the action, made her wonder if he had been doing precisely that. Ava reminded herself that while they had once been very close, the Henry standing before her was a stranger, and she should remember that. 'Then how did you—'

'Know that this one has a soft spot for Granger?' Henry patted Myrtle and stood up. 'I spotted you walking here, in the distance, a couple of weeks ago. Granger seemed to know you both pretty well.'

Ava felt her own cheeks colour. 'I'm sorry. As I said, I do know it's private property.'

'Ha!' Henry laughed. 'Since when did that ever stop you? Come on. I'm sure you know the way to the lake, every bit as well as I do.'

Ava smiled at the reference to their conspiratorial past.

Chapter Eleven

They walked at first in silence, their steps leaving footprints in the dew. Myrtle pulled on her lead, her tongue hanging out as she panted.

'Do you mind if I let her off, she's used to …' *Roaming free on Bramlington land.*

Henry looked at Ava with the hint of a smile. 'Of course not, do what you normally do. Don't ever feel inhibited because I'm here.'

'Thank you.' Ava stopped, so she could release Myrtle to explore the smells made by the animals who had trodden the same path the night before. With the dog free, Ava and Henry walked on, talking about the early morning light and the changing landscape of the woods. While Ava had often thought about what she might say, or feel, seeing Henry again, she never imagined it would be so easy or feel so right to be back in his presence. Her mind felt more enlivened as they discussed the decaying oak tree, the paths they had once trodden being hidden by brambles, and the growth of the deer population in the surrounding parkland. They were kindred woodland spirits, once crowning themselves the lord and lady of the Bramlington estate, with halos of woven willow, decorated with ivy.

Ava didn't know if it was because she had finally addressed the matter of sorting her mum's belongings, the release of the tears she had held on to since her mum's funeral as she had cried long into the night, or the fact Henry was back, that was making her feel so light – but she didn't want to overthink it. She just knew she could feel a sense of freedom inside she had forgotten, and that she would be happy for this moment, with her, Henry and Myrtle walking in the woods, to last forever.

When they reached the lake, Myrtle continued, her nose to the ground, as she wandered around the water's edge, while Henry and Ava paused, taking in the sight before them. Ava had visited the lake on occasion, but it was only now, seeing it in Henry's presence, that she recognised how starkly it had changed since last they were there together.

The water looked cold, deep and murky. Not at all like the lake they had swum in as children. In her memory it was aquamarine, inviting and glistening in the summer sun. But now, even the central water fountain had given up. The naked, eternally youthful boy with his rounded cheeks, curly hair, and dimpled arms holding a dolphin, looked defeated by time – green from the weather and unable to muster even a dribble of water. Looking at the lake now, it was hard to imagine they had ever felt the urge to dive in. It was a stark reminder of the time that had passed.

'Created in the eighteenth century and left to ruin in the twenty-first!' Henry sighed, rubbing his hand through his beard.

'We swam in it, just over a decade ago. This isn't irreversible. It's just neglect.'

'It's more than that—'

'It's beautiful,' Ava insisted, and she meant it. In her mind, the place of their youth was still there. It just needed to be rediscovered; she didn't want to hear it being dismissed out of hand.

Henry didn't respond. Instead, he turned to face her, his brow furrowed. 'Ava, since my return to Dapplebury, I've wanted to talk to you.'

Ava went to speak, but Henry continued, 'I need you to know how sorry I am for what happened.'

'Henry, really it's—'

'I should have stood up for you on the day my mother discovered us, and I didn't. You were my best, my only friend. My time with you, in the woods and here, was everything to me. You kept me sane and then … I stood by. I should have defended you, us.'

'It was a long time ago.'

'Don't say that like that makes it all right.' Henry held her arms, his eyes searching hers. 'It wasn't all right, and I want you to know I won't let you down again.'

Ava looked into his imploring eyes, feeling his ragged breath against her cheek.

'Henry—'

As Myrtle barked, both Ava and Henry turned to see Granger trundling out from the trees behind them. At first, Ava smiled, readying herself to find the dog a treat, but as Ted followed, she hesitated. She had known the gardener for many years since she and Henry were children. He had turned a blind eye to her visits, both then and now. She didn't fear his approach, but she did fear the grave expression on his face, and the increased pace with which he was closing the distance between them, causing his awkward gait to be more pronounced. She knew something was wrong. 'I should go!'

'It's just Ted,' Henry said, his frustration at the interruption clear from his tone. But as Ted's ashen face came more clearly into view, Henry ran to meet him.

The dogs and Ava followed.

'Henry … you're wanted up at the house. It's your father.' Ted shook his head. 'I'm sorry lad.'

Ava noticed the sadness in the older man's eyes as he spoke and felt an ache in her chest for him and for Henry.

'Go. You have to go,' she urged.

Henry looked at her, clearly torn between wanting to stay and the need to leave.

'Run on lad, I'll follow,' Ted added, seemingly misinterpreting Henry's reluctance to leave.

'You have to go,' Ava repeated.

Walking a few paces backwards before turning, Henry took off at a sprint back along the path and through the trees. Granger and Ted followed behind. Calling Myrtle to her side, Ava bent to hold on to the dog's collar and slipped her lead on. They stood alone, as the woods fell silent, in the wake of the commotion. Ava shuddered. Goosebumps pricked her skin, and she knew she was feeling what Flo would describe as the chill wind of change.

Chapter Twelve

'I'm just not sure it's the right time.' Ava looked across the bar to Gino, who was visibly crushed at her not sharing his enthusiasm.

Mary put her rhubarb gin down on the bar. 'But you can't deny February fourteenth is the ideal time to celebrate Valentine's Day. And combining that with an Italian themed night to launch the more suitably named "Around the World in Eight Gourmets" initiative does make sense.'

'Yes, of course, it all makes sense,' Ava conceded. 'But I just think with Lord Bramlington passing and much of the village still in mourning, we should give it a bit more time.' Ava gestured towards the elderly gentlemen at the end of the bar. The two men had been readily sharing their connections with the late Lord Bramlington with all who would listen for the past two weeks. Picking at the edge of her bar mat – made moist by the condensation slipping down the outside of her Coke – she continued, 'It just feels ...'

'Like the whole village needs to lift its spirits?' Mary enthused.

'Trovate sempre il tempo per dedicarvi alle cose chi vi rendono felici.'

Both Ava and Mary looked at Gino, awaiting the translation.

'Always find time for the things that make you feel happy to be alive!' He smiled, before continuing, 'Good food, good friends, love and—'

'Money in the till?' Mary laughed before dodging the bar towel Gino threw at her.

Shaking his head, Gino conceded, 'OK, that too. But I think we could all do with a lift, don't you? Spreading some love might be what we ... the village needs.'

'And, I'm not one to gossip,' Pauline butted in, having

clearly been listening to their conversation, 'but I've heard *he's* back.'

'Who?' Gino, Ava and Mary responded in unison.

'Him. The son and heir. Think about the timing.' Pauline looked expectantly at the speechless trio, before continuing, 'It's obvious, he's only back for one thing.'

Ava felt her throat tighten as she pictured Ted's ashen face and Henry sprinting towards the trees. *To say goodbye to his father? To make amends for the past.*

'The funeral?' Gino asked.

Pauline tutted and shook her head. 'Not the funeral, well yes the funeral, but the title, Dapplebury House, the estate …'

'That's three things,' Mary offered.

Pauline rolled her eyes. 'Yes, all of that, but when you think about it, it all comes down to one thing …'

The three friends looked at Pauline, while she moved in, looking around conspiratorially.

'The money!' She hissed. 'You mark my words. He'll be raking us all for what he can get before he jets off back to America and—'

'Back to America? Who said he's going back to America?' As all eyes turned to her questioningly, Ava sat up, uncrossing her legs as she adjusted her position on the barstool. Swallowing past the tension in her throat, and readying herself to justify her outburst, Ava hoped her voice would come out less trill as she began. 'I mean, he might not. He might stay. We can't just assume he'll go. He could be back to—'

'Not if past actions are anything to go by, and not what I've heard,' Pauline stated matter-of-factly, before heading off to serve a customer at the other end of the bar.

Ava's stomach twisted as she was hit by the implications of the barmaid's words, and the knowledge that people didn't call Pauline "The Oracle" without good reason; her intel was generally spot on and her predictions usually right. Ava didn't know which filled her with more dread, being raked for money she and All Critters Great and Small couldn't afford, the notion that Henry might be capable of that, or the fact he might return to America. Realising that her paper straw had become as dampened as her spirits, she removed it from her glass and drank down the last of her Coke.

Mary looked between Ava and Gino. 'Well, if what Pauline says is true then we've a bloody miserable time ahead and so no time to lose. If we want to turn this village around, I vote we get on with our plans. Worst-case scenario: we'd have tried, and it'll be us three dressed as gondoliers eating pizza and—'

'That's not what Italian—'

Mary held up her hand, shutting down Gino's interruption, before blustering on, 'As I said, worst-case scenario: us three dressed as gondoliers, eating pizza, together on Valentine's night.'

'Mary's right,' Gino affirmed. 'We've got nothing to lose.'

'And best-case scenario – the night will be a success, you'll both make a bit of money, I'll get a date, and we'd have started to lift the spirits, and revenue, of the village before Pauline's voice of doom predictions come true!'

Being won over by her friends' enthusiasm, Ava held up her hands in surrender. 'OK, I'm with you. Let's do it. Whatever the fate of the village'—*whatever Henry's plan*—'we need to stay focused and kick some life back into this village. We need to put money in our tills and show what we're made of. Let's show the new Lord Bramlington what he'd be missing if he returned to America.' Having spoken the words with conviction, Ava didn't question her motives.

'Yes!' Gino punched the air. The sparkle in his dark eyes showing how happy he was to have Ava and Mary on board, as much as his infectious smile. 'We'll need to move fast. Put up posters—'

'Get Pauline on board, she'll get word round in no time,' Mary suggested.

'I'm on it,' Pauline called from midway down the bar.

'How does she do that?' Mary whispered.

'It's a gift.' Pauline winked, causing all three to giggle as if having been caught doing something they shouldn't.

Gino lifted Ava's glass, gesturing to see if she wanted another drink as he spoke. 'I've already sorted the menu, and Chef's on board with it. If you can give out a voucher when people buy an outfit from you, I'll honour it with a free dessert.'

'That's great, thank you. If you're sure. With Valentine's just a week away, I'll have to see what I've got at the shop.' Ava took her replenished glass.

'Stripy tops?' Mary suggested.

'You're so not funny!' Gino folded his arms, shaking his head.

'I'm sorry. I can't help it. You're so easy to tease.' Mary smiled.

'I'll do a range. Bold statement jewellery and patterned pieces as well as more demure outfits, for those wanting to go more minimal chic.'

Mary and Gino looked at Ava, eyes wide.

'What? I've done my homework too, you know.' She giggled. 'Besides, if all else fails I'll put the green, white and red sections together.'

'Ha, you two make yourselves laugh.' Gino feigned insult, before lifting his glass. 'So it's a goer?'

'Yes!' Mary and Ava lifted their glasses, clinking them against Gino's to seal the deal.

As Mary went to put her glass down, she hesitated. 'Do you think we're being too couply? What about those who haven't got someone to spend Valentine's with?'

'Like Flo,' Ava suggested.

'Hmm.' Gino pondered. 'We want to include as many people as possible.'

'I know! We could have a single but happy to mingle table.' Mary wiggled her eyebrows. 'We could invite the new Lord—'

'No!' Ava and Gino spoke together.

Realising her cheeks had turned inextricably pink, she hastily continued, 'As you said, this could end up being us three and a pizza, that's—'

'Not what Ital—' Gino attempted to interject.

'Good point.' Mary nodded. 'Let's see how this one goes first and invite him to the next.'

Gino shook his head. 'I can't imagine the new Lord Bramlington coming to The Brown Dog, can you?'

Ava smiled. She found that so much easier to imagine than Henry raking the village for all its worth. She just hoped she was correct, and that she wasn't letting her judgement of the man be swayed by her memory of the boy she had grown up with.

Chapter Thirteen

With Valentine's night looming, Ava was taking a more root-through-and-take-what-works approach to sorting donations than she usually would. She'd had to set aside her desire to tackle things systematically and, despite the fact it didn't sit comfortably with her, it was beginning to pay off. She had managed to create a display in the window that she felt captured Italian chic and style mixed with the spread-some-love theme she hoped would set the tone for the evening. As much as she was on board with getting the Around the World in Eight Gourmets initiative underway, she didn't want to appear uncaring should anyone – *anyone at all* – in mourning for the late Lord Bramlington, pass the shop. It was the right thing to do for the community, or at least that's what she told herself each time she questioned her motives.

Sorting, steaming and pricing enough items for the Italian sale rail was her next task. Shoes, bags and accessories had proven easy to source from the hoards of donations in the back of the shop. But at a time when chunky knits were predominant, Ava was looking for sleek silhouettes to tempt her customers. It was a challenge, but she wanted to do all she could to make the venture a success. Not only for Gino, but the village, and All Critters Great and Small too. The winter was always a quieter time for the rescue centre. But the busy silly season would soon be upon them along with its annual influx of calls to rescue chicks fallen from nests – or rooftops in the case of gulls. Having dealt with nearly six-hundred birds in the previous year, Ava knew, ensuring they had funds in the bank to see them through was a priority.

As it was, Mary's offer to help at the shop had been thwarted when she'd been called out to a swan that had crash-landed on a damp road. The early morning reminder that such incidents accounted for around thirty rescues a year had given Ava added enthusiasm for her task. The rescue centre couldn't survive on goodwill alone. With the increased publicity she hoped to garner if their new website and social media pages came to fruition, there would inevitably be an increase in awareness of their work, and calls, as well as donations. It was, as her mum would have said, "a skinny fox in a hen house" situation; there'd be gains and losses.

As Ava's phone vibrated on the side, she glanced at the screen. Seeing she had a message from Mary, she picked it up and read: *An impact injury to the beak. Poor thing in shock. Pain relief, antibiotics, no breaks. I'll see you when I'm cleaned up.*

While Ava's theory for such events followed her mum's in that she believed the swan had mistaken the road for a lake or river, Mary went with the possibility of turbulence caused by heat variants from different surfaces as the bird had come into land. No matter which was correct, the swan had landed on a surface it hadn't expected, and blood on white feathers had a way of creating a massacre effect – even if only dripping from a beak injury. The thought caused Ava's stomach to churn.

The haemophobia that had affected her for as long as she could remember meant the sight, and sometimes the thought, of blood, caused a physical reaction she couldn't control. It was the reason she was unable to take a more active role in the animal rescue centre. Her domain was fundraising via the shop, initially to help out while also working at a local art gallery, but later, as her mum became ill, on a more permanent basis. Since her mum's passing, overseeing the finances and all things related to keeping the charity afloat left her little time for anything else. Visiting the rescue and rehabilitation centre itself, housed in a field to the north of Dapplebury, rarely happened through choice.

Ava sent Mary a text, telling her she was pleased the injury was minimal and telling her there was no hurry as she was enjoying the time to be creative.

Having stepped back from the mountain of clothes she had strewn across the sorting table, Ava noticed the time and put the kettle on, in readiness for Flo's mid-morning cup of tea. But as she turned back to the sorting table, Ava noticed a box on the floor and a Gift-Aid label with Ted's name on it. Her curiosity piqued, she picked it up.

Lifting the box onto the table, Ava picked at the corner of the parcel tape, before pulling it off in a single strip. Prising the interconnecting flaps of cardboard open revealed a layer of scrunched up newspaper depicting recent news. Ava lifted it out and was surprised to see a series of parcels each wrapped in yellowing tissue paper, sealed with tape that, from its colour, suggested it had been in situ for some time.

'OK Ted, what do we have in here?' Ava lifted the first of the packages. 'I'm guessing … photo frame. The chunky ornate style.' From her charity shop experience, Ava was convinced guessing the item inside a wrapped package could be her *Mastermind* subject. Though she had come across a few surprise items, she was usually right. 'Bingo! Oh blimey, Ted, where did you get this beauty?' Ava looked at the gold frame in her hand. It was intricately decorated, and, though she'd have to have it checked to confirm her suspicion, it looked and felt valuable.

Ava whistled. She had seen Ted's humble cottage on the Bramlington estate. Her annual Christmas card delivery, and collection of holly to decorate Critters' Cottage, always resulted in them sharing a pre-Christmas tipple, but she had never seen anything so opulent in Ted's home.

Taking out the rest of the packages, she tugged at the tissue paper on the corner of each, revealing six frames, each of varying size but of a similar style. 'Wow!' Reasoning that Ted almost certainly received them from the Bramlingtons – a Christmas gift, a bonus, or long service gift for his dedication, perhaps – Ava knew she would have to drop them round to the antique dealer to help her decide on a suitable price. They might even need selling at auction, as her mum's ornaments had, fetching a tidy and unexpected sum.

With the kettle having boiled, and the clothes for the Italian night still to source, Ava knew she should prioritise the jobs in hand. But there was no point having valuable items sitting in the back of the shop. Not when there were injured swans in need of treatment, Quill Smith and friends to rehabilitate and return to the wild, as well as the numerous other casualties the charity currently had in its care.

Curious as to the value of the frames, Ava carefully stacked them up. It made sense to pass them on for assessment as soon as possible. She could nip next door, leave them in the care of the antique dealer and return to her other chores. Carrying them through the narrow corridor to the front of the shop, Ava jumped as Flo rang the bell for assistance, and the frames almost slipped from her grasp. Her heart thudding, she took stock, gathering herself as she dared to open her eyes and check she still had hold of all six packages. *Phew!* Continuing on her way through the shop, Ava promised Flo her tea would just be a moment and reminded herself to put up the posters she had worked on. She also knew she must thank Ted for his very generous donation.

Chapter Fourteen

Henry walked Granger around the central block of shops in the village, the dog's paws padding along the damp pavement. He knew he needed the air and the walk more than the dog, who had been traversing the grounds of Dapplebury House all day. But Henry had grown fond of having Granger at his side; the dog provided welcome company, at a time when he felt more alone than he could ever recall before.

Henry knew that All Critters Great and Small would be in darkness, and yet he still felt a swell of increasing disappointment with every step that drew him closer to the shop. He hadn't consciously decided to seek Ava out, but as he hadn't seen her on any of his early morning runs since the day of his father's death she frequently occupied his thoughts. Despondent at the sight of the empty shop, he looked at Granger. 'At least I've got you, hey boy?' He patted the dog's flank, before looking up and reading the sign on the shop window: "*Ci vediamo stasera!* Italian Night at The Brown Dog, 8 p.m. Don't forget to claim your free dessert".

Translating the Italian as see you tonight, and seeing the sign, surrounded by hearts, reminded Henry of the date. *Valentine's Day*. He shook his head and looked back to Granger. 'You're not as good-looking, but you're probably more sincere than my usual Valentine's dates.' He smiled.

Having checked his watch and seeing it was after eight, he decided to walk Granger past The Brown Dog. At least an Italian night sounded less like an excuse for a fancy dress party than he had found on his last venture into the pub.

As he walked along the cobbled street, Henry welcomed the chill evening air that nipped at the bare skin of his newly shaven face. Being out made him feel alive. His days had started to merge into one, with his time spent accompanying his mother to various functions, or trying to familiarise himself with his father's business as he attempted to get his head around the complexities of running the estate. By night his thoughts always slipped to Ava. He knew his early morning runs were motivated by the hope of seeing her, as much as wanting to maintain a level of fitness, and the need to clear his head.

In contrast to the rest of the village, The Brown Dog looked warm and inviting. He could hear the upbeat tones of Italian folk music, mixed with laughter. Lights shone through the etched glass windows, the slither that afforded a glimpse inside showed it was busy. The people looked happy, some were smartly dressed, while others were wearing green, white and red. *What is it with these people and their need to dress up?* Being in the vicinity of the pub, he could almost taste a cold beer and wondered whether to go inside. Rubbing his hand around his chin, he decided against it.

When he slipped into the pub on his first night back in England, he had purposely done so anonymously, now, local coverage of his father's death and the fact he'd succumbed to a shave and haircut meant he would be recognised. Aside from the fact he was only interested in talking to one person inside, Henry knew the people of the village were enjoying themselves. He didn't want to give them cause to stop. His father had been well liked amongst the villagers, upon seeing him, no doubt they'd want to offer sympathy. *Or worse*, he told himself. *They might tell you what they think of the heir to the estate leaving and not returning until the well-respected Lord Bramlington was on his deathbed.* Henry shuddered as a chill crept down his spine. He'd have to face the villagers soon enough, and he knew what he'd have to say would see him plummet further in the popularity stakes than he probably already had.

Preparing to head home, Henry noticed a sign on the door: "No date? No worries. Come and join our single and ready to mingle table!" He rolled his eyes, wondering whom Ava was

inside with. *The barman? Would she be on the singles table?*
The thought that she could be inside, chatting to someone
else, laughing and looking at them the way she once had him,
was … frustrating.

He wondered what she would think of him if word got out
about his initial intentions for the Dapplebury estate. Henry
pushed the thought from his mind; he had let Ava down
before, the idea of ever seeing that look in her eyes again was
too much to contemplate.

Chapter Fifteen

As she finished the last of her "chorizo spaghetti carbonara", Ava looked around the bar and dining area feeling a sense of achievement as she recognised outfits from the charity shop. While many opted to wear green, white and red, it was clear some had embraced the spirit of the evening and the look she had hoped to achieve – going for elegant and stylish outfits, along with the matching accessories she had promoted. She watched several vouchers for free desserts being exchanged and hoped Gino had done what he'd said and accounted for the discount in his pricing. Her takings were up in the lead-up to the Italian night; she didn't want him to be out of pocket.

'I'm stuffed!' Mary put down her cutlery and sat back in her seat. 'I never should have gone for the mushroom lasagne after the broad bean and feta arancini!'

'Did you enjoy your meals?' Gino approached their table by the fire, with a smile.

'It was de-lish, but I'm not sure I've got room for pud.' Mary patted her stomach.

'Really? There's a vegan, blueberry and coconut panna cotta. I thought you would—'

'It sounds great but, honestly, if I eat another thing I'll burst.'

'I'd take it as a compliment because nothing normally stops her from having dessert.' Ava smiled.

'She's right! I don't know what you've done to me with your Italian comfort food, but I feel ready for my PJs. My usual vices have been replaced with a longing to curl up in bed with a good book!'

Ava let out a giggle. 'So much for partying the night away with someone from the single and ready to mingle table.'

'I know, who knew carbs would be my only Valentine's date?' Mary laughed. 'I'm going to waddle home.'

'I can walk you ladies home when I'm done here,' Gino offered.

'No. Honestly, I'm going to head off in a mo. I've got an early start tomorrow.' Mary picked up her bag. 'But Ava, you should stay. Gino can walk you home.'

'No, I'll come with you.'

'You will not. Look at this place. It's buzzing, and you two should enjoy the rest of the evening. It's a success. You've made it a success. Full stomachs, happy people, even Flo has pulled'—Mary pointed to a very jovial Flo, animatedly chatting to Ted on the singles table—'and I hope plenty of money in the till for you both. It's been wonderful.'

'And not a stripy T-shirt or pizza in sight.' Gino beamed proudly.

Mary stood and kissed Gino's cheek. 'Honestly, I never thought there would be – you're too passionate for that.'

Gino blushed, rendered momentarily speechless by the compliment.

'But teasing you is too easy and'—Mary picked up her drink and drained the last of her wine—'too much fun!' She leaned down to hug Ava. 'Well done, everyone looks amazing!' She kissed her on the cheek and whispered in her ear, 'Let Gino walk you home. You two look so happy, and it's Valentine's night.'

Ava felt the heat rise in her cheeks and hoped the music and general hubbub meant Gino hadn't heard. As she watched Mary leave, Ava realised she felt happy. The joy in the room was infectious. She knew the uncertainty in the village meant there could be a tough time ahead, but Mary and Gino had been right; a night out was much needed, and it was good to see so many happy people enjoying themselves. The locals had come out to support the event, and that meant a lot.

'Around the World in Eight Gourmets is off to a promising start.' Ava smiled at Gino. '*Congratulazioni!* Oh, blimey, sorry. Is that lowering the tone?'

'No, why would it? It's congratulations in Italian.'

'Really? I literally swapped the end of the word for *zioni* and hoped for the best!'

Gino rolled his eyes. 'And there I thought you'd learnt some Italian.'

'I had. And if you don't mind, I'll definitely have some *dessertzioni.*'

Gino looked at Ava, mock indignation on his face. 'Really? You're doing that?'

Ava went to speak again but giggled. 'No! Even I can't keep that up. Sorry. But I would like to try the panna cotta though, please?' She smiled. 'But I'm paying. I already had this outfit.'

'You will not!' Gino insisted. 'Pud's on the 'ouse,' he added in an attempt at a Cockney accent, as he walked away.

'Pah!' Ava chuckled. 'Phil Mitchell meets Gino D'Acampo!'

As Gino turned out the lights and locked the pub door, the church clock was striking midnight. Being an hour after the last of the revellers left The Brown Dog, the village streets had fallen silent. The air was cold, but Ava was still feeling the warmth of the pub, as well as the warm glow of success from how well the evening had gone. That, and the alcohol she had consumed, was making her cheeks feel positively rosy. She and Gino walked companionably along the street, the only noise coming from their shoes against the cobbles. The clouds from earlier had cleared revealing a velvet sky, speckled with countless stars. Her eyes having adjusted to being outside, Ava looked up and smiled. 'There are so many stars tonight. Look, they're actually twinkling.'

'Did you know ...' Gino paused, looking directly at her.

Ava stopped and looked into his darkened eyes, readying herself for a beautiful Italian phrase about the night sky that, given her current giddy state, might just melt her insides.

'... they're not actually twinkling?'

'What?' That was not what she had expected to hear.

71

'We think they're twinkling but that movement you see, it's caused by turbulence in the atmosphere – the light from the stars is refracted in different directions – making us think they're twinkling.'

'Blimey, has a less romantic sentence ever been spoken by an Italian?' Ava scoffed, folding her arms as she continued to walk towards Critters' Cottage.

'Sorry!' Gino fell into step alongside her. 'I've always had a fascination with astronomy. Some boys liked football or playing on the PlayStation – I liked looking at the stars.'

Ava paused for a moment, looking at Gino. 'How did I not know that?'

'You didn't ask, and, mentioning it seemed a bit … What's that word?'

'Nerdy?' Ava asked with a smile as she continued walking.

'Yes, nerdy. I have told you I'm more of a late-night than early morning person, though.'

'Yes, you have,' Ava conceded, not admitting she had assumed he was referring to an overactive nightlife of a different sort. She thought about the times they'd spent talking. Despite the fact they'd spent long hours chatting, Ava realised she had rarely asked him about his life, passions and ambitions. He had been a good friend to her as she had come to terms with her mum's illness and death, but she wondered how much of a good friend she'd been to him.

'Gino.'

'Yes?'

'I wasn't really upset about the star thing … I mean, you've shattered my illusions. "Twinkle, Twinkle Little Star" will never be the same again, but I don't mind,' she teased, directing Gino towards the shortcut that led through the grounds of Dapplebury House. 'And I'm sorry I didn't know that about you … You can tell me more … about the stars and stuff, if you like.' Ava unfolded her arms, her hand accidentally brushing Gino's as she let it swing by her side.

'Ha, OK! The stars and stuff.' Gino laughed. 'How much did you drink tonight?'

'Hmm, more than a bit but less than a lot,' Ava confirmed, sure that the light feeling she could feel in her head was due to the success of the night.

'So you want to talk about the waxing gibbous moon?' Gino spoke with an amused tone as he pointed at the moon that was less than a full circle but larger than a semicircle.

'The waxing what?'

'You must have done the phases of the moon at school! The waxing gibbous moon.'

Ava shook her head. 'Honestly, I don't remember ever hearing that before.'

'It's the phase between the first quarter and the full moon.'

Ava paused looking at the moon, seeing the mix of light and shadows, and biting her lip to stop herself pointing out that she often imagined seeing a face looking back, even as an adult. 'To me, the night sky has always been a thing of wonder. We are lucky living here, with so much countryside surrounding us. There's hardly any light pollution. When I take Myrtle out on a cloudless night, I'm treated to an astronomical show—'

Gino opened his mouth as if to speak, but Ava continued.

'—but I make up my own constellations, and when I see a shooting star, I make a wish. I am a romantic at heart.'

'Have your wishes ever come true?'

Ava looked through the darkness in the direction of the lake. 'Hmm. Up until recently I would have said no, but now … Well it feels more like a work in progress.'

'So, you have something in common with the waxing gibbous moon, even though you didn't know it.'

'I do?'

'Yes, it's the phase when the moon is almost at its full potential, it is not there yet, but it works towards it … and then *perfezione!*'

Ava giggled. '*Perfezione?* Really, did you make that up?'

'No. It's true. It's all true. The waxing moon is thought to symbolise femininity – intuition, creativity and wisdom.' Gino smiled. 'So you see, you must seize your moment, Ava Flynn. Now is a good time to make your wishes come true.'

'Really?' Ava asked.

Gino stopped walking and gently held Ava's arm.

She turned to face him, taking in the sight of him. The light from the moon was causing a slight glint in his sincere eyes.

'Tonight was a success, wasn't it? I will do the numbers, but it looked like a success to me, and it was your idea and your creativity that made it work. Now is your time, don't you feel it? We are on the cuff of something new.'

'Cusp.' Ava laughed. 'We are on the cusp of something new.'

'Cuff, cusp, whatever, you need to seize your moment.'

Seize your moment. The cold night air had begun to nip at her nose and cheeks. Despite the bright moon, the adjacent woods were shrouded in darkness. All was silent but for the occasional rustle in the undergrowth, and the distant hoot from an owl. Ava thought about the last time she had been in the grounds of Dapplebury House, seeing Henry again, his words, and the fact she hadn't been able to get him out of her thoughts since. She'd no idea if Gino was humouring her or not, but she welcomed his words and their confidence-boosting gesture. She looked into his eyes.

'Gino, you're a sweetie, and I am *absobloominlutely* going to appreciate you more.' With that she leaned up and kissed him on the cheek. As she opened her eyes, she spotted movement in the night sky. 'Look, quick a shooting star! Make a wish—'

'But it's a—'

'Make a wish, please. Just think about the thing you want most.'

Gino looked to the sky, closed his eyes and then looked down at Ava. 'There, I did it.'

'And? What did you wish for?' Ava looked at him, excitement in her eyes.

'I'm pretty sure that's not how wishes work.'

'But that's exactly how friends work.' She laughed, taking his arm in hers as they continued to walk towards Critters' Cottage.

Chapter Sixteen

Henry did up the buttons of his charcoal blazer, flexed his arms and pulled his shirt cuffs down to just below the line of his tailored sleeves. He rubbed his finger over his cuff links, engraved with the Bramlington family crest, and swallowed. It had been a long day; visiting each of the estate's tenants was taking its toll. All were sympathetic about his father's death and wanted to share their memories of the man they considered a friend.

Having been under the watchful gaze of his ancestors – immortalised in oil on canvas – as he had grown up, Henry dreaded and feared the responsibility of the expectations placed upon him by birth. Learning the extent to which his father had let the estate slip towards financial ruin, had, at first, felt a relief. From a distance of over five-thousand miles, the solution had seemed simple. Being home, his perspective had changed; seeing Ava and reconnecting with the estate meant the reality of all that was at stake had become starkly evident.

Henry decided that taking the flak for the forthcoming rent increases – intended as phase one of his newly established plan to save the estate – was preferable to marring the memory of the man so many, himself included, held in esteem. Aware he had run away and turned his back on his responsibilities when his father needed him, Henry had promised he would do all he could to reverse the fortunes of Dapplebury House and its estate. As he saw the peace his presence and words brought to his father's final moments, Henry determined if his actions were too little, too late, he would be the one to go down in the tomes of history as the man who led the estate into ruin. He had been willing to do that when he had been foolish enough to hatch plans to sell, so why not now, for better reasons? Since being back, he had realised he was ready to take on the responsibilities that he should have done long ago. The knowledge that had he stayed, he might have eased his father's burden in his final years would always remain with him. Preserving his father's memory was paramount. He owed him that.

While Henry hoped reflecting on the past and looking towards the future with those he had met, might lay the foundation for greater acceptance of the necessary rent increases soon to come, he was under no illusion that the people of Dapplebury would accept the reality quietly.

That knowledge did nothing to make his day any easier, and neither had the watchful gaze of his late father's personal assistant, who insisted on accompanying him as he visited Dapplebury's tenants. Henry always knew he would inherit his father's title and the estate, but Mrs Jenkins, who had assumed the role of his PA, came as a surprise. A well-presented woman in her late fifties, she possessed a stealth-like ability to move around Dapplebury House in silence, unnerving Henry with her frequently unexpected appearance at his side.

Leaving All Critters Great and Small to last on the list had been intentional. Ava filled his thoughts on many occasions over the previous weeks. He had frequently taken his run at sunrise in the hope she would be on the path towards the lake, but she'd not appeared. Granger stayed around Dapplebury House, not taking off into the grounds, and so Henry resigned himself to the knowledge she and Myrtle had stayed away.

Knowing he was going to see her imminently caused nerves to twist in his already knotted stomach. He wished he could have spoken to her privately before this day. But with so much to organise, to understand and take on, the time had slipped by. He had wanted to forewarn her that to save Dapplebury, the village would be facing difficult times ahead, when he had seen her at the lake, but the importance of the conversation and the opportunity had disappeared with Ted's arrival.

Aware that dismissing Mrs Jenkins before they visited everyone on the detailed list she'd produced would cause questions he wasn't prepared to answer, Henry found himself heading into the charity shop, his PA at his side.

Recognising Flo, he offered a smile.

'Ted's nephew, my Aunt Fanny!'

Seemingly unaware that her opening expression caused the customers in the shop to turn and Mrs Jenkins to recoil, Flo continued, 'Look at you, all cleaned up and looking every bit as handsome as your father. You know you could have told me. I'm the soul of discretion!' Flo tapped the side of her nose with her finger.

Sure that wasn't true, Henry couldn't help but laugh. 'Thank you.' He liked Flo and felt he owed her an explanation. 'I'm sorry about before.'

'No problem'—Flo winked—'I've seen that programme *Undercover Boss*. I know how it works.'

Henry walked to the counter, a quizzical expression on his face as he looked at Flo.

'You know when those in high places go undercover to assess those who are at grassroots. Was I being filmed? Did I do OK? Thank goodness I asked if you were a Gift Aider!'

Mrs Jenkins coughed, raising her eyebrows above the rim of her glasses.

Deciding it was best not to explain, Henry returned his attention to Flo. 'No, no. I had just been away for so long I thought I should check out the village. But today I'm here on official business.'

'Yes, of course, I should have known. I was sorry to hear about Lord Bramlington – we all were. He was a good 'un, and he'll be sorely missed. We prayed for him at Sunday service when we heard.'

Henry swallowed. 'Thank you, my mother and I appreciate everyone's kindness.' He had said the words so many times they felt as if they were on repeat.

'And how is Lady Jayne, I mean, Lady Bramlington? You could tell love had grown from fondness with those two. If only the same could have been said for Charles and Di.'

Henry had no idea what Flo was alluding to but imagined she was a woman who could spend hours conversationally meandering through a maze of tangents.

'She is greatly saddened, of course, but taking comfort from the tributes she has received.'

Flo went to speak, but Henry continued, 'Is Miss Flynn here, today?' Instantly he wished he hadn't added today as it made it seem he'd noticed her absence before.

'She's—' Flo stopped and motioned for Henry to move aside while she served a customer who was purchasing a card.

Left in suspense, Henry glanced at Mrs Jenkins, who was checking her watch. Seizing the opportunity, Henry smiled. 'It's got late. If you'd like to go, please do. I'm sure you have places to be.' He had no idea what places; Mrs Jenkins was a closed book to him, beyond her work as a PA.

'No, I'll—'

'Really. It's fine. Take the car. I'll walk back. It's been a long day, and I'd like the air.' *And a moment to breathe without the scrutiny of a PA, the driver she insisted they used for official estate business, and half the village.*

'If you're sure, Your Lord—'

'Of course, and please, call me Henry.'

'Yes, Your Lordship.'

Henry sighed, and moved back to the counter as the customer – card in hand – followed Mrs Jenkins through the door.

Flo looked at Henry. 'She's out the back, getting through some of the stock mountain.' Flo smiled before waving her hand towards the back-room door. 'Go on. You know the way.'

As Henry walked towards the door, his head felt light at the prospect of seeing Ava.

'Oh, and Your Lordship.'

'It's Henry, please.' He turned back to Flo, his cheeks reddened at the formality in the mention of his title.

'Oo right oh then, Henry it is.' Flo chuckled. 'I just wanted to say – you look so much better without that disguise.'

Not having the heart to tell her that the beard, collar-length hair, and clothes had all been his own, Henry nodded his thanks and smiled. As he walked through the door and along the corridor, still brimming with stock, he could hear Ed Sheeran playing on the radio, and Ava humming along. When she came into view, he took a fortifying breath before speaking.

'Hello.'

Ava dropped the bag of donations she was holding and swung round. 'Henry! Sir? Lord? Oh, bugger! Which is it? Sorry. I never expected … and you look … you look so shiny and … posh!'

Henry laughed out loud, as Ava's cheeks coloured. He liked the fact, being a redhead, she could never disguise her blushes as they spread over her naturally pale skin.

'Good posh or bad posh?' Henry rubbed his hand round his clean-shaven chin.

Ava looked at him, appearing to ponder the question. 'Good, definitely good.' She smiled before seeming to correct herself with a frown. 'I was very sorry to hear about your dad. This must be a very difficult time.'

'Yes. Thank you …' About to go into his well-rehearsed response, Henry breathed. This was Ava, he didn't want to pretend to be anyone but himself with her, and he certainly didn't want her to feel she needed to treat him differently. 'It's … it's been bloody awful, to be honest. But you know that.' He gestured to the newspaper clipping regarding Ava's mum that he had seen on the noticeboard on his previous visit, before continuing. 'You've lost your mum.' He saw the flicker of sadness in Ava's eyes and wanted her to know he understood. 'I'm sorry to hear that. I know ... well, I know no matter what, it hurts.' He pulled at his tie, sliding the knot down and opening his top button before pushing his hand through his hair.

Fixing her gaze in his direction, Ava walked towards him, making his heart thud against his chest. His mind jumped to places he realised she never intended, as she leaned around him to take a reel of price labels from the shelf behind him. He let out a breath and wondered if she noticed. Labels in hand, Ava hesitated in front of him.

'Did you come here to talk about the loss of our parents and how sad that is?' She looked at him, the question reflected in her eyes.

Henry inhaled her fresh, clean scent – *orange and bergamot* – her proximity making him think about all kinds of things that had nothing to do with a sensible conversation, parents or responsibilities. 'No.' He looked at her full red lips, wishing he had got to kiss them more than that once.

'Good! So how would you feel about getting out of here? I need to check on Myrtle and, if she seems up to it, I was going to take her for a walk in'—Ava offered a hesitant smile, chewing her lip a little before finishing her sentence—'your woods?'

Henry laughed, releasing the tension from his body. 'That's the best suggestion I've heard in a long time!'

Ava looked at him. He had forgotten how her eyes lit up as she smiled.

'I'm so pleased you said that because if you'd opted to stay and talk instead of going for a walk, I'd have had to put you to work on some of this.' She gestured to the pile of random items on the sorting table, before heading towards the office, scribbling a note, and taking her jacket from the coat stand.

Henry walked to the table. 'I'm not sure I'd be much good to you here. Sorting things at Dapplebury House is enough of a headache.'

'Don't you have help?' Ava returned from the office pulling her scarf from her pocket and circling it around her neck.

'Hmm my mother, and the enigma that is Mrs Jenkins.'

'Mrs Jenkins?' Ava asked, turning off the clothes steamer and the radio.

'Yes, my inherited PA. In fact, if you've got a bell I can attach to her, or some clogs I can give her, you'd be doing me a—*BLOODY HELL!* Mrs Jenkins, how long have you been standing there?'

Henry jumped, his heart hitting the back of his throat, as he registered the woman in the doorway as if he'd conjured her with the mere mention of her name.

Apparently unperturbed by the fact she'd almost given him a heart attack, Mrs Jenkins looked between Henry and Ava, suspicion in her steely eyes, as she opened her black patent, snap-top handbag, took out a cloth, removed her glasses and wiped them.

'I neglected to remind you. Ms Flynn is, of course, the tenant of two properties on the estate – this shop, and the land and buildings they call Critters' Lodge.'

'Yes, thank you. I am aware of that.' Henry offered a tight smile and a nod, curtly dismissing Mrs Jenkins who he half expected to disappear in a puff of smoke, opposed to turning on her heels and walking back along the corridor towards the shop.

Ava grimaced and put her hand over her mouth in an attempt to stifle a giggle she couldn't hold back. Her laughter was infectious and made Henry feel more relaxed than he had since returning to England. There would be a time to talk rent increases – that had to be done. But all he could think about was having some time alone with Ava. He hadn't lied when he said her suggestion of a walk was the best he had heard in a long time. And he didn't want anything to spoil that.

Chapter Seventeen

When they reached Critters' Cottage, Ava turned to Henry. The sight of him in his classically styled suit, pushing her "Princess" black Pashley bike up the gravel path, made her smile. 'You didn't have to push my bike for me, but thank you.'

'You're most welcome, my lady.' Henry faltered. 'Sorry, I meant because of … I didn't mean …' Embarrassment coloured his cheeks as he positioned the bike next to the porch and kicked down the stand.

Ava screwed up her nose. 'It's fine. I knew what you meant.'

The awkward moment having passed, Henry smiled.

Ava invited him to follow her into the porch. Ducking to avoid the lintel, he wiped his feet on the paw-print welcome mat and began removing his shoes.

'Oh, blimey, keep them on. Really, it's fine. Myrtle never takes her paws off, but I still let her in!' Regretting the obscure response, Ava returned her attention to unlocking the door, looking for the distraction of the dog as she opened it.

'That's funny. Myrtle normally comes to greet me.' Ava looked at Henry, concern in her eyes, which changed to relief as the spaniel sauntered out of the lounge. Spotting Henry, Myrtle increased her pace, her claws tapping against the flagstone floor in a frenzy of excitement as Henry bent to say hello.

'Myrtle, you scared me!' Ava shook her head. 'She's been acting so strangely lately.'

Leading Henry and the excited dog into the living room, Ava couldn't help but think how shabby it looked. She hadn't altered any of the decoration since her mum's passing. She kept it tidy, but it had been rustic to start with and not in a trendy way. As she gestured for Henry to take a seat on her mum's floral sofa, Ava realised her sketchbook was on the coffee table, her drawing of Myrtle visible. Before she could move it, Henry picked it up.

'Still drawing? It's a great likeness.'

Ava took the pad, flipping the front over to close it, embarrassed at Henry seeing her work, and the memory of the sketchbook she knew she still had, full of drawings of him she'd made during some of the long hours they had spent alone in the woods. 'Not really, just the odd scribble.'

'That looks much more than a scribble to me. You always were talented.' Henry smiled.

Talented. Ava's cheeks turned pink at the compliment; she hadn't thought of herself in that way for a long time. She tucked the sketchbook out of the way in a pile of papers and magazines, stacked at the end of the sofa.

Thanking him, she decided she needed a moment for the flush in her cheeks to dissipate. 'I'll … just get sorted, but I won't be long. Are you OK waiting with Myrtle?' Ava gestured for him to take a seat.

'Of course.' Henry slipped off his jacket, revealing broad shoulders and defined muscles in a waistcoat and white fitted shirt, before sitting down.

Ava tried not to stare. Having avoided Dapplebury House, to allow him time and space after his father's death, she wanted to show Henry she was still there as a friend if he needed one. Admiring his muscles wasn't supposed to be part of the plan. Regaining her senses, she headed upstairs.

Having put up her hair, Ava considered the idea of changing into jeans, but with Henry in a suit, walking in her navy, daisy-print skater dress and black ankle boots seemed more fitting. Once in the grounds of Dapplebury House, they could stick to the cleared paths and avoid the thicket and brambles. She checked her make-up, and tried to steady her pulse that had been racing since the reality of having Henry Bramlington in her living room had started to sink in. It wasn't his title that was playing with her mind, but the glint in his eyes and his warm, genuine smile, that she had always been drawn to. That, and the memory of how much she once wanted him. Ava shook her head. *That was a long time ago.*

Trotting back downstairs, attempting to look casual, Ava's curiosity was piqued as she heard Henry on the phone. His voice was hushed, but there was no doubt from his tone that he was angry. She couldn't discern much of what was said, but from the occasional word it seemed Henry wanted more time and it all had something to do with someone called Dixon. It wasn't a name she recognised. *And time for what?* She couldn't make it out. Reaching the final stair, she paused before stepping hesitantly into the hallway.

Peering around, Ava could see Henry, still sitting on the sofa, the angle at which he held his phone meant he couldn't see her. The tension in his posture was evident, and she wondered if she ought to go back upstairs. Whatever the conversation was about, it was clear he never intended her to hear it. Myrtle was sitting next to his black leather brogues, her head cocked to one side as she watched him. Despite the distraction of the telephone call, Henry placed his hand reassuringly on the back of the dog's head, stroking her. Myrtle appeared to appreciate the gesture, before spotting Ava and barking. Henry turned as Ava snapped back into action, attempting to look as if she hadn't been eavesdropping.

'I'll be in touch.' Henry pressed to end the call before looking at Ava.

The haunted look in his eyes removed all the bluster she had prepared in her I-didn't-hear-anything stance, and she let out a breath. 'Is everything all right?'

Henry sat forward, his forearms on his thighs as he lowered his head. He looked defeated. With Henry's attention elsewhere, Myrtle jumped up to make herself comfortable in the armchair, circling and nudging at the cushion with her paw before slumping down.

Unsure what to do or say, Ava took the seat next to Henry.

His knuckles were white as he wrung his hands, and she could see the tick of tension in his jaw.

Turning to her, he held her gaze before speaking. 'Not really, but I am going to do all I can to make it right.'

Ava nodded, still unsure what to say.

'You believe me, don't you? No matter what people say about me, I want you to know … to always remember that.'

'Yes.' Ava didn't know what he was referring to, but at that moment, seeing the vulnerability in his expression, she felt she could promise him anything.

'You know me, Ava. The real me. I haven't seen you in over a decade, and you're probably the only person that actually knows me at all. How crazy does that sound? And while you know I never wanted all of this'—he gestured to his suit and cufflinks—'you know how I feel about the land, the woods, the heritage of that. That's what's in my blood. Not the title and the pretence—'

'Henry, it's OK. I know. I know all of that. I do.' Ava wanted to reassure him; without hesitation, she slipped her hand over his.

Henry looked at her, his green eyes darker than she had ever seen them.

She bit her lip, a wave of desire surging through her as she became his single focus. She swallowed. His gaze slipped to her mouth before his eyes met hers once more. She felt the quickening of her pulse throughout her body and leaned in, inching slowly … until their lips met.

The feeling of his lips welcoming hers, made her want more. She fought back images of the last time they had kissed: the goosebumps she felt despite the heat of the day, their skin, wet from their swim, touching as they shared explorative kisses; an intense longing for more. She'd thought about this moment for a long time.

Opening her eyes and bringing herself back to the present, Ava leaned back, just a bit. Henry offered her a lopsided, flirtatious smile, while his desire-filled eyes held all kinds of promises. She smiled back. The Henry before her was every bit a grown man and they were no longer children about to be caught and chastised.

Henry sighed, before speaking. 'Ava, I'm sorry. I shouldn't ha—'

Realising he was misinterpreting her pause, she stopped his words with a kiss. She didn't want the moment to end; if he spoke about what he should or shouldn't do, if they applied rational thought, then the spell might be broken. Holding on to his loosened tie, Ava pulled him towards her, pressing her lips more firmly to his. He responded, meeting her kisses with his own, as his hands moved around her waist, and up her back. With a single movement, he removed the clip from her hair, sending her auburn curls tumbling around her shoulders and releasing the fresh, clean scent of her shampoo.

Sliding his hand into her hair, he drew her closer. 'Ava.' Her name sounded ragged as he spoke it, sending sensations through her body.

Urged on by his obvious need for her, she responded, unbuttoning his waistcoat and removing his tie before kissing round the smooth line of his jaw and neck. Sliding her hand over the cotton of his shirt, she felt the honed body she had envisaged in her thoughts since being pressed against him on the grass. She swallowed before unbuttoning his shirt, and sliding her hand down the centre of his firm chest and stomach, meeting the fine dark hairs above his belt line. He inhaled, before shifting so that she could straddle him. Kissing her, his hands moved to the outside of her thighs, slipping beneath the cotton hem of her dress. Ava held her breath, anticipation building as his hands moved higher. She felt lost in the moment, her mind spinning with desire until a shout from the kitchen caused her to freeze.

'Ava!' The shout came again.

While Myrtle scampered from the comfort of the chair

towards the unexpected but familiar voice from the back door, Ava and Henry sprung apart.

'Oh my God, it's Mary!' Ava leapt up, her cheeks flushed.

Henry looked at her wide-eyed – his hands hurriedly attempting to do up his shirt buttons. 'Who's Mary?'

'What the …?' Before Ava could answer, Mary had reached the lounge, stopping and doing a double take as she took in the scene before her. Myrtle wagged her tail in an effort to get her attention.

Henry pulled a cushion into his lap.

A look of confusion flicked across Mary's face before she smiled. 'Oops sorry!'

Ava was sure the extent of the heat in her cheeks meant they were turning purple. She pulled the hem of her dress down and pushed her hands through her hair, attempting to regain her equilibrium enough to speak. Her mind spun as she tried to assimilate what might have been with the situation she now found herself in. *So much for not being caught!* Ava looked from Mary to Henry. He was clearly coping with the turn of events so much better than she was. While her mind was in chaos, he sat with a bemused grin tugging at his lips – still red from the fact they had been thoroughly kissing her just moments before.

'Mary this is Hen … Lord Henry … I mean Bramlington … Bramlington Henry … Oh Lord! I am making a mess of this!' Ava buried her head in her hands.

Henry laughed and looked at Mary. 'Henry. Just Henry is fine. I would normally stand up to shake hands but …'

'Not a good time? I get it.' Mary giggled before backing slightly out of the room.

'Oh, God! Let's go into the kitchen.' Mortified at the whole situation playing out before her, Ava took Mary by the arm and led her towards the kitchen, glancing over her shoulder and raising her eyes to the ceiling at Henry as she went.

Once away from the chemistry-charged atmosphere of

the living room, Ava pulled Mary closer to her, her voice an urgent whisper. 'What are you doing here?'

'I could ask you the same.' Mary matched Ava's tone, wiggling her eyebrows before continuing. 'And with the newly crowned Lord Hotlington. You bloody dark horse you.' Mary giggled.

Ava ignored her, deciding now wasn't the time for explanations about Henry. 'I live here, what are you doing here?'

Mary pulled the note Ava had scribbled before leaving the shop from her pocket and unfolded it. 'You never leave the shop during business hours unless I force you to. I popped down to speak to you, read this and thought there must be something wrong. "I won't be long. It's a beautiful day for a walk!" It sounded too cheery. I thought it was a coded message or something. A plea for help, maybe.'

'What? Why? Nobody does that.' Ava looked at Mary, deciding it was best not to ask where she might have got such a notion from. 'Besides, I'm always taking Myrtle for a walk.'

'Yes! At normal-people-are-still-asleep-o'clock, not two hours before closing – mid sorting stock. It's not like you. This'—Mary gestured back towards the lounge—'is all so … not like you! I mean Ava you were … with Lord Hot—'

Henry coughed, making his presence known. They both spun to see him standing in the doorway, his shirt buttoned, tie and waistcoat back in place, looking unflustered, and in Ava's opinion, as she noticed his still ruffled hair, thoroughly gorgeous. Realising she and Mary were both staring at him – gaping like a pair of guppy fish as Flo would put it – Ava broke the silence.

'Yes … Lord Hot—' She stopped, giving Mary an admonishing look for putting words into her muddled mind that were all too ready to tumble out. 'Henry and I were about to walk the dog.' Ava looked at Myrtle as if she might corroborate her words and provide a plausible alibi.

Henry folded his arms, looked at Myrtle and then at Ava. 'I think she's pregnant.'

Mary gasped, putting her hand to her mouth, before looking pointedly in Ava's direction.

Ava put her hand protectively over her definitely not pregnant stomach. 'Not me! You don't mean me, do you?' Instantly wishing she hadn't added the ridiculous question to her statement when her being pregnant would have required a miracle, Ava cringed.

Henry beckoned Myrtle to him, who obliged happily. 'I mean this one. I think she's pregnant. I was going to mention it when you came downstairs but—'

'You got distracted?' Mary suggested having clearly found her voice.

Not by what you're thinking, Ava thought, remembering the phone call Henry received.

Henry stroked along the dog's abdomen; Myrtle wriggled with excitement at receiving his attention.

'You said she hadn't been herself. My guess, seeing her today, and comparing her to the bitches I've seen at our kennels, is that she's pregnant.'

'Myrtle? How?' Mary looked at Ava, her expression a mix of shock and confusion.

'Really? And you're the animal expert!' Ava looked from Mary to Henry, her mind still trying to process the information. 'Has Granger not been done?'

Henry stopped stroking the dog and raised his eyebrows. 'He's a stud dog.'

'Who's Granger?' Mary asked.

Ava ignored the question. Her mind was trying to catch up with the possibility that Myrtle could be pregnant. The dogs had often wandered from the path she walked to explore the woods, sometimes being gone for twenty or more minutes. *Would they have had time? Wait ...* 'But he's retired.'

'Yes, that makes him old, not incapable.' Henry stood up.

Mary looked between the two of them. 'She asks again, who's Granger?'

Henry walked to the table and touched the top of a chair. 'Do you mind?'

Ava gestured that it was fine for him to take a seat and turned automatically to put the kettle on.

'Granger is one of my family's stud dogs. A chocolate Labrador whose pedigree you can trace back for generations.' Henry spoke with an amused tone, as he settled himself at the table.

Mary whistled, taking the seat next to him. 'Go, Myrtle, you minx!'

Ava couldn't believe that both Mary and Henry seemed to find the prospect amusing. 'But Myrtle was all grown up when I got her. I've never owned one puppy, let alone a whole litter.' Ava prepared a tray, with a pot of tea, three cups and matching saucers, a jug of milk and a bowl of sugar and took it to the table.

As she sat and went to speak, Henry's phone rang. He excused himself to the back garden to answer it. Myrtle followed in close pursuit.

Ava attempted to lean over far enough so that she could peer out of the window without being spotted. But her attempt to fathom any clues as to the nature of the call was scuppered; distracting her, Mary tugged on her arm and drew her in closer.

'Yes?' Ava swallowed, she wasn't sure she was prepared for questions about her and Henry, or that she wanted to share memories of their times in the woods with anyone else, even Mary.

'Is it the fact Lord Hotlington is here or the prospect of Myrtle being pregnant that has made you decide it's a teapot and best china occasion?' With that, she burst into giggles.

Ava looked at the tray and couldn't help herself, giggling too, at the obscure sight before them; teabag tea made in a mismatch of mugs was their norm. She couldn't recall the last time she used her mum's best china, and yet there it was, sat primly on a tray before them. 'I have no idea. It seemed like the thing to do.' As she recovered herself and wiped the tears from her eyes, she looked at Mary. 'In all seriousness, I am worried. Myrtle is my baby, my only family now. What if anything goes wrong? I can't imagine what I'd do if—'

Mary reached across the table and took Ava's hand. 'You've got me, and you'll see, Myrtle will be fine, and you'll be fine. If you have any issues, you've got connections to help you – a vet and a team of volunteers all used to caring for animals. And don't forget you know more than you think. You've helped or at least seen your mum raise fledgelings, badger and fox cubs, hoglets … and more, I'm sure. Wild or domestic, the pregnancy and birthing thing is not so different. And there's Gino.'

At the mention of his name and the memory of what his wish had been, and her determination to help him fulfil it, Ava's cheeks coloured.

'And I'll be here,' Henry interjected.

Ava and Mary turned in unison as Henry walked back towards the table.

'I won't walk away from this responsibility. I'll come to appointments with you, pay for anything you need, and, of course, that includes the vet's bills.'

Mary's eyes boggled.

Ava nodded, smiling at Henry. 'Thank you. I knew we could depend on you.' In all honesty, Ava hadn't even got as far as considering any such thing, but Henry seemed to need reassurance that she believed he wouldn't run away and she was happy to give it to him.

Mary paused, teaspoon hovering above the teapot, as she looked between them, her expression incredulous. 'You do both know it's the dog who's pregnant, don't you?'

Ava averted her gaze from Henry's. 'Of course.' She

attempted to laugh, but even she didn't recognise the too-light sound that escaped her constricted throat.

Henry coughed, sat down and set about pouring milk into the cups. Thanking him, Ava thought of the moments before Mary had walked in on them, and wondered if she would have stopped to be careful, or if Henry had come prepared. He'd said she was the only person who knew him and yet, it occurred to her, that she had no idea what he'd done during his absence from Dapplebury. It was true there was so much they shared, but undeniably there was also the void of time between them.

Now, at least, Myrtle had given them a reason to spend time together. Ava could seize her moment, as she originally intended when she'd asked him along for a walk, and get to know the new Lord Bramlington. And not just in the physical sense – though that prospect remained tantalisingly tempting as she recalled the touch of his hands upon her skin and his firm body beneath hers.

The Tea having been poured, Mary raised her cup, her pinky finger at an exaggerated jaunty angle, causing Ava to give her a kick under the table.

Undeterred, Mary said, 'Pedigrees are all well and good, but they're not always healthy. Adding in a mix of something new can be a good thing … Look at the royal family – even they've seen sense.' She winked at Ava before adding, 'To your grandpuppies. Unexpected but on the way!'

Ava took a sip of her too-hot tea. 'Let's get confirmation from the vet first.' Feeling grateful that, with all that was whirring through her mind, she had said something sensible, she looked at Henry and added, 'Let's definitely not tell your mother about this!'

Chapter Eighteen

Ava took the keys from her bag and unlocked the shop door. Mary followed her inside, precariously carrying two takeaway cups. After the night she'd had, Ava welcomed the smell of the strong coffee emanating from them. Since taking Myrtle to visit the vet, Ava's head had been whirring with all the things she needed to consider concerning the dog's health.

'Flipping heck, they're hot!' Mary put the cups down on the counter and shook her glowing fingers. 'But, I thought you might need it. I know I do.'

Ava picked up the post and relocked the door to avoid customers trying to drop off donations or coming in for a browse before she was ready. 'Thanks. Sorry, I forgot to ask. How was last night?' Ava thought about the telephone call Mary had received. There were scant details but enough to know there was an incident involving a deer.

'Well let's just say if it had been Christmas, we'd have made the papers.'

'Really, why?'

'Think antlers and garden lights!'

'Oh. Was the deer all right?'

'Yes. A couple of apples for distraction and a sharp knife and he was off into the night. Talking of going off into the night, Quill Smith and his pals are in the pre-release pen. It's been pretty mild, so we'll be releasing them soon.'

Ava turned on the strip lights that flashed and buzzed into action. 'Isn't it still early for that?'

'No, they're healthy and the temperature's right. With the hedgies moving on we'll lower expenses and gain the room for emergencies.'

Ava always liked to hear of the animals being released back into the wild and made a mental note to ensure they recorded the event. The charity's new website was being developed in the skilful hands of one of the volunteers, and she hoped it would provide a forum for sharing such events. 'Well, I'll miss hearing how Quill Smith is doing, but I can't deny I'm all for lower expenses.'

Ava picked up her much needed coffee and headed towards the back of the shop. While they had tea and regular coffee-making facilities of their own, they determined long ago that some days required a coffee hit in the form of a double shot espresso that only the local café could provide.

Drink in hand, Mary followed, while Myrtle stayed to have a sniff around.

'I'm sorry I couldn't come with you to see Bill yesterday. Did Lord Hot—'

Ava looked at Mary, a smile in her eyes. 'Henry came with us, yes. It was very kind of him. He must have so many other things to be concentrating on right now, and it wasn't like the vet told us anything he didn't already know.

'She has to have limited exercise, no rough play, and, at this stage, ten per cent more food. I feel so bad. How could she be seven weeks pregnant and I didn't notice? What kind of owner am I?' Ava leaned against the sorting table and picked up her coffee, inhaling the strong aroma, before taking a sip that burnt her tongue. 'Gestation is only around nine weeks for goodness' sake!'

'Don't beat yourself up over it. Some women give birth without knowing they're pregnant.'

'Really?'

'Yes, and if you don't believe me ask Flo. She spent a long time telling me about a programme she'd seen on TV – I think she might have meant it as a warning for me, or something. Anyway, the thing is the women and their babies were fine, and Myrtle will be too. And now you know, she can get all the love, support and treatment she needs.'

'Henry said I could supplement her diet with cottage cheese

or sardines, and maybe some cabbage or broccoli. Honestly, that seems like I'd be punishing her.'

'Ha! I'm not sure she'd see it the same way.' Mary drank her coffee, looking at the noticeboard, before turning back to Ava. 'Whatever you supplement with, you just need to get the balance right. Fat puppies will be hard to deliver, and you don't want that for her.'

Myrtle sauntered through from the shop, and Ava looked at her big brown eyes and button nose. Even with guidance from Bill, the vet, and having Henry's support and advice, she was feeling the responsibility of keeping Myrtle and her brood healthy.

Mary put her cup down and beckoned the dog to her. 'Anyway, you know I'm not only here to check on Myrtle. Though, of course, I'm excited to hear your news. Congratulations Miss Myrtle, and don't worry, I will make sure your mummy has you spayed after this.' Mary looked from the dog to Ava.

'OK, you can say it. You told me so. But when I got her she was so fragile and ... and well, I obviously never thought this would happen.' Ava gestured to Myrtle and took a tentative sip of her coffee.

Myrtle looked between Ava and Mary, seemingly aware that they were talking about her; the picture of innocence.

Mary rubbed behind Myrtle's ears, before looking at Ava, her eyebrows raised. 'The thing is, as your friend, I feel I should point out that playing with a stud is a risky business, that can, as Miss Myrtle will attest, result in pregnancy!'

Ava put her hand over her mouth while she attempted to swallow her coffee before she sprayed it across the room. 'I am aware of that. Thank you.'

Mary grinned and continued, 'And talking of studs. I left you at the Italian night, all rosy cheeks and fluttering eyelashes, with Gino, and then, the next thing I know I find you in your cottage entangled with Lord Hotlington. About which I have oh so many questions I don't know where to begin, so I am going to stop talking and you can start!' Mary pretended to zip up her mouth and raised her eyebrows expectantly.

Ava shook her head and moved the donation bags left on the floor from the previous day into the appropriate pens. She needed to move the conversation away from the subject of Gino before she gave anything away, but equally, she didn't want to discuss her relationship with Henry. 'Don't you have work to do? Aren't there sick and injured animals just crying out for your attention? I, for one, have a shop to open!' Ava took out her keys and rattled them. 'You know if I don't open on time, it will encourage fly-tipping. And we all know nobody leaves their best donations on the doorstep, especially not on a day when the local tip is closed. The dump it and run brigade will rejoice at the opportunity to leave their tat unseen.' Ava went to the safe and took out the float; on top of it was a note from Flo saying all was well when she closed up, and that the man from the antique shop had dropped an envelope off for her.

'That's a brilliant excuse but neither Myrtle nor I are going to let this go. We need answers.'

Ignoring Mary, Ava pulled the envelope out from underneath the money, turning it over in her hands.

'You all right?'

'Yes … I'm fine. Just intrigued.' Ava began to open the envelope. 'I took some frames to the antique dealer, and he's dropped this round.'

'Is that unusual? Don't they normally correspond by letter? I rather hoped they still used ink and a quill pen?' Mary laughed before looking at Ava and adjusting her tone. 'How do they normally get back to you?'

'Normally I just pop back and they tell me an evaluation. This must be—'

Ava pulled a note and photograph from the envelope and did a double take as she tried to process what she was seeing. Recognising the smiling faces of the two women pictured, each with a child in their arms, her heart skipped a beat and she felt a flurry of palpitations in her chest. 'It's …' Her words trailed off, her mind still attempting to make sense of the image in her hand.

It wasn't who was in the picture she had trouble comprehending; it was why they were being pictured together. She recognised her mum and, of course, herself – not only from her mop of red curls but also from the toy in her dimpled hands. *Raspberry Rabbit.* With a cheeky grin showing four milk teeth, she imagined her age to be about one, while the dark-haired baby, wrapped in a blue crocheted blanket, in Lady Bramlington's arms, must surely be Henry. Both women looked relaxed, their heads tilted together, their expressions happy.

Mary put down her coffee. 'Well, don't keep me in suspense. You're stringing it out longer than one of those talent show hosts. *It's …?*' Mary added dramatic emphasis to the final word as she spoke.

'Confusing,' Ava muttered as she scanned the note: "This was behind the mount in one of the frames. Thought you would want it. Exquisite pieces by the way. I suggest you go for auction, rather than via the shop. Let me know".

'Ava, seriously, what is it?' Mary went to Ava's side and looked at the picture. 'Is that you and your—'

'Mum. Yes.'

'And is that—'

'Lady Bramlington.' Ava attempted to gather her thoughts. 'And Henry. But I don't understand. This picture was in a frame donated by Ted. Why would Ted have it?'

'Look, there's something written on the back.' Mary took the picture from Ava, turning it over.

'Best friends and babies,' they read aloud in unison.

'What?' Ava took the picture back from Mary. 'What do you think it means?'

Mary looked at Ava. 'Well I'm no detective, but I'd say it means your mum and Lady Bramlington were best friends. Either that or you and Henry were, but that seems less likely as you both look tiny.'

Ava felt heat rise in her cheeks. She knew she and Henry became best friends, but as babies? No. Theirs was a friendship formed in secret in the woods. The picture was perplexing. 'But my mum never mentioned ... You know what she was like about even going on their land. And the only time I ever recall meeting Lady Bramlington she was cross, no, bloody furious at ...' Realising she was going to reveal too much about her past with Henry, Ava corrected herself. 'Bloody furious at me trespassing.'

She looked back at the picture. Her mum and Lady Bramlington were clearly content in each other's company as they held their babies on their laps. Her mum had never mentioned knowing Lady Bramlington, and yet the photograph was discovered in a frame, the fading of the picture suggesting it had once been on display. *So it had once been a treasured memory to someone. But who, Ted?* 'If they were once best friends, then something happened to alter that, but what?'

'Oh my God, you're his love child!' Mary gasped, her hand going to her mouth.

'Ted's?' Ava looked at her incredulous.

'No, not Ted's, Lord Bramlington's. Lady Bramlington found out and'—Mary's eyes went wide as if a sudden realisation dawned upon her—'which would make you and Henry—'

'No! It definitely doesn't.' Ava pushed away an image of her straddling Henry on her mum's floral sofa. 'Have you seen my hair? My complexion?'

'Yes!' Mary dropped her shoulders, the deflation of her fanciful idea reflected in her demeanour.

'All very much from my dad!' Ava pulled at one of her curls that sprung back into place as she released it. 'Connor Flynn might have died when I was two, but his genes very much live on in me. Believe me, I've seen the pictures.'

Mary looked at the photograph. 'Ah bugger, so you're not the secret heir to the late Lord Bramlington then? You're not going to step up, claim your inheritance and save the village.'

'No, I'm really not.'

Hearing the bell ring as the shop door was opened, Myrtle went to investigate.

'That'll be Flo. She's got the spare keys.' Jumping into action, Ava pushed the photograph and the note back in the envelope. 'I'll put the kettle on.'

Mary lowered her voice, 'OK, but what's your theory then?'

Ava filled the kettle with water before putting it on its base and clicking it on. 'I don't have one. But I'll start with Ted.'

'If that's about that photograph, Ted'll be no use to you.' Flo looked round the corner.

Mary looked at her, eyes wide. 'How do you—?'

'I asked what was in the envelope. You said always check what people bring in, no electrical, no previously used safety equipment, no videos, no nightwear or fancy dress without a safety standard. Definitely no underwear and to ask about Gift Aid e-v-e-r-y time.'

'I was talking about donations, not private correspondence.'

'I know, but best to be thorough.' Flo winked.

Mary took a mug from the mug tree, taking over the tea making since Ava stood motionless in the wake of Flo's comments.

'So you know what's inside?' Ava asked.

'I know it's a photograph, donated by accident amidst a set of fancy gold frames. When he hinted at the value of the frames, I put two and two together. It had to be the donation in Ted's name. Am I right?'

'Yes.'

'Bingo! Miss Marple has nothing on me!' Flo giggled.

'But what do you mean in Ted's name?' Ava asked, attempting to keep Flo's mind on track.

Flo folded her arms. 'Well, it wasn't Ted who brought the donation in, it was him, in disguise. He had me fooled for a while but—'

'Ted in disguise?' Ava was getting more confused by the minute.

'No!' Flo laughed, unfolding her arms and slipping off her coat. 'Lord, hold up, he said I could call him Henry. Oi get me, hobnobbing with the Bramlingtons.'

Ava went to speak, but Mary interjected.

'So the donation was from Henry, but he Gift-Aided it from Ted, why would he do that?' Mary raised an eyebrow at Ava, suspicion clearly on her mind, before looking back to Flo.

'I told you he was in disguise.' Flo walked through to the back office, hung up her coat, left her bag and walked back towards the two dumbfounded women, a wide grin on her face. 'Undercover boss and all that. Checking out the local businesses. He had a beard, long hair, nothing like when he was here yesterday.'

Ava pushed away an unhelpful image of how Henry looked when she saw him yesterday. 'So the donation was from Lord Bramlington?'

'Yes – but I can call him Henry. And when I asked him if he would Gift Aid them'—Flo looked pointedly at Ava—'he didn't want to give the game away and said they were from Ted, his uncle.'

'Ted's his uncle?' Mary asked in surprise. 'My God, this is turning into one of those crazy chat shows where everyone's got a secret, and it turns out they're all related!' She poured the boiling water into Flo's mug and finished making her tea, barely taking her eyes from Flo.

Ava reached for her coffee. Her mind was too muddled

with everything that had gone on in the last twenty-four hours to take this all in.

'No! Ted's not Henry's uncle.' Flo laughed.

'But you said—'

'I said, he said, he was – as part of his disguise. It's very simple. I don't know why you two aren't keeping up.' Flo tutted and shook her head, picked up her mug of tea and began to walk back towards the shop. 'Come on, Myrtle, you and I best get the shop open. I think these two have feathers in their heads today!'

'Well, that clears up one bit of the mystery. The donation was from Henry. But the whole disguise thing. That's a bit odd, isn't it?' Mary pondered.

Ava thought about seeing Henry in the woods and knew that the beard and long hair hadn't been a disguise, at least not in the sense that Flo thought it was. As for knowing he had donated the frames, Ava was unsure if her mind felt any clearer from knowing that fact. She drank down the last of her coffee. 'Do they make a triple shot coffee in the café at all? I think I might need something stronger.'

'Yes. But wait, what if Henry donated the picture on purpose? Maybe he wanted you to find it,' Mary continued, seemingly unwilling to let the subject go.

'No, that makes no sense. I looked at the frames and I missed it. If he wanted me to find it, he'd have left it more prominently or … or just shown me.'

'OK, so you need to find out what Henry knows.'

Ava nodded, unsure that Henry would be any wiser on the subject than she was. If he knew about the connection between their parents, he had never mentioned it. She had already been through her mum's things and found nothing, and that meant the only person left to ask was Lady Bramlington herself. *And that won't be happening any time soon.*

'Or you could go public, ask around. Flo obviously hasn't

102

seen the picture, or she would have said something. You could show her, or maybe Pauline—'

Ava felt a cold shiver down her spine, her eyes flicking to the picture of her mum on the noticeboard. 'No. I'd like to keep this between us, for now, if you don't mind. Whatever the reason, my mum kept her connection to the Bramlingtons from me. Until I know why I'd rather not go public.'

'An excuse to go undercover with Henry!' Mary winked.

Chapter Nineteen

Henry strode out onto the driveway and checked his watch. He had three hours before his meeting with Dermot Dixon. With tension pulsing through his body, running seemed the preferable option to going back over the proposal he had spent long hours preparing. As the letters alerting tenants to the future rent increases had already gone out – Mrs Jenkins was nothing if not proficient – Henry knew he had to get phase two of his plans underway. Securing a deal with Dixon meant he'd be able to reassure the people of Dapplebury that the increases would be balanced against plans for future jobs, affordable housing and, ultimately, continued revenue for the shops and other establishments.

Seeing Granger approaching, a glint in his deep, brown eyes, Henry smiled. Whenever he felt at his most alone in his battle to save Dapplebury House, the estate and village, Granger was there to offer silent support and companionship.

'You're a good boy, aren't you?'

The Labrador welcomed the pat on his flank, his tail wagging.

Henry bent and checked the laces on his trainers, pulling them in a little tighter, before standing; the chill morning air was refreshing.

Trying to clear his mind, he set off, the gravel crunching under his feet until he turned and headed into the woods. Granger followed closely behind. Since his arrival back home – *home*; the word was beginning to feel right – Henry had hacked down some of the overgrown brambles, and started to make his mark on the land once more, with trails forming where he ran. As well as a means to keep fit and release his frustrations, the exercise served as an escape from the confines of Dapplebury House, and the watchful eyes of his mother, and Mrs Jenkins.

Welcoming the seclusion, he wondered how he had been able to exist in Los Angeles, one of the busiest cities in the United States. Of course, he'd never planned to live in Los Angeles. Having obtained a Geography degree from the University of Cambridge he'd spent a year travelling – a trip inspired by his refusal to connect with the reality of his situation and the expectations of his parents. He never imagined his journey would lead him to volunteering in Sri Lanka where he discovered a passion for meditation, self-healing, hypnotherapy and wellness. Or that a connection made during that time would see him turning his passion into a career as he accepted a job opportunity offered in Los Angeles. It all seemed so far removed from life in the village of Dapplebury, in the south of England, and in his youth and determination to forge his own path, he had welcomed that.

Trees flicking past him as he ran, Henry could hear his own ragged breathing as well as that of Granger, who despite his age, kept up with the pace. Thinking about his looming meeting, Henry's mind whirred with the telephone calls, emails and conversations he had entered into with Dermot Dixon.

The man, who Henry recently discovered had the stout build and tenacious personality of a terrier, had done his homework. When he contacted Henry in Los Angeles, he'd been full of talk of taking the responsibility from his hands, and of turning Dapplebury House into luxury apartments. The deal he was offering was attractive; his approach and timing impeccable. Barely a day passed since he'd been back, that Henry hadn't been grateful for refusing to enter into any official agreements until after his father's death. Well, now he had passed on and Henry was ready to make a deal. It just wasn't the deal that Dermot Dixon was expecting.

'Wish me luck, Granger! We need this to work,' Henry panted. He was all too aware that if his negotiations didn't go to plan, he risked reneging on his promise to his father, losing Dapplebury House and the estate. And then there was Ava. No matter what the outcome of his meeting, he risked losing her. She loved the grounds of Dapplebury House every bit as much as he did, but without being able to tell her how desperate the situation was, would she be able to forgive what he was about to do? Henry picked up his pace and fisted his hands, his nails digging into his palms as he ran.

He had to have faith that she would understand. He couldn't contemplate how different life in Dapplebury would be without her as a friend. *Friend?* Who was he kidding? He wanted them to be so much more than that. Since their recent trip to the vet with Myrtle, he frequently recalled the way Ava chewed her lower lip when she was worried or unsure, the crease of her nose when she was curious; her smile that reached her eyes when she was happy. And her desire-filled eyes that connected deep within him when she had thanked him as they said their goodbyes. It all filled him with a hope he didn't dare to entertain until he sorted the estate and dealt with the ramifications of the deal he was about to make.

Shaking his head did nothing to push the image of Ava from his mind. *Stay focused!* Zipping up his jacket as the breeze gusted through the trees causing their boughs to creak and their leaves to shudder in whispers, Henry ran on. Despite his best efforts, he recalled his all too brief moment with Ava at Critters' Cottage, before Mary arrived and before Myrtle became their priority. He remembered the intoxicating scent of Ava's hair as it had fallen around her shoulders, the touch of her soft, smooth skin; and how he had wanted more, so much more. The memory caused a longing he couldn't remember ever having for any other woman, and an ache in his chest he was sure wasn't the result of his run.

Coming through a clearing in the trees, he reached the lake and paused to regain his composure, his hands on the taut muscles of his thighs. Just moments behind, Granger followed, slumping down on the grass, his dripping tongue hanging to the side of his mouth, his rapid panting causing his whole body to quake. Henry crouched to pat him, before looking up across the murky depths of the water. Recalling Ava's words when they had stood there together – *This isn't irreversible. It's just neglect* – Henry knew she was right. But everything came with a price, and he didn't yet have the money to pay.

Henry growled in frustration, throwing a stone into the water and watching the ever-increasing circles spreading on the surface in its wake. Having worked tirelessly to come up with an alternative to put to Dixon, all Henry could do now was hope; hope the deal would come to fruition and hope Ava would understand, and forgive him.

Chapter Twenty

'It's not the finest food, that's all I'm saying. Only the French say French cuisine is the finest. Ask anyone, and they will tell you, the honest flavours of Italian will win out every time. Traditional recipes handed down over generations. We respect our ingredients. We let them speak for themselves.'

As Gino had been speaking for a good ten minutes on the merits of Italian over French food, Ava wondered if he was actually going to let anything or anyone speak for themselves.

'You see, a meal to us is—'

'Gino!' Ava held up her hand. While she appreciated his passion, she feared how long he might go on if left to continue his rant.

'Yes?' Gino looked confused by the interruption.

'The point is, you can't host a French-themed night with you denigrating the star of the show – the French cuisine. Otherwise, you should have called your venture Around the World in one perfect cuisine and seven not so good ones!' Ava waved to the waitress and asked for the bill, before taking out her purse.

Gino slunk back into his seat, sighed and shook his head. 'So, you think it's too late to change the name?'

Ava noticed the teasing glint in his eyes and threw her napkin at him. 'What are you like?'

Gino picked the napkin up and placed it on his plate. 'The night will be a sell-out. You'll see. I'm a professional. Didn't I make the English night a success?'

'Fish and Chip Friday wasn't exactly a hard sell or the truest representation of English cuisine.'

'No. But it was popular. You can't deny it.'

Ava thought about the Friday night they had spent, enjoying fish and chips in the pub while listening to classic pop songs. 'No, I can't, but it does make me fear what you're offering for the French night.'

'Chef is taking the lead, offering traditional French cuisine.'

'That'll be nice.'

'Besides ... I can always offer an Italian alternative.'

'You're terrible.' Ava laughed, accepting the bill from the waitress with thanks.

'Hey, it's my turn to pay.' Gino reached across the table, but Ava pushed his hand away.

'No. It's definitely mine. Besides, next time Mary will be with us. I'm getting a good deal.' Ava shrugged her shoulders and placed cash on the table. 'It's a shame she had to work today.'

'Did she, really? I was worried she hadn't come because you told her what we—'

'No, really. She's taken some abandoned kittens to a local fosterer.'

'Kittens?'

'Yes, you'd be surprised how often people call about domestic strays and rescues. I guess they just want someone to help the animals and they know we won't ignore them. We do what we can, passing them on to the best place for them.' Ava stood up and slipped her fleece on. 'And remember, I promised I wouldn't say about the other.' She smiled at Gino, pleased that she had managed to keep her lips sealed, even though she and Mary usually shared everything.

'Good. Thank you.' Gino smiled, relief clear in his eyes. He stood to do up his jacket and followed Ava to the door as they chatted.

'Sorry, it's a bit of a rushed breakfast today. I've left Flo putting up a Mother's Day display. She offered, and while I normally do the displays, I was grateful.' Ava scrunched up her nose and shrugged her shoulders. 'I thought we should mark the weekend, before I get sorted with the French theme on Monday.'

As they stepped out onto the pavement, Gino took hold of Ava's hand, drawing her attention to him. 'If you don't want to be alone tomorrow, you can come to my house. You know my Mamma loves you.'

'Thank you, that's very kind, but really, I'll be fine.' Ava smiled, appreciating the kindness in Gino's eyes as much as his gesture.

Her mum had been gone eighteen months and Ava missed her everyday. Her second Mother's Day without her would be difficult, of course, but she also knew it was one day in the forever she faced without her. She felt the loss of her mum today, she'd feel it tomorrow and she knew it was a pain she'd still feel as she took her own final breath. Mother's Day might pass with little more than a numb feeling of emptiness while smelling a similar washing powder to her mum's on clothes donated to the charity shop, or hearing her mum's favourite song, could have her in floods of tears.

Flo had once told Ava that grief is as unpredictable as the sea, some days the waves come in gentle ripples, while others they rage with a force so wild it feels they might consume you; the secret, she said, was learning how to stay afloat. In the past eighteen months, with the help of her friends and the Flynn spirit that was very much alive inside of her, Ava had learnt that was true.

Gino released her hand, and the two of them walked side by side, towards the charity shop.

Ava took in the sight of the daffodils growing in planters outside the café. March was in full swing; the days were getting warmer, and spring was coming. There was a time of change ahead, and for the first time in a long time, she felt ready to embrace it. 'Besides, I have to stay home tomorrow, I have an expectant mum to look after. Myrtle needs me.'

'Of course, how is she doing? Taking it all in her four-legged stride?'

'She certainly is. She's looking rounder!'

'You haven't told her that, have you? I once made a similar comment to my eldest sister, and I'm lucky I lived to tell the tale.'

'Ha, of course not. A lady never wants to hear such a thing. She's on limited exercise, and she's not supposed to jump which is ... *What the*—!' Ava froze as she took in the sight before her.

'Oh no, isn't that ...?' Gino's eyes went wide.

'But I told Flo ... I gave her ... I don't even know where they ...' Ava closed her mouth, aware that she was no longer forming coherent sentences. Instead, she shook her head and looked bewildered at the display of sex toys in the charity shop window. It was something she never imagined she'd see, and something that was made so much worse by the fact that the only one of her instructions Flo seemed to have followed was to hang the sign she had left, prominently above the display. Ava's cheeks flushed as she read the words aloud, 'Treat yourself and relieve the tension this Mother's Day!' Ava put her hand to her forehead, wishing the ground would swallow her up. 'Oh, God!' She ran inside, Gino following.

'Quite a bold statement you've gone for this year!' He laughed.

Flo welcomed Ava with a broad smile. 'Aren't they wonderful?'

'No! They're really not.'

'But you said to go for it with a relax on Mother's Day theme.' Flo looked between Ava and Gino, clearly disappointed at their lack of enthusiasm.

'But I left yoga mats, detox books, calming CDs, not ... I mean ... where did you ...?' Ava decided she might not want to know where the offending objects came from and left the sentence hanging.

'They were donated this morning. Wasn't that great timing! They're so much more fun to look at than yoga mats and CDs.'

Gino burst out a giggle, resulting in an admonishing look from Ava as she tried to hold it together.

'Flo, do you know what they are?'

'Of course I do. I might be old, but I've not lost my marbles yet. I keep up with the latest trends. I read magazines. They're back massagers! And, how great is this? The woman that brought them in said that big one is suitable for in the shower, while that smaller one is handbag sized. Who'd have thought!'

'I never thought … Did you Ava?' Gino teased, while Flo continued.

'But my favourites are those shiny balls. They keep your fingers nimble – great for rheumatism if you move them around in your hand. Wait I'll show you—'

'No! Please don't,' Ava interjected.

'It's no bother. I thought about getting them to take along to Knit and Natter this week. They could all do with—'

On hearing that, Ava succumbed to the giggles she could feel building inside and joined Gino as they each let out a peal of laughter. Flo looked between them, clearly discombobulated by their reaction.

Attempting to regain her composure, Ava spoke, 'Bless you, Flo, and thank you for … this.' She gestured to the display. 'But the thing is—'

'They're all new, and Gift-Aided!'

Ava could tell Flo was proud of her achievement and didn't want to upset her. She had to handle this carefully, but while she was trying to think, Flo continued to speak.

'She'd bought them on impulse and then decided she was no Anastasia … Anastasia Steele. I'll admit, I don't know who that is, but she must be like Jane Fonda back in the day – she had us all in leotards and leg warmers, and wearing those things on your wrists.'

'Zip ties?' Gino suggested, mischief in his expression, earning him a punch on the arm from Ava.

'Sweatbands,' Flo corrected, looking between Gino and

Ava. 'Honestly, what did you two have for breakfast? I don't know what's so funny!'

Ava couldn't help herself and burst into another fit of the giggles. Gino leaned closer to Flo and whispered in her ear. Ava had no idea what he said, but judging by the shade of crimson Flo turned before she burst into laughter herself, Ava assumed she had been enlightened.

'Well, I never. Who'd have thought? Imagine if I'd taken them to Knit and Natter. And to think, she stood there nice as pie!' Tears ran down Flo's cheeks as she saw the funny side.

'I think we'd better remove them, don't you?' Ava managed, attempting to get her giggles under control. As she went to fetch a bag to dispose of them, her phone rang. Seeing it was Mary, Ava pressed to pick up the call, hoping to share what had happened. But before she could speak, Mary's voice came out in a rush.

'Ava, you need to come here now. I'm at the Lodge.' Her tone was insistent.

'What is it? Are you OK?'

'I am. But your boyfriend's not going to be. I am going to bloody kill him!'

'Boyfriend? Wh—'

'Lord Gitlington! There are some men here, surveying the land or something. Ava – he's going to sell it.'

'What?' Ava's head spun.

'Are you OK?' Gino's voice came from behind her.

She swung around. 'Gino, I need a lift to Critters' Lodge. Can you take me? I don't think I can ride my bike.' Her hands were shaking. Critters' Lodge was the heart of the charity, its rehabilitation and rehoming centre. Losing that would set them back decades, to a time when her mum did what she could at her cottage and often had to send animals on to other centres. She had to get there and find out what was going on.

Chapter Twenty-One

Mud splattered up the sides of the red metallic paint of Gino's Audi A3. Ordinarily, Ava would discourage him from driving so rapidly down the country lanes, but today the urgency in Mary's tone made her welcome the speed.

'There has to be a simple explanation. It doesn't seem like something the Bramlingtons would do. I'm sure there's been a mistake.' Gino gave Ava a brief smile before turning his attention back to the road.

His tone was reassuring, but Ava had an uneasy feeling about the whole situation and wrung her hands in her lap. It didn't seem like something the late Lord Bramlington would do, but Henry, how well did she really know him now? If he were acting under his mother's bidding, Ava didn't know what he was capable of. As they drove through the gates of Critters' Lodge, she undid her seatbelt, and was getting out of the car and heading towards the entrance before Gino had finished parking. Ava could see two official-looking men talking at the side of the building; presuming them to be party to whatever was going on she gave them a hard stare. She wanted to speak to Mary, and to establish some facts before speaking to them.

Having clearly been awaiting their arrival, Mary strode out of the door, drawing Ava's attention. For a person so rarely fazed, Ava couldn't help but think her friend looked flustered. The flush on her cheeks and neck was unsettling.

Taking Ava's arm, Mary led her to the door. 'Your boyfriend is selling this land!'

Ava looked over her shoulder to see if Gino was following. 'He's not my boyfriend, and we have a tenancy agreement.'

Mary nodded in the direction of the men Ava had glared at. 'Well, according to them, they're here to survey for development purposes.' Mary led the way inside.

Catching up, Gino followed.

Aware of her proximity to the treatment rooms, Ava felt her stomach flip. She needed to stay focused on the matter in hand. She tried to look directly ahead, but the smell of disinfectant, mixed with the aroma of sick animals, played with her senses and took her back to her childhood when her mum would bring injured animals home to their cottage. She swallowed.

'So Lord Gitlington, all sweet and helpful the other day is planning to sell the land from underneath us. He didn't mention that when he was promising to stick by you, did he?'

'Stick by Myrtle, not me,' Ava managed, her mind whirring.

'The charity won't survive, and these animals need us!' Mary's words were fuelled by anger and passion, reminding Ava that Mary had been her mum's apprentice. Reaching the office door, they went inside.

'Here, take a seat.' Pulling over the office chair, Mary encouraged Ava to sit down.

'Hasn't he been away? Perhaps he didn't know the lodge was here.' Gino shut the door behind them.

'Of course he knew. It's been here for years. It would have been here before he went away,' Mary hissed, as she fetched Ava a plastic cup of water from the cooler in the corner. 'Well, I'm not going to stand for it. Lord Snakelington might own this land but, as Ava said, we have an agreement to use it, and that means those men outside have no bloody right to be here!' Mary glanced in Ava's direction as if to check she was OK before heading for the door.

'Wait. What are you planning to do?' Gino held on to her arm.

'Hit them with a shot of tranquiliser?' Mary raised a defensive eyebrow at Gino, before pulling her arm free.

'Mary, listen to me. Use your head,' Gino implored.

Mary lowered her voice. 'Seriously, Gino, if you're not going to be on our side and use some of that Italian passion I know must be in there somewhere, then you can bugger off back to your car—'

'OK! OK!' Gino held up his hands and met her gaze. 'I'll help you get rid of them. But, we are not tranquillising them.'

Ava was grateful to hear Gino step in, applying some common sense, while she attempted to get herself together.

'So what's your plan, then?' Mary challenged.

Gino took a breath. 'We'll hose them!'

'What?' Ava couldn't believe what she was hearing, but as her body was trembling, she wasn't sure she would be able to stop them.

Mary faltered, looking at Gino, before smiling. 'Genius! Let's do it.'

As the door shut behind them and the room fell silent, Ava could hear the thud of her heartbeat and felt the prickling of sweat on her skin. She inhaled for the count of seven and exhaled for the count of eleven several times over, in an attempt to regain her equilibrium. Once she felt in greater control of her faculties, she stood and looked around the office with an increasing sense of achievement at having made it this far. She was inside Critters' Lodge.

The furniture, some she recognised as being selected by her mum, some new, was functional. The whiteboard on the wall was filled with information about the animals currently in care, reminding Ava why she was there. Mary was right, just as her mum had always been: the animals needed them and it was their job to care for them in a crisis.

Noticing the countdown to the launch of their new website, also on the board, Ava felt a new wave of determination. The loyal volunteers had come through for the charity, as they always did. They were applying their skills to the task – sorting through the newspaper clippings, creating the new website – working towards the imminent deadline. She couldn't let them down any more than she could let the animals down. *Publicity!* Publicity was what she needed, not only for the website but also for their current plight. Ava's pulse raced, as much from the post adrenalin rush of entering the lodge as her determination to put a stop to the sale of the land.

She hadn't been caught trespassing this time. The charity's claim to remain on Bramlington land was legitimate. They had long rented the site, albeit for what her mother had called a charitable discount, and they were not going to be ousted without a fight. Whatever Henry's reasons, selling the land from underneath them, and without explanation, was unforgivable.

'I've made it this far'—Ava looked at the picture of her mum hanging on the wall—'and I am not going anywhere without a fight!' With that, she put her hands on her hips. She felt empowered by the determination that coursed through her. Her relationship with the charity had, at times, been tumultuous, and while she was proud to keep her mother's legacy going, she often wondered whom she was doing it for. But standing in the office of Critters' Lodge she knew, this was her fight, and the Bramlingtons were not going to win.

Hearing a commotion outside, she rolled her eyes. Publicity for whatever tactics Mary and Gino were currently using to remove the surveyors from the land was not what she needed. She knew she would have to go outside and address the situation. Shooting the messengers, either with a tranquilliser or a hose, was not going to help their cause. She had to take control of the situation, remove the real trespassers and take on the orchestrator of their current situation. Henry. Ava looked at the door. She knew exactly what she had to do, and she knew the time was now. She just needed her legs to co-operate and move from where they were firmly rooted to the floor, to manoeuvre herself back out past the treatment rooms to do it.

Chapter Twenty-Two

Pacing the small back room of the village hall, Henry tried Ava's phone again. He could scarcely believe the turn of events. He had left his meeting just hours before, buoyed by the fact he'd reached, at least in theory, a solution that would give the village and the estate's dwindling funds a significant boost. It had all gone well. While nothing had been signed, he and Dixon had shaken hands on the deal. On both sides, there were checks and formalities to complete; a process that should have taken long enough for him to broach the subject with Ava and discuss the ramifications of his plans. Now it seemed she wouldn't speak to him.

Why, in the time it had taken him to drive home – albeit via a diversion to the family churchyard to share his thoughts on the meeting with his father – Dixon had taken it upon himself to send his men to Critters' Lodge, Henry had no idea. Ava's mum and her charity were treasured among the people of Dapplebury. Looking like the man about to destroy all that she had worked for was a hard place to come back from. And now, news of their actions had spread. As formal notifications of the rent increases had been received, Dixon's men had added fuel to the fire of discontent that was already simmering in the village. Despite all that was said on the day he had visited the estate's tenants, Henry knew adoration for his father and sympathy at his passing wouldn't be enough to ease tensions now changes were afoot.

Henry looked at himself in the mirror. He was losing the natural tan that came from living in Los Angeles. His life there seemed further removed than the reality of the time that had passed. Henry thought how different things might have been if he'd stayed in Dapplebury and shook his head. *At least you're here now. At least you're trying to put things right.* His thoughts were small comfort when the chaos of the afternoon implied he was stuffing it up at every turn.

Six o'clock approached. The people of the village were gathering at the impromptu meeting Mrs Jenkins organised to "nip tensions in the bud" having heard the barmaid from The Brown Dog intended to call one of her own. Henry appreciated the intel and the organisational skills of the PA who'd managed to find a venue and invite the entire village in a timescale that would have fazed most mortals.

Moving into the wings of the stage, Henry could hear the chatter in the main hall and pushed his hand through his hair. Peering through a gap in the curtain, he could see familiar faces in the crowd. Not one to miss out on the opportunity to be at the centre of any business pertaining to the village, the barmaid, Pauline as Henry now knew she was called, was serving tea via a hatch at the side of the room. *No doubt with a slice of her hastily formed opinion on the side!* Henry searched the awaiting crowd for Ava, but couldn't see her.

As those not yet seated began pushing their way along the rows of chairs, Henry knew the time of reckoning was near. With the stage set in the village hall, and him waiting in the wings – *cast without doubt in the role of the villain* – Henry realised he was about to get heckled more than the hideous am-dram society in all the years he had been made to watch their productions with his father.

'I'll introduce you.' Mrs Jenkins walked past him, and Henry knew he had to stop her.

'Wait! Don't ...' He shook his head. It was too late. Mrs Jenkins was centre stage, and he wondered if anything could have possibly made him look more pretentious than having a woman who carried her handbag in the style of the Queen, introduce him.

'People of Dapplebury.'

Oh, God!

'I give you Henry ...'

Oh no! Don't—

'William Edgar De Byron, Eighteenth Baron Bramlington.'

And she did! Henry felt his cheeks blaze red. Didn't village halls have a trapdoor? Something, anything, to come to swallow him up into darkness, and allow him an escape. With that introduction, he might as well have instructed Mrs Jenkins to put him in the pillory and hand out the rotten fruit and veg!

The hall fell deathly silent, and Henry heard himself swallow. Clearly pleased with her efforts, Mrs Jenkins walked off stage, satisfaction in her eyes as she offered a courteous nod as she passed him. He should have known; she loved to brandish a title. Henry walked out, the sound of his footsteps too loud against the wooden stage. All eyes were upon him. He steeled himself, in readiness to speak.

But, as the door to the back of the hall swung open, everybody turned in unison. Henry looked up to see Ava, limping in, wincing with each step, her ankle bandaged. His embarrassment quickly turned to concern. If any of Dixon's men had hurt her, he was going to kill them, and hang the consequences. The fact she was being supported by the barman from The Brown Dog, who had his arm around her waist, did nothing to ease the tension Henry could feel welling inside. The wounded look in Ava's eyes that he was sure wasn't as a result of her ankle, twisted his already knotted stomach.

'Ava, you're hurt!'

All eyes swung back to the stage.

Aware he was being scrutinised, Henry coughed and spoke again. 'Miss Flynn.' Jumping down from the stage he met her midway into the hall, as he continued, 'Miss Flynn, let me help you to a seat.' His eyes searched hers, willing her to know he meant her and her mum's charity no harm. *Though there was bound to be short-term heartache, you knew that.*

'I'm fine. I can stand!'

'But—'

'She said she's fine.' Mary walked around from behind Gino, propping up Ava's other side, preventing Henry from being able to help.

'Here love, sit down.' Flo beckoned to Ava, making everyone in her row move along to make room, before looking at Henry and tutting loudly.

Aided by her friends, Ava shuffled into the seat, while whispers of how she hurt her ankle spread around the hall. The words "his heavies" repeatedly echoing as Henry tried to regain his composure. Henry had heard enough. He wanted nothing more than for this to be over so he could speak to Ava alone. He needed to explain his actions, in as much detail as his promise to his father would allow, and he wanted to find out how her ankle had been injured. He jumped back up onto the stage, keen to stop the crowd turning into a mob; he had to allay their fears and get them to leave as soon as possible.

'Please, if I could just have your attention.' The acoustics in the room made his voice seem too loud; he swallowed and started again. 'Thank you all for coming.' All eyes were upon him as everyone sat, waiting, watching. Henry wished he had asked Mrs Jenkins to turn off the electric wall-mounted strip heaters that were throwing out an unnecessary heat adding to the intensity he could feel in the room and shining an orange glow, directly in his eye line. *Honesty, go for honesty!* 'I have one thing I want you to know, and that is, I have nothing, nothing, but the best interests of Dapplebury House at heart.'

'Exactly, Dapplebury House! And sod the rest of us,' an elderly gentleman called out from the back of the hall. 'You heard him. It's all about Dapplebury House.'

Oh no! Henry recognised the error as soon as the words left his mouth. 'No! That's not what I meant. Dapplebury estate, the village at large. I have nothing but the best interests of Dapplebury at heart. To me, they are synonymous.'

'Speak English!' Pauline called out.

'The same,' Henry corrected. 'Dapplebury House, the grounds, the wider estate and the village – to me they are one and the same.'

'All yours for the taking!'

Henry couldn't see who made the remark, but similar jeers from around the hall followed. Hearing enough, he lifted his palms in front of him, an attempt to stop the heckling and a sign of surrender. 'I am not here to take anything. Rent increases, along with the sale of some land to the north of the village, are necessary moves to secure the future of Dapplebury, to see it prosper. To secure your homes and livelihoods.'

'It's all lies. Your father will be turning in his grave!'

Henry faltered at the comment. As he'd visited his father's grave earlier, he'd thought how, for the first time in a long time, his father wasn't wracked with the worry of maintaining his reputation, of the risk of losing the estate, and of leading the family name into financial ruin. He was very much at peace, a peace Henry knew he could have helped him find during his too-short life if only he had returned from America earlier.

'That's not fair!'

Henry looked up at the sound of Ava's voice, and the crowd fell silent as she awkwardly got to her feet. Gino stood to balance her, and Henry noticed the look of thanks she gave him.

'We all know the village is in trouble. We've known it for a long time.'

Henry welcomed the voice of reason. And the fact it came from Ava, after Dermot had revealed his plans too soon, gave him hope. *She'll still listen.*

'I can't condone Lord Bramlington's methods, especially not regards the sale of the land housing Critters' Lodge.' She looked at him directly, and disgruntled murmurs spread around the hall.

Henry cringed. Hearing her address him so formally cut as much as her wounded expression and sentiment.

'But you can all rest assured I will fight to save All Critters Great and Small, our rescue centre is the heart of all that we do. We will not roll over. We'll renegotiate terms, pay higher rent, if that's what it takes.'

It won't be enough. Henry knew the pittance paid in monthly rent by the charity for the land Critters' Lodge was on, and he knew it was unlikely they could afford the premium such a piece of land could command.

'We'll do more fundraising. We'll bring people into the village.'

Ava looked to the stage. Henry felt the penetration of her eyes upon him as she spoke about the work of the charity and the years it had been established. Henry wanted to speak out, to reassure her that his plans included a strategy for safeguarding the future of All Critters Great and Small. Critters' Lodge was just a building – it was the people and the work they carried out that made the charity what it was. He hoped she would see that. But he knew now was not the time. He needed to speak to her alone; he needed to be sure she would agree, and, what he expected to be the greatest challenge, he needed to get his mother on side with the whole concept without revealing the fact his father had almost led the estate into financial ruin.

'But, Your Lordship, we need to know if you mean what you say. We need to know you won't run away when the going gets tough. We need to know you're here to stay.'

His mind and attention was drawn back to Ava as she addressed him, his title sounding too formal as she spoke it. Henry swallowed. He adjusted his cufflinks, feeling the family crest, as he met her eyes. He could see the fire that blazed behind them, and the determination. She was challenging him. This was the Ava he knew. This was the Ava he had always loved.

'I am here to stay.' He spoke the words with conviction and hoped Ava would know he meant them for her. *Honesty!* At a time when he had so much to keep to himself, honesty was a welcome relief.

Chapter Twenty-Three

Unable to stand, or speak any longer, Ava sat down. She wasn't sure if the tremble in her muscles was caused by the pain in her ankle, or the fact, in a room full of people, Henry had managed to make her feel that he was speaking directly to her. Pushing her stray curls back from her heated cheeks, she breathed.

On the journey to the village hall, she planned a speech. She wanted him to know she was a force to be reckoned with. All Critters Great and Small had a tenancy agreement with regard to Critters' Lodge; they had been established on the land in question since demand for their services had outgrown her mum's cottage. The original stable block on the site had been converted for use and the prefabricated buildings that housed the office and treatment rooms had been added over time. They were not trespassers on Bramlington land. They had rights, and she would fight for them.

But, as she had seen Henry, standing, a man alone while the rest of the village compared him to his late father, her heart had softened. As she spoke, her determination had waned, and the clarity of her convictions blurred. She knew what it was like to live up to a parent who was held in such high esteem, to people who only ever saw the good – the façade presented to and for them. Empathy had a lot to answer for. That, and the glass of whisky Mary had administered to help with the pain in her ankle, were playing havoc with the clarity of her mind.

While others around the hall took up the mantel of asking for promises and reassurances regarding Henry's commitment to the village, Ava watched. As much as he had always insisted he didn't want the role that came with his title, there was no doubt that it suited him. Of course, she could still see her Henry, the one she grew up with – who came alive in the grounds of Dapplebury House. But now, there was something more.

While she initially felt sorry for him, as the meeting progressed, it was clear he was taking control. Listening and responding to each of the concerns raised, he was calm and patient, and yet persuasive and strong in his convictions. Perhaps her empathy had been misplaced. While she often felt out of depth trying to live up to her mum's reputation, it seemed Henry was more suited to his father's role than she ever imagined. The thought once again reminded her how little she knew him now.

Looking around the hall, she could see the tide of dissent was turning in his favour. Even Gino was nodding, and Pauline's jeers had stopped as Henry spoke of increased revenue for the struggling businesses and the need for affordable housing. With many of those in the hall being parents and grandparents, he was hitting home the point that too many young people had been forced to leave the village in search of homes and jobs.

Ava had to concede, the new Lord Bramlington was persuasive in his comments and ... *bloody handsome in his suit.* She shook her head. *Damn that whisky!* She needed to stay away from such thoughts. She knew she needed to stay focused; she had to remind herself of all that was at stake. Despite the fact she once loved and trusted Henry, he had let her down, not standing up for her against his mother when she had so desperately wanted him to, and she needed to remind herself of that. The charity had to stay paramount in her thoughts and actions. Of course, changes had to be made to save the village, and it was clear from the tone in the room that anger was turning to acquiescence, but it wouldn't be at the expense of her mother's legacy. She would see to that.

Ava wasn't surprised when Henry began to conclude the meeting. *Quit while you're ahead. Why give the dissenters time to regroup?* But as the crowd began to stand to leave, their situation no different to when they came in but their minds appeased, Mary stood, whistling for their attention.

'Right, now on to The Brown Dog! Let's go and make plans. Promises are all well and good but they don't put food into hungry mouths, or heal the sick and injured.'

Ava leaned across to her, pulling on her jacket to get her attention, before whispering, 'What are you doing?' Ava agreed they couldn't trust words, and that they needed to take action to help secure the future of the charity and the village, but with her ankle throbbing, she also knew she needed to take a moment to restock and recover. 'Why are you talking like a politician?'

Mary leaned down, a glint in her eye. 'I'm not. I'm talking like an animal welfare officer. You didn't think I was talking about people, did you? I'm with you. Let's up our fundraising efforts, prepare ourselves for higher rent. And let's get the village ordering pints down at The Brown Dog. That'll put some money in the till, too!' Mary winked at Gino.

Beaming, Gino pulled Mary towards him and kissed her cheek. 'You're a star!'

'With this lot heading to The Brown Dog, we best get a move on!' Pauline called to Gino from across the hall.

Before responding, he turned to Ava, asking her if she could manage.

'Of course. Mary will help me, won't you?'

'Yes … yes, of course.' Mary stopped staring at Gino and turned her attention to Ava.

'Can I help?' Henry stood before them, his hand outstretched to Ava.

Meeting his gaze, Ava noticed for the first time that he was wearing the same tie she'd pulled loose when he'd visited her cottage … She shook her head. 'No.' She needed to clear her mind and while they had business to discuss, she knew now was not the time. It had been a day of revelations and she was under the influence of whisky, albeit for medicinal purposes. 'No. I'll be fine, but … thank you.'

Mary stood by Ava's side. 'You don't need to thank him. This wouldn't have happened if it hadn't have been for his heavies.' Turning to address Henry directly, Mary continued, 'I've got her. You've done enough today, don't you think?' Mary pointed at Ava's bandaged ankle.

'Ava, I'm sorry … I never … I'll sort this out.' He spoke the words sincerely, before turning to leave. Amidst the commotion of people moving from their seats, Ava saw a glimpse of Mrs Jenkins following, hot on his heels. Henry was reaching for his phone before he got to the door.

Ava looked at Mary. 'I'm not sure blaming him for my ankle when we need to negotiate rent is a good idea.'

'He deserved it!' Mary shrugged.

'But if I'd just left the lodge via the door, it wouldn't have happened.'

'True, but you got in via the door and that's a huge deal. Leaving by the window – well that's something to work on.' Mary smiled.

Chapter Twenty-Four

Even with Mary's support, hobbling over the cobbled street was proving harder than Ava had imagined. More than once she wondered if she would have been able to convince Henry to carry her, before shaking the image from her mind. She needed to sleep off the effects of the whisky, and she knew resting her ankle would make sense. She had too much to do to be out of action for long. She had to take care of herself. The charity needed her now more than ever. And Myrtle needed her; she could only rely on the kindness of her neighbour to look after Myrtle for so long. And Ava wanted to be with her, especially as her due date drew near.

'I think I should go home—'

'Let's just look in and then I promise to get you home. You did a great job at the meeting. I think if you just take a moment now to rally the troops, we'll have the village well and truly on side. With everyone facing their own rent increases, we need to keep their sympathy. Charity donations are non-essential when it comes to cutting back. We have to remind them we need them.'

'I suppose. But I'm sure you'd do a better job than me. I'm not sure I can feel my nose.'

'What?'

'My nose. I mean I can see it, I just can't feel it.' Ava crossed her eyes. 'It's definitely there.'

'Are you OK?'

'I think so ... Wait, can I normally feel my nose?'

'What? No. Maybe ... It's not something anyone ever thinks about.' Mary paused, looking into Ava's eyes as they reached the door of The Brown Dog. 'I had no idea one glass of whisky would affect you so much.'

'Me either, though maybe it was the second or it could have been the third.' Ava giggled.

'What? When—'

'There was the one I had before I climbed out of the window.'

'Wh—'

Ava flapped her hand. 'I knew you'd have some in your drawer. Mum always did for, you know, emergency purposes. Then there's the one you gave me for my ankle, and the one I swigged when I went to the loo before we left the village hall.' Ava slipped the half-empty bottle of whisky from her bag. 'I thought it might help with the walk over here.'

'I'll take that.' Mary took the bottle. 'Let's get you inside. Fresh air and alcohol don't mix.' Mary helped Ava hop up the step and into the pub, before motioning to a seat near the bar. 'Let's sit you down, and I'll get you some water. You've eaten, right?'

'Yes! Breakfast with Gino. *Ooo* Gino, we've got a secret!'

'Have you?' Mary responded with a teasing tone as she helped Ava into her seat.

'Yes. And, oh, wait—' Remembering the image of Flo's inappropriate window display, Ava began to giggle. 'There were sex toys, big ones, small ones, jiggle balls.'

Mary looked at her, her head flicking between Ava and the bar, where Gino was serving. 'What, you … and Gino? But what about Henry?'

Ava manoeuvred herself into a comfortable position. 'Hmm, Lord Steal-the-land-from-under-me-but-looks-bloody-gorgeous-in-or-out-of-a-suit-tra-la-la-lington?' Ava pulled a face and contemplated what she had said. 'That sounded better when you were doing it!'

'Yes, don't do that again!' Mary screwed up her nose and shook her head. 'You're positively drunk. Look at you!' Turning to order a large glass of water from Gino, Mary asked him to stash the bottle of whisky behind the bar.

Ava waved, before winking conspiratorially at Gino.

Mary let out a breath. 'It seems one glass of whisky turned into half a bottle. We got outside and—'

'The fresh air catalysed with the alcohol.' Gino shook his head.

Ava looked at them both standing at the bar, staring in her direction. 'I see you both judging me, but I'm not drunk. I'm just a little light-headed, and my nose is missing.'

Mary put up her hand before Gino could speak. 'Don't ask!'

'But other than that, I'm good. I even remembered I needed to stay focused.' Ava smiled. 'Wait, what did I need to stay focused on?'

Mary passed her the water. 'Saving All Critters Great and Small. We're here to get this lot on side. Henry's promises are all well and good, but we can't lose Critters' Lodge. The animals need us.'

Ava sat back and smiled. 'You remind me of my mum.'

Now Mary's cheeks flushed. 'Thank you. I'll take that as a compliment. Now, you sit there, nod and smile and leave the talking to me.' She took a breath.

'Good plan!' Ava put her thumbs up, while Mary stood on a chair to get the attention of the villagers.

Chapter Twenty-Five

Despite Mrs Jenkins' attempts to follow him, Henry told her to return to Dapplebury House. She had done more than enough for one afternoon. He thanked his hypnotherapy training for teaching him how to read people and to stay calm under pressure, without it he might not have been able to bring the crowd back on side after the way she'd introduced him. The skills he had learnt stood him in good stead for life – he'd told his parents that many times when they thought he was wasting his time.

With every passing day in his new role, Henry was more determined to do it his way. He would take the Bramlington title and Dapplebury House into the future, but it had to be on his terms. Yes, he had a responsibility to the past, to tradition, and expectation, but he had no intention of living shackled to archaic notions of how the estate had to be managed and run.

Having called Dixon's office, Henry knew the man's location. He wanted their conversation to be face-to-face. He wanted the man to know, in no uncertain terms, that he had crossed a line. Going to Critters' Lodge without permission was out of order; telling Ava about the sale before he'd had the chance to, was out of order. And the fact Ava had ended up injured was not only out of order, it was going to cause somebody's head to roll.

While having a title had its drawbacks, it also came with a certain amount of gravitas; gravitas that was going to be yielded in full throttle at whoever dared to hurt her. Yes, he needed Dixon's deal in order to go ahead with his plans for the estate, but he was also well aware that Dixon would be gaining plenty by way of reputation and future work if all went well with the contract.

As he pulled up outside the office, Henry felt the tension in his clenched jaw and neck. Getting angry wasn't generally his style, but the sight of Ava with her ankle bandaged had infuriated him. That and the eager Italian constantly at her side. 'You better have a bloody good excuse, Dixon!' Getting out of the car, Henry strode towards the office door.

Chapter Twenty-Six

Ava filled the kettle, trying not to put too much weight on her ankle. Once she was home, snuggled up with Myrtle, she had been able to rest it and sleep off the effects of the whisky. While her ankle still throbbed, she was surprised and grateful that her head didn't. Mary had left a note saying Flo was happy to open the shop and other volunteers had offered to cover while Ava's ankle forced her to be out of action. It was really kind, but she had no intention of staying away from the shop longer than was absolutely necessary. Not only would she go stir-crazy having to sit and rest, but the jobs that needed her specific attention would mount up.

About to message Mary, to thank her for delivering her home and for talking to Flo, Ava saw a missed message on her phone, saying Mary was on a call involving a bird stuck in a chimney. Smiling, Ava sent the message of thanks and wished her luck. The last bird Mary had rescued from a chimney turned out to be a jackdaw, who came out of the ordeal unscathed, unlike the homeowner's white carpets and furniture. Mary found it all funnier than she probably should have, but thankfully the charity wasn't held responsible for the damage.

Seeing she also had a message from Gino, Ava scrolled to it, suddenly cringing as she recalled mentioning his secret. She bit her lip for fear that she'd let it slip while under the influence. *You wouldn't have, would you?* Reading, her eyes went wide. *Oh no, oh, no!* Unable to take in the full implications of his words on first reading, she read it again. This time, saying the words aloud. 'Looking forward to the inaugural Bramlington Festival. Hope you've given yourself enough time to organise it. And I never imagined you'd be up for skydiving! When I said seize your moment Ava Flynn, I never imagined you'd seize it quite so *fully.*'

'What?' It had to be a joke. Surely she didn't put herself forward for any such thing. She already had so much to do. How could she possibly organise a festival too? And skydiving? She would never volunteer for that. She couldn't manage jumping out of a window without causing herself an injury, let alone an aeroplane at whatever hideous height people jumped from. Gino had a warped sense of humour. Ava knew it had to be a joke – he was teasing her because she'd been inebriated. Resting her phone on the kitchen counter, she put it on speaker and tried to call him while she got herself a mug from the cupboard and the milk from the fridge. There was no answer. Rather than leave a message she decided to send him a text. A grin spreading across her face, she asked if he thought skydiving while dressed as a hedgehog might help raise more funds for the charity. 'Ha, two can play at the teasing game!' Laughing, she finished making her tea and filled Myrtle's food bowl before placing it on the floor.

At this late stage, the dog was supposed to be having sixty per cent more food than usual according to the vet's guide, but she'd been fussy over the last couple of days. Ava stroked her as she sniffed at her bowl, not committing to taking a bite. 'I don't blame you. I'm not sure where you'd put it.' Myrtle's abdomen had become rounded; the movement of the puppies was frequently visible as they jostled for space and the poor spaniel had started to walk with a waddle. It was no wonder she had reached the point of panting with even the slightest movement.

Ava had bought a whelping box in readiness for the puppies' arrival. She had also sourced and purchased everything on the "supplies list", including a torch – in case of night-time toileting, despite the fact her phone torch would have sufficed; and a new set of scales – as if her hardly-used kitchen ones wouldn't have been good enough for the new arrivals. At least having the items made her feel ready, or at least as prepared as she was going to be considering the unexpected-pregnancy-

and-now-pending-labour circumstances. And while she was pretty sure she'd be able to cope with the blood from the birth, partly because Myrtle would be her priority in the situation and partly because she knew fresh and spouting blood was what generally caused her issues, it was good to know Mary would be there as her "birthing partner" as they had been calling it. While Henry had offered, Ava didn't want to risk having a meltdown in front of him. Besides it would hardly be appropriate now. Taking her tea to the table, she thought about the events of the day before and knew choosing Mary over Henry was the right decision.

Henry had previously been to see the vet with them, and while he had been friendly and supportive, he hadn't mentioned his plans for Critters' Lodge and that hurt. Ava knew she needed to speak to him and negotiate new rental terms. Giving up the land was not an option she would contemplate, and he had to know that. She also knew she needed to quash any other feelings she had for him. His actions had proven how little she knew him. After they had got carried away when she brought him to the cottage, they had shared a few chemistry inspired moments – looks that lingered, touches of hands that made her want more – but nothing had happened. Ava shook her head. *Thank goodness.* She didn't want anything to complicate her need to fight to save Critters' Lodge.

Sipping her tea unthinking, she burnt her tongue. '*Bugger!*' Putting her mug back on the table, she decided to have a shower before contemplating the day ahead. Ensuring Myrtle was safely ensconced in her whelping box, Ava headed upstairs.

Chapter Twenty-Seven

Having left Dermot's office with every bit of his anger turned to curious amusement, Henry had driven to the charity shop in search of Ava. Finding it in darkness, he had gone to The Brown Dog, but having won a small battle amongst the villagers, he didn't want to reopen the debate about the future of the estate. He'd stood outside for a while, and heard the throng of voices within – his reality a metaphor for how he had always felt in the village. At least growing up, he'd shared the feeling of being on the outside with Ava.

Going home had felt empty, but sitting down with his mother to inform her of his intentions before somebody else did, had felt good. Of course, she had argued, and even attempted emotional blackmail as she told him how disappointed his father would be. But the awareness that she didn't know the mess the estate was in made him push the accusations aside. He knew she was still grieving, and that change was always going to be difficult. But this was *him* running the estate. Doing it his way was the only way he could achieve that.

Having woken early, he'd gone for a run in the grounds of Dapplebury House. Disappointment at not seeing Ava and Myrtle was, he knew, ridiculous; the dog would be on limited exercise, and Ava had an injured ankle. But no amount of running was going to remove her from his mind, and so he found himself standing in the porch of Critters' Cottage, hoping she would be home. He pushed his hand through his hair and then round his chin, wondering if he should have returned home, shaved and freshened up before seeking Ava out. He shook the thought from his mind. The fact was, there wasn't anybody else he wanted to see, and nowhere else he wanted to be.

As he rang the bell, Myrtle barked. Henry listened for movement inside, hoping Ava would be home. He knew she could be determined and stubborn. *She's probably gone to the shop, despite her injury.*

'Ouch! Oh, bugger.'

Hearing Ava's voice from inside, Henry felt a rush of relief that quickly turned to guilt at making her walk to the door – she continued to grouse. When at last she opened it, she was wearing a towel, her hair in a messy bun with water droplets covering the top of her breasts and shoulders. Henry swallowed. He could smell her fresh, clean scent and wished he had taken a shower before turning up on her doorstep.

'Henry, now is not a good time.' Ava tucked herself behind the door and fixed him with a glare. 'We clearly have a lot to talk about but—'

'Yes, we do.' He could see Ava was reluctant, but now he was in her presence he couldn't help but lead with the thing utmost in his mind. 'A hose? You used a hose on Dermot Dixon and his men?'

Ava's cheeks coloured a little, but she cocked her eyebrow in a show of effrontery. 'They had no right to be on the land, and you had no right to send them!' She flicked a loose, unruly curl back from her face.

'Woah!' Henry held up his hands. 'I didn't send them. Honestly, I didn't. And considering the array of weapons you have access to at the lodge, I think they were lucky to get away with being hosed.' Henry laughed. 'But, what I don't understand is why you leapt out of the window, and then let me, and the rest of the village, think the worst.' He raised his eyebrow, goading her to respond.

The look on Ava's face told him, he had her. Hosing Dermot Dixon and his men from the land All Critters Great and Small rented was one thing, brazenly lying, albeit by omitting to tell the truth, was another. Henry watched as the flush of her cheeks burned brighter and spread to her neck. She must have felt it, as her hand moved to her throat, drawing his eyes to the smooth skin of her neck.

'I leapt out of the window because ... because ...' She hesitated. 'It's really none of your business. The fact is, you were planning to sell without even mentioning it to me, and you know losing that land would have a devastating effect on the charity—*oh, bugger!*' Ava winced in pain as her impassioned speech led her to stand tall, her injured ankle bearing the brunt of the action.

Henry felt guilty. 'Seriously, they took it upon themselves to go to the lodge.'

'So you didn't send them? You're not selling?'

'That's not what—'

'So you are going to sell the land out from under us?' Ava looked at him, confusion in her expression.

'It's not like that.'

Ava readied herself to speak, but a yelp from the kitchen drew her attention. Without hesitation, she left the door and limped as quickly as she could towards the sound.

Concerned, Henry followed.

Myrtle was in her whelping box, panting, her head low, circling before laying down.

'It's started.' Henry had seen many bitches in labour, and there was no doubt Myrtle was ready. Her breathing was rapid; agitation was evident in her every move.

'I need to phone Mary.' Ava searched for her phone, but as she found it, her concerned expression turned to panic. 'No wait, she's on a call.' Her gaze darting from the phone to Myrtle to Henry, she continued, 'What shall I do? She looks so uncomfortable.'

'Myrtle's going to be fine. You just need to comfort her, tell her she's going to be OK. She needs you. This is her first time, so she's going to be distressed, but you'll see, with each pup she'll gain confidence.' Henry kept his voice low and even.

He held Ava's gaze, encouraging her to match his steady breathing. He offered her a small smile. And tried not to think about the fact Ava Flynn was barely a foot away, in a towel.

Her complexion looked paler than usual, her concern for Myrtle evident in her eyes; he had to resist every instinct to pull her into his arms. *Like she'd let you. Focus on the dog; that's what she needs.* Seeing she was regaining her composure, Henry broadened his smile. 'Which end do you want to be?'

'What?'

'The reassuring, stroking her head, offering calm support end, or the watch the delivery end?'

'Definitely the reassuring end.' Seemingly remembering she was still in a towel, Ava hesitated and folded her arms over her chest. 'But I'm—'

'You've got time to get dressed. It could be hours before the first pup puts in an appearance.'

'Right. Yes, and Mary might make it by then.'

Henry hoped not. While Ava could be feisty, what Henry had seen and heard of Mary had convinced him she was volatile, and he really wanted to speak to Ava alone, about the future.

After checking on Myrtle, Ava hurried upstairs. Henry shook his head, unable to believe he had just sent her to cover herself up when she'd been looking so perfect in that towel. Deciding to distract himself, he tipped away her cold tea and made them each a fresh one.

When Ava reappeared in the door, her hair was loose; she was wearing jeans and an All Critters Great and Small sweatshirt that made Henry think she'd selected it on purpose to make a point.

'I hope you don't mind. I made us tea.' He wasn't going to be drawn into talking any further about Critters' Lodge. Not now. If talks didn't go well, she would ask him to leave, and he didn't want that, not when she needed him. *Who are you kidding?* The fact he felt more like himself just by being near her, made him pretty sure he was the one in greater need.

As she went to check on the dog, Ava's eyes flicked to the mugs of tea on the side. 'No pot.'

'Sorry, was I supposed to …'

Ava crouched near Myrtle. 'I didn't mean to say it out loud.'

Her attention remained entirely on Myrtle, but her cheeks had coloured and Henry was sure she was avoiding making eye contact with him. *Was the pot such a big deal?*

Seeing the paraphernalia on the kitchen table, he decided to change the subject. 'You've certainly got everything you could possibly need.' He held up a pair of forceps contained in their sterile packaging and a bulb aspirator.

'It's from the list the vet gave me. I wanted to be prepared – forewarned is forearmed and all that.' She stroked Myrtle's head as the unsettled dog continued to pant. 'Mary was able to supply some of it from Critters' Lodge.'

Being Myrtle's first litter, Henry knew they could be in for a long day, and as much as he didn't want to get into a discussion about the land sale right now, it was clear something needed to be said. He wanted Ava to remember the birth of these puppies fondly. The atmosphere of unaddressed animosity wasn't going to allow that to happen.

He leaned against the kitchen side. 'Look, I know we have lots to talk about. And I have a whole lot of explaining to do. But Ava …' He waited for her to look at him. 'Do you remember I asked you to have faith in me, to remember, no matter what, that you know me.'

She nodded.

'Well, I promise you won't lose Critters' Lodge. The charity will be safe.'

Oh, God! The look of relief and the smile she gave him, twisted his insides. He knew she thought he meant the land was safe. Before he could say more, she was standing and closing the distance between them.

'Thank you!' She pulled him into a hug before kissing his cheek and stepping back.

He tried not to let the feel of her skin and the scent of her hair mess with his faculties.

'Sorry, I … it's just a relief.'

Henry saw the colour spread across her cheeks.

'And we'll pay more rent, fundraise more. I always knew we'd have to once—'

Myrtle yelped, drawing their attention back to her. *Saved by the dog!* Explaining his plans more fully was for another time.

Ava was back by Myrtle's side instantly. 'Is she OK? Shouldn't she see the vet or something?'

Henry looked at Myrtle. 'I'd say she doesn't have long. There's no need to move her. We just need to let nature take its course.'

Ava nodded, concern evident in her eyes, and Henry admired how, despite her apparent nerves and concern for the dog, she was determined to remain calm and to be the comfort Myrtle needed. Ava knelt in front of the whelping box, pulled back her hair and tied it into a messy bun. Her words were calm and steady, but Henry could see the slight quiver of her hands as she stroked Myrtle's head.

The dog panted rapidly and lay down – the intensity of her contractions visible on her flank. While her chocolate brown eyes stayed wide, she hung her head low. Knowing the first pup was imminent, Henry knelt next to Ava. He could feel the warmth of her proximity and heard how her breathing matched Myrtle's, quick at first, and then silence as she willed and urged the first puppy to come out.

'It will be OK.' He said the words as if to Myrtle, meaning them for Ava.

Ava exhaled as Myrtle began to pant again. 'Henry, what if there's … Will there be much—'

'Blood?' he finished.

'I didn't know if you'd remember.'

'How could I forget? I cut my hand and you were the one getting all the attention for passing out.' He spoke in a hushed tone.

Ava grimaced, responding with a whispered, 'Sorry.'

'Don't be. I held you while shouting for Ted, willing the colour to come back in your cheeks. In those few moments … I knew …'

'What? What did you know?'

'Holding a scythe by the blade was a bloody stupid idea.'

Ava let out a giggle and stopped herself as Myrtle let out an alarmed yelp.

'She's OK. The first pup is coming, look.'

Ava's eyes remained fixed firmly on Myrtle. 'Really?'

'Yes, it's OK. It's safe to look.' Henry pointed at the puppy as it emerged enwrapped in its sack, confident that Ava would be fine. The only evident blood was different from the rich red blood that had caused her problems in the past.

Ava slowly turned her head. 'Oh my goodness, you clever girl,' she whispered, her eyes wide as she took in the sight.

While time seemed to stand still, they watched and waited.

'Should we do something? Shouldn't it be breathing by now?'

'She knows what to do, give her a chance.' Henry spoke in a low, hushed tone.

Myrtle turned, licking the small pup, in an attempt to remove it from its sack. Henry and Ava watched intently, waiting to let nature take its course. When at last the sack was clear, the pup – with closed eyes, tiny paws, and a disproportionately big, pink muzzle – breathed and made a small squeaking noise. Both Ava and Henry let out a breath in relief and smiled.

'It's perfect.'

Henry watched Ava, silently; her expression was a mix of wonderment and pride. He could see tears welling in her eyes.

'Look, it's moving.'

As she spoke, Ava took Henry's hand in hers to draw his attention back to the moment. He swallowed, welcoming her touch and the opportunity to share this perfect moment.

Together, they watched as the small pup began to crawl towards its first feed, the behaviour as instinctive and natural as it felt to Henry to have Ava by his side, their hands touching.

Chapter Twenty-Eight

Over six hours Myrtle's five puppies had been delivered safely with just two of them needing intervention. Henry had stepped in each time, rubbing, encouraging, aspirating and coaxing the reluctant puppy to breathe. Myrtle had been a star, and all were feeding well. Ava felt emotionally and physically drained. She and Henry sat on the floor, watching the new mum and her litter.

'Thank you so much for today. I couldn't have done it without you.' Ava looked at Henry, the emotion of the day getting the better of her and tears welled in her eyes.

Henry offered her a smile before reaching up and wiping a tear from her cheek. She felt the brush of his hand against her skin.

'Thank you for letting me stay and help,' he spoke in a whisper, his green eyes appearing darker in the evening light.

As he met her gaze, she realised she had moved in a little closer, drawn towards his touch. She swallowed. They didn't speak, the attraction between them clear. She felt a blush spread across her cheeks and neck and a growing desire within that told her how much she wanted him. She leaned in until their lips touched, lightly at first, a gentle kiss, followed by another and another. His soft lips against hers sent sensations rippling through her body. These tender kisses felt more intense than their lust fuelled moment on the sofa the last time Henry had visited. Ava felt heat burn deep within and ached for him, as she drew him in closer, making their kisses deeper. His stubble, a sign of the long day they'd shared, felt rough against her skin, and she welcomed the sensation. When he pulled back, his breathing was ragged, and she missed the feel of his lips on hers. He put his forehead to hers. 'I need to go. I've got to shower.'

Ava took a breath. The rasp in his voice made her want him more. She didn't want him to leave; she didn't want the moment to end.

'You can shower here.' She moved back a little, biting her lip. Trying not to think of Henry, in her shower, water pouring over the firm torso she had all too briefly felt before.

'Really?' Henry looked at her, unsure.

'I'd like you to stay.'

'Good. Because there is nowhere else I'd rather be.' He spoke the words with the hint of a smile tugging at his well-kissed lips, before leaning forward and kissing her nose.

Ava tucked her hair behind her ears and watched as Henry stood and slid off his T-shirt.

Oh!

'Don't suppose you have anything that will fit, do you?'

Ava shook her head silently, aware that she had All Critters Great and Small sweatshirts in a variety of sizes in a cupboard upstairs, but to say so would bring up the charity and she wanted to keep this moment strictly personal. 'I could wash it. I'm going to wash the towels and … stuff.' Mindful of her ankle, Ava stood, taking the T-shirt from Henry. Her legs felt stiff from the hours spent sitting on the floor or crouching by the whelping box.

'Really? You don't have to.'

'I know.' Ava smiled, turning towards the washing machine to prevent her eyes lingering on his torso.

Before she could move away any further, Henry caught hold of her arm, pulling her towards him. Unsteady on her ankle, Ava turned and spun into his chest. He wrapped his arms around her and kissed her, lifting her onto the kitchen counter in an easy movement. Ava felt the hard worktop underneath her. Returning Henry's kisses, she moved her legs to accommodate him standing between them. Feeling his bare skin beneath her hands, and the ripple of his muscles as he moved, a wanton moan escaped her; an action that caused him to shift position and pull her hips closer to him. Pausing for a moment, Henry's breathing was ragged and Ava could see the rise and fall of his chest as he tried to compose himself.

'Ava Flynn, I wish I had the words to tell you how I feel about you.'

Ava smiled. 'I quite liked you showing me.' How had she ever thought she could quash her feelings for this man? Being with him always felt right.

Henry laughed before planting a final kiss firmly on her lips. 'I'm going to shower.'

Ava watched him walk through the hallway before she turned to Myrtle. 'Blimey girl, this is turning out to be one crazy day.'

Myrtle cocked her head.

'OK, I know, it's been particularly crazy for you.' Ava slid off the kitchen side, being careful to place her weight on her good ankle. She laid Henry's T-shirt over the back of a kitchen chair and began to pick up the towels they had used during whelping. As she bent to put them in the washing machine, the back door opened. Ava tried not to show her disappointment at Mary showing up unannounced. She usually loved her friend's impromptu visits, but the day had felt special; sharing it with Henry, alone, had made it even more special and she really wanted to see where the evening might lead them.

'You haven't been answering your phone, so I'm here to see if you're OK.'

Ava felt guilt wash over her. 'I haven't? I mean, no. I haven't.'

'I was worried with it being Mother's Day, so I thought I'd come and keep you company.'

Ava Flynn, you are the most ungrateful friend ever! Ava smiled at Mary and felt terrible for inwardly regretting her showing up. 'I've been distracted. Look.' Ava led Mary to the whelping box to show her Myrtle and her puppies. 'Aren't they gorgeous.' She spoke in a proud whisper as they watched the brood, their velvet bodies and soft pink muzzles jostling for position as they fed.

Mary gasped. 'Oh my goodness, look at you, Miss Myrtle. You're a mumma now. Happy Mother's Day!' Her tone was light as she addressed the dog and looked over the puppies. Turning back to Ava, Mary continued to smile. 'Congratulations, Grandma!' She pulled Ava into an unexpected hug before stepping back, searching her face and assessing her. 'Are you OK? Why didn't you call me? I would have been here.'

'She started this morning. I knew you were on a call and didn't want to disturb you.'

'So you did it all alone. Were you OK?'

'Yes, I was fine … but I … I wasn't alone.'

'Did Gino come? I thought he was taking his mum out. Wow!' Mary folded her arms and returned her gaze to the puppies. 'You know you're special when he lets his mamma down for you.'

'No. It was … Henry.'

Mary turned to Ava, her expression incredulous.

'He was great. He's been here all day. He saved two of them. I'm not sure I could have done it without him.'

'You could have. You would have phoned me.'

Ava was taken aback by the change in Mary's tone – a jolt out of the serenity of the evening.

'But Henry was here.'

They heard a noise from upstairs.

Mary's eyes flicked to the ceiling before looking back at Ava. 'And is he still here now? Is that him?'

'Yes, he went to shower.' Ava regretted saying it the moment the words left her mouth.

'What the hell, Ava! Are you literally sleeping with the enemy?' Mary cocked her eyebrow, and as she caught sight of the T-shirt draped over the back of the kitchen chair, her expression turned to a disapproving glare that suggested she wanted an explanation.

'Not here, come to the lounge.' Ava was not going to have raised voices near Myrtle and her puppies, and she could tell Mary wasn't going to be easily appeased. When she got to the lounge, she turned to her friend, but it was Mary who spoke first.

'What the hell are you doing? I don't know what I'm more shocked about, that you would do this to Gino, or that you are doing it with the person who wants to undo everything we've worked for! Seriously, Ava, I don't know what is going on with you. How could you? What would your mum—'

Ava held up her hand. 'Don't, don't go there.' Ava took a breath. Mary was, without doubt, a wonderful friend, but she had also been her mum's apprentice, and while Ava loved her, the fact she sometimes made claims about what her mum might think, feel, say or do, as if she didn't know herself, hurt. Ava was tired. She very much still wanted to be wrapped in Henry's arms, and she really didn't want Mary to tell her how she may or may not be letting her mum down. Mother's Day was hard enough, without throwing guilt into the fusion of emotions.

Ava looked into Mary's eyes and spoke in a hushed tone. 'The charity is safe. Henry has assured me of that. And as for what I am doing, or not doing with him, that is none of your business. But as I told you, he has been here all day. He helped deliver the puppies and—'

'Then you thanked him, by what? Getting cosy behind Gino's back?'

Ava was taken aback by Mary's words. 'What are you talking about? Why would Gino care who I see or what I do with Henry?'

'Ava! My God, you've changed since Lord Shagling—'

'Stop with the names. You know he's called Henry!' Ava looked at Mary exasperated. Maintaining a lowered voice and cool façade was becoming increasingly difficult in the face of her erroneous barrage of accusations.

'OK, so since *he's* been back, you've been behaving strangely. You're less committed to the shop. I've tried to stay neutral about it, but you stupidly let your dog get pregnant when there are more puppies in the world than owners to love them. You've slept with Gino and done goodness knows what with sex toys, and now you're cheating on him with L— *Henry!*'

Mary made air quotes as she spoke his name, while Ava's mind scrambled in an attempt to fathom the implications of her words.

'You've got it all wrong.'

Mary looked at her, eyes wide, disdain etched in the tightness of her jaw and her tight lips. 'By all means sleep with him if it saves the charity, but don't do it behind Gino's back. He deserves better than that.'

Ava attempted to take a breath. Her chest felt tight. She had never seen Mary so angry.

'Mary stop! You know I love Gino but I—'

'I am going to go.' Henry spoke the words from the doorway of the lounge, as both women turned to look at him. His hair was wet from the shower, and he was dressed and wearing his T-shirt that Ava had left on the chair in the kitchen.

She could see confusion in his expression and hurt in his eyes.

'It's been a long day. I'm glad I could help.' He swallowed. 'Good luck with the puppies.' His eyes flicked in the direction of the kitchen, towards Myrtle and her litter before he added, 'I'll write, about Critters' Lodge, but, as I said, it will be OK.' With that, he turned and left.

Ava attempted to call him back, but in a few strides he was through the hall and had shut the door behind him. She felt hot tears sting at her eyes. How could the most wonderful day of her life have turned to this? Mary had goodness knows what opinion of her, and Henry … She didn't know what Henry had heard but whatever it was, it had caused an expression in his eyes she wouldn't forget any time soon.

Ava took a breath. She and Mary had argued over small things in the past. Ava knew it was all part of loving someone passionate about her beliefs and individual sense of right and wrong. But this felt different. Mary had gone too far. She turned to face her, forcing herself to lift her chin.

'You've got it wrong. You've got it all so wrong.' Ava saw a hint of uncertainty flick across Mary's face.

'It looks … it looked … I thought.'

'I think you've made it clear what you thought. And if that is truly your opinion of me, then I think you should go.' Ava swallowed against the tightness in her throat. She didn't want to lose her friend, but she knew she had to stand up for herself, and for Henry. They'd spent too long living in the wake of others' opinions of them. She knew she loved him, she always had, and if he felt the same for her, she was determined not to let anyone stand in their way. Not this time.

'Ava! I'm sorry, but you've got to admit … you know—'

Ava cocked her eyebrow, halting her friend mid-sentence, as she emulated Mary's disdain filled expression of earlier. Ava felt thankful her bravado was making her appear more together than she felt. She was tired, she physically ached from the tension she'd held in her body for much of the day, and she longed to be back in Henry's arms – in their shared moment of serenity after the puppies had been safely delivered.

Instead, she was reeling from Mary's words. The responsibility of the charity shop and keeping her mum's legacy alive was a lot to bear. And maybe Mary was right; perhaps she had let that slip a little over recent weeks, but she was loyal, and she was trustworthy. She had kept her promise to Gino; she hadn't done anything to let him down. Despite what Mary might think, she loved him as a friend and welcomed the closeness they'd come to share. *Friends are the family you choose*. Mary's words, shared at less complicated times, slipped into Ava's mind.

Mary took a breath, and began again, 'He was in your shower. His T-shirt was discarded in the kitchen. You've been behaving ... You look ... I don't know, different!'

'So what? I must have slept with him?' Ava scoffed, despite being aware that the incredulity of her tone belied her earlier actions. If they had been left alone, she knew she wouldn't have held back.

'Did you?'

Ava turned her back on Mary and walked towards the window, trying not to show the pain in her ankle. 'That's none of your business.'

'But Gino—'

Ava turned to look at Mary. 'Gino and I are friends. You know that.'

'Friends? Really? That's not what you said at the pub when you were off your face on whisky. Ava, I know!'

'What do you know?' Ava wondered what she had let slip, and searched the fug of her memory for conversations of the previous evening.

'I know ... I know about you and Gino ... and the sex toys. You said—'

Ava laughed as it occurred to her what Mary was referring to. With her emotions in turmoil, she giggled, while Mary looked at her in disbelief at her reaction.

When she managed to control herself, Ava took a breath. 'I was talking about Flo!'

'What?'

'I was talking about Flo and the sex toys.'

'Flo?'

'Yes, it was Flo who used the sex toys.'

'With Gino?' Mary screwed up her face, the anger of earlier replaced with confusion.

'No. Oh, God, no! Definitely not. It was just another of her spectacular mix-ups, involving a donation she shouldn't have accepted. I'll explain later.' Ava felt some of the tension lifting from her body at the turn in the conversation.

'Oh really? Thank goodness. I mean, I'm a modern woman but—'

'But you're hot-headed. You jump to conclusions and you are a complete pain in my—'

'But you love me, and you know I only do it because I care.' Mary's expression softened, and Ava saw the slightest hint of a smile in her eyes.

Ava shook her head and blew out a breath. 'I do, it's true. You and Gino, you're my family now.' Ava sat at the end of the sofa, urging Mary to sit down too. 'But you have to know, Henry is important to me too. We've shared things, experiences that I've never told you about.'

'You're not talking about sex toys now are you?'

Ava giggled. 'No! I'm talking way more personal than that.' She smiled.

'What?'

Ava shook her head. 'Let's put the kettle on, and I'll explain everything if you'll listen and stop jumping to conclusions.'

Mary blushed, picked up a cushion and hid her face in it. 'Ugh, OK. I promise.' When she looked up, she smiled. 'You do know I'm only like that because I care.'

'I know, and I'm grateful for it … most of the time.'

Mary threw her cushion at Ava.

Ava threw it back. 'Let's get that kettle on.' She stood, and steadied herself on her stiff legs, taking care not to put too much weight on her ankle. 'And while the kettle's boiling you can make yourself useful and check on the puppies. Myrtle will need to go outside, and I want a minute with her.'

As Ava walked back towards the kitchen, Mary touched her arm, causing her to turn.

'I'm sorry about what I said. I know how much Myrtle means to you.'

Ava nodded her head, silently accepting the apology. 'I know her being pregnant was down to my inaction, but I want you to know, I will take great care of her and her puppies and they will all be loved. Even if I've got to keep all five of them myself.' Ava really hoped it wouldn't come to that, but her determination to take care of them all was genuine. She had known that the moment she had seen them enter the world.

'I know that, really, I do.'

By the time Ava had finished talking, it was late. They had drunk their tea and moved on to, and half-emptied, a bottle of wine before Mary sat back and readied herself to offer her thoughts.

'Bugger me.' She shook her head and let out a breath. 'So this is the opportunity for a new beginning for you both, a second chance against the odds. I mean, I'm not one for a big love story or anything, but ...'

Ava wondered if that were true and what it meant for her friend.

'... but it sounds like you two were always meant to be together. Some, not me, of course, might say you're soul mates. So why didn't you go after him? Why didn't you follow him when he left earlier and tell him to ignore your crazy ranting friend?'

'Because, in the moment, staying here and sorting things with my crazy ranting friend felt like the priority. I don't know what I would have done if you'd gone when I said you should go, but I'm glad you didn't.'

'I'm not that easy to get rid of.'

'Ha, no. But, honestly, I think that's a good thing.'

The hint of a blush spread across Mary's cheeks. 'I know I've already said it, but I am sorry for the things I said. I was out of order.'

'So long as you know I'd never do anything to hurt Gino. I appreciate him as a friend, but that's all there is between us.'

As Ava said the words, she knew how lucky she was. Mary and Gino were close friends, who had been there for her since the loss of her mum, and she loved them for it. Being an only child could be a lonely place sometimes.

'I know that. I do. It's mad. I am only a little older than you and yet working so closely with your mum has kind of made me feel responsible. She used to talk about you and worry about you a lot. I think some of that rubbed off on me. Like I was an apprentice in looking after you as much as the wild animals in our care.'

'I hope you aren't suggesting that's the same thing.' Ava giggled. 'Besides, I can look after myself.'

'So can they. They just need a bit of help, sometimes.'

'OK, admittedly losing Mum knocked me, and I do appreciate you looking out for me. But I am a Flynn through and through. I can be tough, and I've been feeling more like my old self lately. I think that might be why I've been behaving differently. I'm remembering who I am. Testing what I want, instead of feeling like I am struggling in the wake of losing Mum and trying to live up to what she might have wanted. Does that make sense?'

'Yes. It makes complete sense.' Mary pulled Ava into a hug. As she pulled back, she looked at their empty glasses. 'I'd top us up, but you'll need a clear head tomorrow.'

'Tomorrow? Why, what's tomorrow?'

'The day you go and get your man.'

'What?'

'You have to speak to him, Ava. Tell him how you feel. I am in no position to give advice. I keep a three-date rule—'

'You don't have sex until the third date?' Ava's tone was disbelieving.

'No, I never go on a third date. It stops things getting serious.'

'So you really aren't in a position to give advice,' Ava teased.

'No. But I do know that relationships live and die on the conversations you should or shouldn't have had. You have to tell him how you feel.'

'But Lady Bramlington—'

'Lady Bramlington has some explaining of her own to do, and you can speak to her about the photograph too. I know it's been on your mind.'

'That's a lot to contend with in one day.'

'And you're a Flynn. You'll take it all in your stride.'

'I know you're right. I need to do it, don't I? Own my feelings and face my fears.'

Mary swallowed. 'Yes, of course.'

'She is the only one who can shed light on that picture, and I have to know what happened.'

'Yes, you do, and you know I've got complete faith in you.'

Ava smiled, her head and heart filled with determination, while a small voice inside reminded her that Mary didn't have quite so much faith in her earlier.

'And when that's all sorted, and you've got your man and Lady Bramlington on side, we'll have to make a start on that festival you've promised the village. I don't know what you were thinking with that!'

Ava's eyes went wide. *Oh no, it's true!* She wondered if she should ask if it was also true that she had volunteered to do a skydive, but decided she was happier remaining in blissful ignorance about that.

Chapter Twenty-Nine

Inspired, no doubt, by guilt for her outburst, Mary had reported for puppy watching duties early. Ava was surprised that she also brought Bill, the vet, along, to check Myrtle and the puppies over, saying he owed her a favour. Ava didn't like to ask what Mary had done to garner the favour. But she welcomed the reassurance that the new mum and her litter were doing well and the news that Myrtle could be spayed in the not too distant future. The ups and downs of watching her precious dog bring new life into the world had been an amazing but also intense experience.

Having spent the night on a makeshift bed next to the refreshed whelping box, Ava welcomed the opportunity for a break. While she longed for an early morning walk, Mary insisted she got a lift from the vet as far as Dapplebury House. Her ankle, while still bruised, was feeling much better, but she knew she should continue to take it easy.

Once she had thanked the vet and waved goodbye, Ava took in the fresh air; it was good to be outside, albeit that the formal aspect of the garden she found herself in was in contrast to the parts of the grounds she usually lurked in. The neatly mowed lawn was lush, while yellow and purple flowers danced amidst the longer grasses beyond. She could hear birds singing in the distance. But the repeated phrases of the song thrush, competing against the more shrill notes of a greenfinch did little to settle her nerves.

Ava couldn't help but think, if only her ankle would have allowed her to walk through the woods, she could have convinced herself it was a typical day, and she wasn't about to confess her love for Henry or confront Lady Bramlington about the photograph. Her stomach would feel less of a tangle of knots. Clenching her jaw a little too tightly, she made her way to the sweeping drive that led to the house. This felt very different from her regular clandestine visits, where she felt shrouded by the cover of the trees.

Walking along the driveway, she felt exposed as Dapplebury House loomed large against the backdrop of the bright blue spring sky. An aeroplane streaked a contrail overhead that seemed out of place when she felt as if she were entering the set of Downton Abbey. Deep red and pink hues of rhododendrons and camellias contrasted against the pale stone of the eighteenth-century building. Seeing the opulence of it all, Ava felt ridiculous for coming to tell Henry she loved him. He was the newly crowned Eighteenth Baron Bramlington, and quite literally lord of all that she surveyed, while she worked all hours in a charity shop, trying desperately to keep her mum's dream alive. Why had she ever felt their plights were similar?

Doubt crept into her every step as the gravel crunched beneath her feet. Perhaps if Lady Bramlington heard her coming she would have her escorted off the property before she could make a fool of herself. There was a cool breeze blowing against her face that played with the strands of hair that escaped her ponytail. Ava had decided to wear black trousers and a jumper, replacing her usual trainers with sensible shoes, but now she wondered if she should have dressed up more. Maybe she should come back another day, wearing something more appropriate. And after she had given it all more thought.

Her steps slowed the nearer she got to Dapplebury House until she stood motionless, divided between turning around, or continuing on the path that was leading her forward. *Go home. Don't be a fool. Go home and tell Mary … what?* Ava thought about the various answers to that question. What would she say? She'd tried, but she didn't have enough Flynn spirit to see her through, after all? She had spoken to Henry, but he didn't feel the same way? Lady Bramlington was right to throw her off the land all of those years ago, as she wasn't worthy of being there after all?

Every scenario made her more determined to see her mission through, not because she was sadistic, but because she knew, if she didn't do this now, they would be the thoughts that filled her mind. She would think them if they came to fruition or not. And so she had nothing to lose. *Except for your dignity and maybe Henry's friendship if you make a complete arse of yourself!* Realising she might have already lost his friendship if he had heard Mary's words of the previous evening she walked forward, her pace quickening. If she achieved nothing else with this visit, she knew she must put that right. Once she reached the door, there'd be no turning back.

As she ascended the worn stone steps to the wooden door that she imagined to be around eight feet tall, she took the picture of her mum and Lady Bramlington from her pocket. 'I hope you understand, Mum. I have to know what happened, and I have to follow my heart. I blame my tenacity on you, so … here goes.' As she lifted her hand, Granger barked from behind her, causing her to jump. Relief flooded through her at seeing the dog, and she beckoned him over.

'Did Henry tell you you're a daddy? Three girls and two boys. Five beautiful Springadors. I know!' Ava laughed. 'I didn't know that was a thing either, until now.' Ava rubbed behind Granger's ears before the realisation dawned that he was a stud dog. 'Oh, but this isn't new for you. I forgot.' Ava shook her head, wondering if it was weird she felt a little deflated at the thought.

'Ah, but Myrtle was – is – special.'

Henry's voice took Ava by surprise. She stood and put the photograph back in her pocket. Her heart was racing as she tried not to think about the words she wanted to say to him.

'Do you think?' she managed as she steadied her breathing.

Henry looked fresh from a run, his hair ruffled and his eyes and cheeks glowing. The hint of a grin played at the corner of his mouth. 'Well, she's the only one he's ever actually courted. I'd say that's special, wouldn't you?'

'I guess it is.' Ava thought about the many times Granger had joined them for their morning walks and the fun the dogs had shared playing together.

'How are Myrtle and the puppies?'

'They're all good. Thank you.' Ava wanted to say that Mary brought the vet to see them, but wasn't sure mention of her friend would be welcome. Instead, she smiled, and as she caught Henry's eye, the two of them shared a moment that sent her back to the previous evening. But it was all too brief, as Henry looked away, breaking eye contact.

'So what brings you here?' The hint of a smile was gone.

'I need to speak to you … and … Lady Bramlington.'

Henry couldn't hide his surprise.

'I have something personal to ask her. God, that makes it sound like I'm going to ask for her blessing to marry you.' Ava felt her cheeks blaze as the words left her mouth. 'Not that I'm going to, I mean, we're not … Wait, do people do that in … posh world?' *Stop talking. Stop talking, now!* Ava felt sweat prick at her skin as her mind scrambled at how to get this conversation back onto safer ground.

'What are you saying?' Henry looked at her, his expression puzzled amusement.

'I'm sorry. Ignore me.' *Please, please ignore me!* She wished the ground would swallow her up, or perhaps one of the camellia bushes; with her cheeks blazing red she was sure to be able to disappear amongst the foliage. 'I'm nervous. All I wanted to say was it's personal, that's all. Sorry for … whatever that was.' Ava felt the picture in her pocket.

'OK. Is it anything to do with the estate or my father? Something I can help you with?'

'No. Thank you. If you don't mind, I'd rather speak to Lady Bramlington directly.'

Henry's curiosity was clearly not satisfied by her vague explanation, but she was grateful when he didn't push for more information. Goodness knows what would come out of her mouth next.

'OK. So shall we discuss Critters' Lodge first or do you want to—'

'Critters' Lodge?'

Granger moved from sniffing Ava's shoes to nudging her pocket for a biscuit; without removing her gaze from Henry, she showed the dog her empty hands. She hadn't thought to bring treats with her. Dissatisfied, Granger sauntered to Henry's side.

'Yes, you said you wanted to speak to me. I assumed you wanted to talk business.'

Ava noticed that Henry's voice had a more formal tone than just moments before.

'Yes, business.' Not wanting to declare her feelings on the doorstep, she was pleased to be able to buy some time.

'Why don't you come with me? I've got to get changed, but if you don't mind waiting we can talk. I'll explain everything, and then I'll take you to my mother.'

'OK.' Now, Ava was curious. While Henry had promised the charity would be safe, it seemed he had more to say on the matter. She hoped it wasn't anything inspired by whatever he'd heard the night before.

As he led her to the back of the building, Ava congratulated herself on not audibly gasping. She had seen it from a distance many times, but its grandeur and scale were infinitely multiplied when up close; she was shocked by the magnitude of it. While the front of Dapplebury House had looked imposing, the view of the back, blazed in light from the morning sun, unencumbered of trees and plants, was simply stunning. Being set on a hill, it overlooked the grounds and estate. She was sure the row of almost floor to ceiling sash windows must offer the perfect vista from every room. Her eyes were wide as she attempted to take it all in.

'Wow! It looks different seeing it up close. More ...'

'Dilapidated?'

'No! More beautiful. It's magnificent.'

Ava looked across to the stretch of woodland, where she regularly walked Myrtle. The lake was beyond but partly obscured by the line of trees. She could see the village and could just about make out the main street where the charity shop was. 'You're the master of all you survey.'

Henry laughed. 'Believe me, it's not all it's cracked up to be.'

'Not just the house, but the grounds. Look, I've never seen them from this vantage point.'

'Natural landscape by design,' Henry joked.

'What do you mean?' Ava kept her eyes fixed on the rolling green space in front of her, thinking how wonderful it would be to sit in this spot and paint the scene.

'Swooping lawns, scattered trees, the woodland and … well, you've seen the ornamental lake'—Henry visibly swallowed—'all pleasure grounds, inspired by Capability Brown in the eighteenth century.'

Ava's mind boggled at the lineage of it all; even the grounds were steeped in history.

Walking along to a large, predominantly glass door in the centre of the building, Henry opened it and gestured for Ava to enter before him. As she went to go inside, she hesitated.

'Do you need to announce I'm here or something? I don't want your m—I mean, Lady Bramlington to—'

'Trust me, she'll be polite.' Henry spoke the words matter-of-factly leaving Ava in no doubt that he intended to see to it.

Reassured, she smiled and stepped inside. Granger followed. The dog's claws tapped against the black and white chequered floor as he walked. The walls were painted rich damask, a contrast to the alabaster skin of the men and demurely posed, flat bosomed women in the portraits that hung in large gilt frames around the walls. Ava felt their eyes upon her.

'Relatives?' Her voice sounded too small.

'Mostly. Do you want to wait in my father's, I mean, my office, or come to my room?' Henry's cheeks coloured. 'I'm only asking because Mrs Jenkins lurks in and around my office.'

Ava grimaced, remembering meeting the woman at the charity shop. 'I'll wait in your room. If that's OK.'

'Well there's plenty of other rooms to choose from, but I'd rather keep you safe with me. If I'd known you were coming I'd—'

'Sorry, it was a spur of the moment thing.'

'I don't mind. It's just not how I envisaged your first visit here,' Henry explained.

Ava couldn't help but smile at the thought that Henry had considered her visiting Dapplebury House.

Leading the way to the grand staircase, Henry turned to Granger and told him to go to his bed. Granger trotted off, and Ava wondered if he actually had any intention of obeying.

As they ascended the stairs, Ava looked at the well-trodden carpet that ran down the centre of the highly-polished staircase. She couldn't help but wonder at all those who had trodden upon it before her. The building, like many of the items in it, had seen significant changes over the years. The generations of Bramlingtons and their visitors – perhaps even royalty, had made their mark. Ava was sure every fibre of the house must have a story to tell. With her mind wandering, she thought of her mother visiting the house. She and Lady Bramlington had been friends; it was highly plausible to think she would have. Seeing portraits of the late Lord Bramlington and Lady Jayne, Ava looked at Henry.

'Are there portraits of you?'

Henry laughed. 'God awful ones of me as a boy.'

Ava giggled. 'Can I see them?'

'No!'

'I bet they're amazing.'

As they reached the top of the stairs, Henry turned to her.

'Amazingly awful and not at all a reflection of my childhood. If I mention a suit and bow tie, a sailor suit and, oh, let's not forget the five-year-old holding a brace of pheasants, you'll get the idea.'

'Oh, dear! I knew you as a boy. They all sound perfectly apt to me,' Ava teased.

'I don't know what my parents were thinking.' Henry shook his head as he led Ava along the east corridor. Here they passed several closed doors before Henry stopped.

'And this is my room.'

He opened the door and gestured for Ava to go in.

She took a breath. 'Wow! I'm running out of adjectives. It's stunning.'

'Hmm, it's feeling more like home than it did when I first came back. I've made a few alterations.'

Ava looked at the space; she was pretty sure the entire contents of her mum's cottage would fit in this room alone.

'I've had it painted and removed anything of historical value so I could take down the awful curtains.'

Ava looked at Henry quizzically.

'I live in a museum. Light is the enemy as far as the family heirlooms and my mother are concerned. Don't get me wrong, I know I have to respect the history of the place, but I have to be able to breathe too. Do you get what I mean?'

'Yes, yes, I do.' Ava looked at the open view, afforded by the large windows that flooded the room with light. She walked across the polished wooden floorboards to get a closer look.

Henry joined her, and the two of them stood, content to look across the grounds until Henry broke the silence. 'I should get sorted. Make yourself comfortable.' As he said the words, realisation seemed to dawn. 'Ava, I'm sorry, I completely forgot to ask about your ankle. Is it OK? Did you walk here? I just made you walk up the stairs.' Henry looked at her, his brow furrowed.

'It's fine, really it is. I can still feel it, and I'll need to rest this afternoon, but it's OK. Thank you, though. It's much better than it was.'

'OK. But here, be sure to sit down.' Henry pulled over a large leather chair and encouraged Ava to sit by the window. Once he was sure she was comfortable, he gathered some clothes from the wardrobe and headed to what Ava assumed must be the en suite.

She heard the shower start and breathed. The fact she was in Dapplebury House, in Henry's bedroom, was a lot to take in. She couldn't let her mind spiral into thinking about what she wanted to say to him, or her conversation with Lady Bramlington. She knew she had to focus on what he had to say about the charity first. *One step at a time.*

Hearing a noise at the door she looked towards it, frozen to the spot. Her heart beat rapidly at the thought that it might be Lady Bramlington. Ava knew being discovered in her son's bedroom was not going to aid her cause when it came to gaining information. Lady Bramlington's reaction at discovering them together at the lake had been extreme; Ava could only imagine how she might react to finding her sitting in his bedroom while he took a shower. The strange noise stopped, and Ava released a breath. Her eyes scanned Henry's room, for what? *A place to hide.* She mocked herself for the thought. What would she do? Get under the large double bed? Hide under the duvet? Slip into the wardrobe, or duck down behind the gym equipment? But as the door began to open, she leapt awkwardly to her feet, ready to make her move.

Chapter Thirty

Having showered, Henry got dry and put on his jeans and a shirt, leaving it open at the collar. His mind was whirring. When he'd returned home the previous evening, he had been confused. He'd been convinced Ava felt the same for him as he did for her, but hearing Mary's words and Ava's confession that she loved Gino, hurt. Ensuring All Critters Great and Small was safe had always been a priority. She didn't need to pretend to have feelings for him to secure its future. He hoped she knew him better than that, and he certainly thought he knew her better than that. How it felt when they'd kissed along with her words "I love Gino" had caused juxtaposing thoughts to echo through his mind for much of the night. And now … now, she was in his bedroom.

Seeing her at Dapplebury House was a surprise that had taken him off guard. In truth, he wasn't sure how to react. He looked at himself in the mirror. *Focus on the charity. That's why she's here.* He hated the thought of her with Gino. But he hated the thought of his life in Dapplebury without her in it even more. He had to play it carefully and not overthink the fact that she had come to Dapplebury House. He also had to try not to wonder why she needed to see his mother; he sincerely hoped she'd not heard anything about the affairs of the estate, and his father's poor financial state.

Steeling himself, he opened the door.

'What the hell are you doing?' Henry looked in Ava's direction, taking in the sight of Granger attempting to be a lapdog, and making a large seat for one look like a very small seat for two in the process.

Ava giggled from under the dog. 'He's keeping me company. I hope you don't mind.'

Looking at Henry with doleful eyes, Granger clambered to the floor and sat on Ava's feet.

Ava stroked his head. 'I thought I could hide behind him if anyone came in.'

Henry couldn't help but laugh. 'Why would you need to do that?'

Ava cocked an eyebrow. 'Let's just say when I heard a noise at the door, I was about ready to …' Henry saw Ava's eyes move to the bed and her cheeks coloured. 'I was about ready to leap in your wardrobe. The fact it was your wayward dog and not Mrs Jenkins or Lady Bramlington was a big relief.'

'Ha, well they'll both have to get used to you being here.'

'Wh-what?'

Henry walked to the other side of the room. *What did you say that for?* 'Would you like a drink? I've tried to make myself as self-sufficient up here as possible. It's my sanctuary from … well from everything else.'

'A mini fridge? You have a mini fridge in your … Would you call this a bedroom or a suite?' Ava looked at him, her eyebrows raised.

'Technically it's a suite if you count the lounge and reading room next door, but this is my bedroom.'

Ava turned to where Henry had gestured. 'There's a door! I didn't see it hidden amongst the panelling. I could have waited through there.'

'I know, I wanted to keep you close.' Henry spoke the words matter-of-factly. No matter what, he was determined that his mother wouldn't treat her as she had in the past. He'd promised Ava that when he saw her at the lake, and he intended to honour that promise. Besides, the other rooms had their original décor and furnishings, and he wanted Ava to see the place that reflected more of him, his tastes and belongings. It felt more fitting. Seeing that she was trying to take it all in, he felt the need to explain.

'I didn't alter this room with money from the estate. The furniture and gym equipment are my own. I got them after the sale of my place in Los Angeles.'

'You don't need to explain to me.' Ava shifted in her seat.

But Henry wanted to explain. He wanted her to know; he wished he could tell her why it was so important that she knew he wasn't squandering the estate's money, but knew he couldn't. 'Sorry.' Henry pushed his hand through his still-wet hair. 'Did you want a drink?'

'Here?'

'Well, we could go for a walk in the grounds and I could show you my plans, but with your ankle, I thought ... And in my office Mrs Jenkins—'

'Then, yes, please, a drink here would be great.'

As Henry went to fetch them both a drink, he felt Ava watching him.

'What did you do, while you were in LA? You've never mentioned it?'

Henry fetched them both a sparkling water and pulled a chair up next to Ava. Granger moved, looking between the bed and Henry, before slumping down on the rug.

'Do you promise not to laugh?'

'Yes.' Ava smiled.

'I was a wellbeing coach, a personal trainer, and I studied hypnotherapy.'

'Oh blimey, you're not going to hypnotise me, are you?' Ava giggled.

'No. I knew you'd laugh.' Henry leaned back in his chair.

'Henry, really, I'm not laughing. Health and happiness are hugely important. Along with success, they're the holy trinity of the twenty-first century. I think it's great.'

'They're all subjective. People have to realise their own needs and potential to be productive – in whatever way that means for them, but I can help with that. It's an amazing thing to guide someone on their journey.'

Ava screwed up her nose. 'You're not going to get crystals out and start chanting are you?'

Henry saw the hint of a smile in her eyes and laughed.

'No, don't worry. You're safe. I much prefer getting out in nature.'

'Now that I knew about you.' Ava thought of the times they had spent in the grounds together, often exploring, but sometimes just sitting or laying together, listening to the sounds of the woods, watching the clouds go by, the two of them lost in the moment and their world. It was calming, grounding and thoroughly intimate.

'Maybe I should have been a lumberjack.'

'I can see that.' Ava giggled.

Henry put his elbows on his thighs and leaned forwards. 'Thanks. At least I could have been more useful around here.'

'You're doing a great job. I saw how you spoke to the crowd at the village meeting. From what I remember, it was an amazing turnaround. Wait, you didn't hypnotise them, did you?'

Henry sat back. The sun was shining in through the window, warming them, and causing red and auburn streaks to shine in Ava's ponytail. He wished her hair was loose. Granger sprawled out, bathed in sunlight, while he dozed.

'No, I just read the room. I told them what they wanted to hear.'

'You lied?'

'No, definitely not! I just phrased things in a way that appeased, opposed to angered them. Understanding people's fears, hopes and motivations are key. That and listening. Reading body language helps, even micro-expressions can reveal how someone is feeling.'

'And do you do that when you're speaking to me? Read my body language.'

Henry saw Ava shift in her seat; she crossed her ankles and laced her fingers in her lap. He didn't like the reaction; he never wanted her to feel anything but relaxed around him.

'It's a habit, but to be honest you're not that easy to read. I think I know how you're feeling, but then you surprise me.'

Or in the case of yesterday's revelation, bloody shock me. Henry had always felt Ava was the one person he could trust; the one person who knew and liked him for who he really was. His absolute belief in that being undermined by what he had heard, caused the hurt and confusion that kept him awake the previous night.

Ava smiled and relaxed her stance. 'Good.'

'Not always for me. Yesterday, I thought—'

'Henry, I do want to talk about yesterday. I don't know what you heard but there are things I want to say. But before I do that, I really do want to hear what you wanted to tell me about Critters' Lodge.'

Henry wondered if, like he had heard Mary say, Ava's feelings for him were dependent on the fate of the lodge. He knew he would have to reassure her it was safe, no matter what. As much as he'd hoped there would be more between them, he wanted Ava to feel for him as he did for her. Henry pushed his hand through his hair and sat up a little straighter, in readiness to speak.

'Ava, you're going to need to keep an open mind.'

Chapter Thirty-One

Ava looked at Henry, wondering what he could mean. The events of the day had already called for an open mind; she was not only in Dapplebury House but in Henry's bedroom. All of these things would have seemed out of the question even a month ago. She looked at Henry and noticed the tick of tension at his jaw. *Micro-expressions.* His green eyes appeared lighter in the sun, and she wished she could still see the longing written in them, from the night before.

'The land Critters' Lodge is on, is prime real estate. I wish I could just forgo the sale but it's just not that simple—'

Ava couldn't believe what she heard after he had promised the lodge would be safe. 'But you said—'

She went to stand up. Granger scrambled to his feet. Henry caught Ava's hand in his before she could rise, and as she turned to him, he held her gaze.

'I said that Critters' Lodge would be safe, and it will. The charity will be safe but not there. I have to sell that land, Ava. I've got no other choice. I wanted to tell you before you heard it from anyone else, but Dixon reacted too soon.'

Henry released her hand. Looking at him, she waited for more of an explanation – her breathing rapid.

'I wish I could tell you more about why I need to sell, but I made a promise that means I can't.'

Ava could see Henry's frustration and felt the sincerity of his words. 'Are you in some kind of trouble?' She sat forward, her eyes searching his.

'No, it's not me. But I need to do this for the estate. It will help me buy time, to sort out how, or what to do next.'

'And the charity?' Ava's voice was uncertain.

'I want to move it here, to the grounds of Dapplebury House. There's a stable block and an old dairy that you could take over. The current office and the treatment rooms are in prefabricated buildings, which can all be moved intact as part of the deal with Dermot Dixon. You'd have more space than you've got now so there'd be room for expansion.'

'That's possible?' Ava opened her bottle of sparkling water and felt the fizz mist her face. She wiped it and took a drink as she contemplated Henry's words.

'Yes, it's what Dixon's men were at Critters' Lodge assessing. They didn't want to agree to our deal without first considering the cost of the move.'

'Oh.' Ava thought about the reception they'd given the men.

'Luckily, Dixon was appeased by the fact you all had no idea about the deal and were acting purely based on passion to protect the charity. I think he was a bit impressed, said it reminded him of something he might do.'

Relieved, Ava smiled. As much as this was a lot to take in, she was aware that despite whatever troubles were causing him to sell the land, Henry was trying to do the right thing by the charity. Nevertheless, she needed a moment to fathom the ramifications of his plan. 'So the charity will be here … Your mum, Lady Bramlington will—'

'Will have to get used to the idea.'

'So that's what you meant about Mrs Jenkins and Lady Bramlington having to get used to me being here.' Ava felt a little disappointed at the realisation and dropped her eyes to Granger.

'Yes. I meant the charity being here in the grounds.'

Ava bit her lip.

'I've thought about opening up the west wing of the house. I'd have to keep some of it private but, as I said, much of it is like a museum and some of the artefacts are notable antiques. It might be a way to generate income. It would create jobs for the locals too. Though I might have to ask you about recruiting volunteers. Mrs Jenkins mentioned speaking to the local colleges and making links with them. There's a lot to explore. Getting revenue is going to have to be my first priority.'

Ava sat, looking at Henry. These were significant changes, changes that would be good for Dapplebury. She was well aware the village needed a boost.

'And perhaps we could open up Critters' Lodge, show people the work you do.'

Ava held up her hand. 'Mary will never go for that. I can tell you now, if you want us here as some sort of sideshow, like a zoo, she'll never agree. The animals in our care need peace and quiet to recuperate away from people. Returning them to the wild is always our end goal. *Rescue, recovery, rehabilitation, and release.*' She chanted her mother's mantra as vehemently as Lily Flynn had always spoken the words herself.

'Of course, sorry. I ... I just thought ...' Henry stood up and looked out of the window, Granger faithfully at his side.

Ava could sense his disappointment.

'Honestly, I thought it would help the charity too – that it might help with fundraising if people saw your work.'

'I can see why you thought it. And if we were a pet rescue, then it might be different. We'd be inviting people in to meet the animals in the hope of rehoming them, but we're not. We're a wildlife rescue. It's different.'

Henry turned and picked up his water, taking a drink. 'But the idea of moving Critters' Lodge here, you think you can agree to that?'

'I'd need to see where you intend to locate us. We'd have to assess the costs—'

'As I said, the moving of the current buildings are included in my deal with Dixon. There'll be no cost to the charity for that—'

'There'll be change of address and other costs. There are always hidden costs with a move. And we'd need to get Mary on side, not just about moving the animals but with her on board it will be easier to persuade the other workers and volunteers. But, to answer your question, I can see why being here would have its advantages. The access is certainly easier, and even if we can't open the rescue centre to visitors, we'd be in a higher profile location. How long are we talking about?' Ava pushed a stray curl behind her ears. As much as this would be an upheaval, she felt excited about it too. It felt like it could be a new beginning, one where she was at the helm of the charity, moving it forward instead of picking up where her mum left off.

'I need to push the deal through with Dixon as soon as possible. Then I can use some of the funds to work on getting this place ready. The publicity alone will take a while.'

'Yes, that reminds me, we have a new website going live soon for the charity, maybe I should delay the launch. We can share the news about the move at the same time.'

'It sounds like we have a plan.' Henry smiled, and Ava could see that he felt genuinely happy with all that they'd discussed.

She stood and put out her hand. 'Shall we shake on it?'

Henry took her hand, and she felt the connection of his touch. She stood just inches away from him and looked from his lips to his eyes. 'Henry, I wanted to … Talking about the charity, it wasn't why I came here today. I wanted to—'

Henry stepped back, breaking eye contact and letting go of her hand. 'Yes, I'm sorry. You wanted to speak to my mother. I'll take you to see her now. She knows some of what we've discussed. I've spoken to her about the sale of the land and opening up the house. She is … reluctant but I've told her we have to move forwards. Keeping a house of this size takes money. She'll come round.'

Ava was trying to gather her thoughts. She'd been ready to tell him about her feelings, but he'd broken the moment. She wanted it to be right, and she didn't want him to think her feelings for him were based on him saving the charity. She decided to wait. They'd be seeing a whole lot more of each other now, and so the right time would inevitably arise.

'I hope so. For your sake, and the charity's.'

'She's less'—Henry shuddered—'than she used to be. Don't worry, I'll take you to her now and if you want I can stay and make sure she listens to what you have to say.'

Ava thought for a moment. Whatever caused the change in the relationship between their mothers might be of interest to Henry too, especially as his mother's reaction to them being together all those years ago had been so fierce. Besides, her stomach was already twisting into knots. Having Henry along for moral support might help steady her nerves. As well as ensure she actually got in the door.

Chapter Thirty-Two

Ava stood in the corridor, waiting for Henry to return for her. He had gone inside the drawing room to speak to his mother in readiness for her to go in. Not hearing raised voices, Ava assumed was a good sign. Granger had been led outside en route to visiting Lady Bramlington, making her feel very alone, with nothing more than a stag's head, staring blankly out across the corridor, and a coat of armour for company. *Never mind Downton Abbey. This is full-on Scooby-Doo!* Ava didn't know which was making her feel more like she was going to be murdered. At least she hoped karma meant the stag would be on her side. She realised she would have to address the issue of having taxidermy from bygone years exhibited within walking distance of Critters' Lodge.

As the door clicked open, she jumped. *'BUGGER ME!'* Ava looked at Henry, her eyes wide, her hand clenched over her mouth as her cheeks flushed.

He didn't bother to stifle his laughter. 'Don't worry. I'm sure she's heard worse.'

Henry held the door open a little wider, inviting Ava into the room. She swallowed, an attempt to encourage saliva into her too-dry mouth. Once inside, she looked at Lady Bramlington; the woman she had for so long vilified in her thoughts looked smaller than she remembered. She was certainly much older and less animated than the woman Ava had encountered by the lake, as she sat, her hair neatly coiffed, wearing a black twinset and pearls. Remembering herself, Ava wondered if she should curtsey.

'Mother, you remember Ava Flynn.' Henry made the introduction and gestured for Ava to take a seat on one of the three two-seater settees in the room, while Lady Bramlington sat in a high backed chair. The duck-egg blue of the walls counterbalanced the bold floral patterns on the soft furnishings and worn-Axminster carpet. A large, age-flecked, ornately framed mirror hung above the open stone fireplace. Paintings depicting landscapes in the style of Turner adorned the walls, and Ava wondered if they were genuine.

The ruched curtains at the window, and the carved lime wood panelling that framed the room absorbed the light, making it appear much darker than Henry's. As much as Ava appreciated the age and magnitude of the surroundings, she could see why he chose to alter his own living space.

Once Henry took a seat, Lady Bramlington folded her hands into her lap and readied herself to speak. 'What brings you here?' She looked between Ava and Henry, cocking a grey eyebrow. 'You have a personal matter to discuss with me, I believe.'

Ava swallowed again. 'I wanted to ask you about, about this ...' Reaching into her pocket she produced the photograph.

'Bring it closer. I can't see from back there.'

Henry looked at Ava curiously as she flicked the picture towards him, before passing it into the hands of Lady Bramlington. The woman looked at it, her breathing becoming visibly more rapid as she turned and read the back.

'Where did you get this?'

Ava wondered if Lady Bramlington's eyes were glistening more than previously. 'It was in the frames, Hen— Lord Bramlington donated.' Ava wished she'd read up on the etiquette of using titles; she had no idea if she were saying the right thing.

Henry coughed and shifted in his seat.

'Donated?' Lady Bramlington looked at him, pointedly.

'They were wrapped in newspaper in the office. I felt they could be put to better use donated to All Critters Great and Small.'

Lady Bramlington seemed halted by the mention of the charity.

'It was a very generous donation. They've gone to auction and along with some of my mum's ornaments—'

'Ornaments? Birds and woodland creatures?'

Ava thought she saw recognition in Lady Bramlington's eyes and wondered if she had gifted them, or was it simply a guess given her mother's work.

'Yes, that's right. They've raised a wonderful amount for the charity, funding vital care for sick and injured animals who have—'

'No owner to look after them in their time of need.'

Ava looked at Lady Bramlington.

'You sound just like your mother, and you look just like your father.'

Henry looked between the two women.

'Yes, I do.' Ava smiled. 'You were friends with my mother.'

'Yes, dear friends.'

'But she never mentioned that. I've been through her things, and there's no evidence of it. Until I saw that picture I had no idea—'

A single tear slipped down Lady Bramlington's face, causing Ava to swallow. Perhaps she had gone too far. Henry moved to his mother's side and placed his hand on hers. She brushed him off.

'Ah, ignore me. There's no point crying over what can't be undone.'

Henry passed her a tissue and moved back to his seat.

'What is it? What can't be undone? If you were once dear friends, what caused you to fall out?' Ava felt her pulse quicken. She knew she was pushing for answers when Lady Bramlington was clearly upset, and possibly still fragile from being in mourning for the loss of her husband, but now she was here, she had to know. Time slipped by as they all sat silently, the room filled with the ticking of the grandfather clock Ava hadn't noticed on her way in.

Finally, Ava spoke. 'When you found me, us, at the lake,

you were furious. You told me to go, forbade me to come onto your land. Why did you dislike me so much? What had I done?' Ava was surprised to feel tears prick at her eyes, a release of the pent-up frustration of that day; she determined not to let her emotion show.

'I'd like to know too.' Henry looked at his mother. 'Before then my life here was tolerable, after—'

'I did it for her!' Lady Bramlington croaked out the words.

'Me?' Ava was confused.

'No, not you – Lily. I did it for Lily. It would have broken her heart if she'd seen you that day. I knew you visited the grounds, often. And I am not a fool. I know you still do. But on that day, I saw the way you looked at each other, the way you were both behaving. I knew you were infatuated with each other, perhaps, even as young as you were, falling in love.' Lady Bramlington shook her head.

Ava looked at Henry, neither of them denying it.

'Why? Why would my mum have hated it? I mean, I know she didn't like me visiting the grounds, but your reaction … There was more to it than trespassing wasn't there? What is it? What happened?' Scenarios fired into Ava's mind, none of them good.

Henry took the picture from his mother, turning it over in his hands as he looked at the image and then the words on the back.

'You have to tell us. Whatever the reason, whatever the secret, it's time to tell us now.' Henry's voice was calm as he urged his mother to speak.

'It never should have happened.'

'What? What shouldn't have happened?' Ava felt a cold shudder run down her spine as an ominous feeling crept over her.

'I killed your father.'

'*What?*' Both Ava and Henry spoke in unison.

'But you can't have. My father died in a car accident. Were

you there when his car hit the tree? What do you mean?' Ava's mind spun.

The door to the room opened, and Mrs Jenkins walked in, carrying a laden tea tray. 'Refreshments, as requested.' She placed the tray on a low, French-polished table in the centre of the room, stood and stared at the three ashen faces before her. 'Shall I pour?'

'Not now, Mrs Jenkins, thank you.' Henry spoke calmly but authoritatively and stood as if to urge her out of the room. Once she left he closed the door behind her. Henry poured three cups of tea, putting sugar in each without asking if it was wanted.

Taking the seat next to Ava, he put his hand over hers. She welcomed the comforting gesture.

'Mother, you're not making sense and this isn't fair to Ava. You need to explain what you mean. I think you need to tell us everything.'

Despite the steam coming from it, Lady Bramlington lifted her tea and took a sip. Ava watched as the woman, looking frailer than her years, readied herself to speak.

'We were great friends, your mother and I. There was something special about our friendship, it was as if we were always meant to find each other. Living here, it's like a fortress. The world goes on outside while you're trapped inside. When I was first married, I was barely twenty-one. I had married the man of my parents' dreams, not my own. I liked him, of course. He was wealthy, titled, good-looking and he could be fun, but I didn't love him, that came later.' She sipped her tea.

Ava moved her hand so that she could squeeze Henry's reassuringly. Her own father died when she was two. While she sometimes felt she had fleeting memories of him – the briefest of images of him locked in her mind – she rationalised that they were inspired by stories her mum shared or photographs she had seen. What she did know for certain was that her parents had shared a great love. For Henry to hear that his own parents didn't must be difficult. But then his world was very different from hers. She only had to look at her surroundings to know that.

He accepted the gesture, thanking her with the briefest of looks, before returning his attention to his mother.

'Lily and Connor Flynn were a breath of fresh air. They were passionate in their beliefs and actions. They both loved the grounds here, like you.' Lady Bramlington looked at Ava.

Ava nodded silently as she sat, enthralled to hear about her parents in their youth, and confused as to where this story was leading.

'I envied them their freedom of mind, body and spirit. Some thought them hippies, but they weren't like those who checked out of life – they lived. I mean really lived, and they had strong beliefs. Their energy was intoxicating.'

Ava began to wonder if she was going to hear her parents were cult leaders. If Lady Bramlington started talking about them chanting or dancing naked around campfires, she was going to have to ask her to move the story on. As intrigued as she was, there were some images she didn't need in her mind. She wanted to hear about the rift – whatever it was that had torn their friendship apart, because, despite what Lady Bramlington thought, Connor Flynn died in a car accident.

'We all became close, and we joined their cause.'

Oh no, they were cult leaders.

'We'd newly taken over the estate, and we wanted to make our mark. What better way than leading it into a new and greener era in which the animals were respected and protected?'

Of course, animal welfare was always their cause. Ava admonished herself for allowing her mind to jump to erroneous conclusions.

'They worked closely with us. Hunting for pleasure stopped. And they worked with Ted to ensure the protection of the animals and their habitats in our grounds.'

Ava wondered why, in all the time she had spent with Ted, he never mentioned that to her.

Henry leaned forward, passing Ava her tea before taking his own.

'And so our friendship grew, as did your parents' charity. When at first your mother became pregnant, we were all delighted. Of course, we wanted a child too, an heir for the estate.'

Ava wished Lady Bramlington hadn't made her desire for a baby sound like a business transaction. She flicked her eyes to Henry, wondering if hugging him would be inappropriate. Reminding herself to stay focused, she turned her attention back to Lady Bramlington.

'Your birth didn't dull your mother's passions in any way. If anything, she fought harder to make the world a better place for you. She could be very rigid in her ideals. We disagreed about some things, but friends do. Eight months later, Henry was born and we were all happy. You were very protective of him'—Lady Bramlington looked between the two of them— 'even then.'

Ava knew her mum was rigid in her ideals, but still having someone else say it made her feel defensive on her behalf. She returned her cup and saucer to the tray having only sipped at her tea. 'And then my father died.'

'Yes.'

'And did you cause his accident?' Henry pushed.

Mirroring Ava, Lady Bramlington placed her teacup and saucer on the tray. 'I caused him to flee into the night, taking you, Ava, with him.'

'What? What do you mean? I wasn't with him.'

'You were and Lily could have lost you both because of my actions.'

'What actions?' Henry pushed his hand through his hair.

'I was in love with Lily. I had been since the moment I met her and she loved me too. I was never in any doubt about that.'

Henry sat back as the air left him.

Ava didn't move, but she felt as if the world around her was shifting.

'For a long time we, of course, did little more than flirt and kiss – secret passion-fuelled kisses. Imagine the scandal if we had declared our love. Imagine what it would have done to your father.' She looked at Henry.

'My mother loved my father.' Ava heard the words as if someone else had spoken them.

'Yes, she did very much. But we shared something more, something deeper. I know that must be hard for you to hear, but it is true. On the night your father died, Lily and I were in the stables, together. We kissed like we had many times before.' Lady Bramlington wiped a tear as it ran down her cheek. 'Things went further. It felt very natural, like the culmination of all those secret moments. Our bodies playing out every yearning we had felt—'

'We get the idea, Mother. What happened next?' Henry's words were impatient.

'It was beautiful, slow, tender.'

Henry shifted uncomfortably in his seat, causing Lady Bramlington to move on.

'As we lay in each other's arms, the cool evening air gentle on our enlivened bodies, Connor found us. He was hurt and shocked. Lily tried to run after him but by the time she had covered herself it was too late. He was in his car and speeding down the drive before she could stop him. You, Ava, were in the car.'

Ava tried to take it all in; it was too much. Her view of her mother, of Lady Bramlington, of her parents' life together, and of her father's death all shifting; and then a fleeting memory flashed into her mind.

'The blood. There was so much blood. I was crying, Daddy, Daddy, but he couldn't hear me.' The room spun. Henry's voice slipped in and out of her consciousness, and Ava welcomed the dark emptiness as it engulfed her.

Chapter Thirty-Three

Ava tilted her head back attempting to see from under the sombrero Pauline had insisted she should wear. 'I knew after Gino's beret on the French night that these evenings would turn into something vaguely stereotypical. I've tried to keep it stylish by offering fashions inspired by the country in the charity shop, but this is what we have come to.' Ava shook her head at Mary's poncho and maracas.

'But look around the room, everyone seems happy. Well, it's hard to tell with that table.'

Both Ava and Mary looked at the table of six, dressed in homage to the Day of the Dead.

'But everybody else looks happy. And the food is, without doubt, a triumph.' Mary took a bite of her cauliflower taco with chipotle romesco. 'Gino has really gone all out on the vegan menu. He's amazing.'

Ava looked at her, a wry smile on her face, before mimicking Mary's enthusiastic tone. 'Amazing.'

'An amazing landlord, that's all I meant. He's an amazing landlord to think of every customer.'

Ava looked around the room. 'Yes, I'm sure he was thinking of every customer.' She took a mouthful of her ground beef taco and waited for Mary to survey the surrounding tables. 'You realise you are the only vegan here, don't you?'

'You don't have to be vegan to order a vegan dish.'

'No, you don't.' Ava was getting frustrated with keeping Gino's secret, especially as she felt sure Mary had feelings for him too. With her own love life in tatters, she really wanted to see her friends happy and wished she hadn't promised not to tell Mary Gino had fallen for her. As she wondered how else she could open Mary's eyes to the lovely man who was so clearly smitten with her, Ava spotted Flo coming in, wearing what Ava was sure had been a picnic blanket for sale at the charity shop, as a poncho. Flo waved and walked towards their table.

'Right, the pups are fed. They've had a little nibble of your table leg—'

'What?'

'Just a few teeth marks, nothing like a bit of history on your furniture. I've still got notches on my—'

'Oh God, do we want to hear this?' Mary interjected.

'On my door frame, from when my boys were growing up, silly. Now they're both over six foot tall. Actually, my eldest has just broken up with his girlfriend. Shall I get him to stop by the shop and—'

Ava raised her hand. 'No! Thank you.'

As Flo settled herself at the table, Mary leaned forward and spoke. 'Flo, you know she's in love with the son of her mum's lesbian lover, but can't now do anything about it since their love affair was instrumental in causing her father's car accident and, as it turns out, her fear of blood.'

'Mary!' Ava was shocked. Despite the fact she'd already shared her parents' past with Flo, after breaking down at the charity shop, Mary's summary of the situation seemed indiscreet, especially in The Brown Dog. 'I'd have thought you of all people would show my parents some respect.'

'I do. Revelations of your mum's secret love affair with Lady B have made her go up even higher in my estimation if that's possible. She really was an amazing woman who followed her passions … in more ways than one. And, as for your dad, it's sad, it really is, but you know I believe in fate. It was his time, Ava. If that hadn't have caused his accident, then something else would.'

'You don't know that's true.'

'And you don't know it's not. But think, Ava. You were in the same accident and you're here now.'

'That's enough, you two. Gossip gets around this place.' Flo looked towards Pauline, serving at the bar.

Both Mary and Ava laughed. To be told by Flo to be more discreet felt like an oxymoron. But Ava was grateful to her for staying true to her word. Flo had kept Lily and Lady Bramlington's secret as she promised she would.

'And all of the parties involved deserve some respect. The past is in the past, the future's not yet written, and the here and now is for the living.' Flo imparted the words as if sharing great wisdom.

'I'm sure I've read that as a meme.' Mary pondered.

'The past is history, tomorrow's a mystery and today is a gift. That's why they call it the present.' Ava smiled.

Flo shook her head. 'No! Not where I was going with that. I just meant you can dwell on everything or you can move forward. You deserve to be happy and those pups won't be around to distract you forever. They're growing up fast. The blighters were running circles around me this afternoon and—'

'Thank you so much for spending time with them. I really do appreciate it. While I was in the shop, I managed to make huge progress on planning for the summer festival. In fact, I wanted to run an idea past you both. I know we're not a pet rescue, but what about having a dog show – with a prize in my mum's honour. What do you think?' Ava congratulated herself on the subtle subject change before Flo started talking about Henry.

'That's a lovely idea. I guess you'll charge for entry.' Mary smiled.

'Yes, but I'll keep it reasonable. It's likely to be children who enter. While the festival itself will be good for the village, the money we raise ourselves will all be extra revenue for the charity. Goodness knows we need it with the move.'

'And how's that going?' Flo directed her question to Mary. Since Ava found it too distressing to speak to Henry herself, she had placed Mary in charge of all matters relating to the relocation of Critters' Lodge. While Mary had been reluctant at first, she welcomed the expansion opportunity as they took over the "fateful" stables as she liked to call them, and the dairy at Dapplebury House. Lady Bramlington had deemed it fitting that All Critters Great and Small's rescue and rehabilitation centre should be on-site and that the unused stable block should be dedicated to Lily's memory.

'Very well, actually. It's an exciting new beginning for the charity. We'll have larger premises, with easier access, but our rent will remain the same.'

'I'm not sure that's sensible on Henry's part. I'm sure the estate needs the money.' Ava thought about her conversation with Henry and his need to sell the land that had housed the Lodge.

Dismissing Ava's concerns, Mary continued, 'Funny how you never questioned why you had mates' rates when you thought Lady Bramlington hated you.'

'My mum always said it was a PR thing, good for the Bramlington image to have a charity housed on the estate and that they'd never dare put the rent up for fear of the trouble she'd cause.'

'I guess that makes sense now. She really could have caused trouble if she'd gone to the papers. It would have been quite the scandal, especially back then,' Flo put in.

Ava looked at Mary. 'And you knew my mum. Her decision to stay would have been based on what was best for the charity. It was always her priority.'

'That's true.'

'And what about the late Lord Bramlington? Did he know about … you know … what happened?' Flo leaned in, her eyes flicking between Ava and Mary.

'When I'd got over the shock, Lady Bramlington said when Mum refused to see them after Dad's death, she told him she was racked with grief and seeing them brought back too many memories, which was kind of true. That and guilt. She said she wondered if he knew, but if he did he never mentioned it to her. Better to live in denial than have your fears confirmed, I guess.'

Flo sat back. 'Better to live knowing than die wondering, I say.'

Ava couldn't help but feel Flo's comment was directed at her.

Mary picked up her taco. 'Have you been on Facebook or something today, Flo? You're a meme a minute.'

'Ha, when the puppies let me.' Flo giggled before offering to get a round of drinks.

As she made her way to the bar brandishing the money Ava insisted she should take as a thank you for puppy sitting, Mary finished her mouthful and looked at Ava.

'The move is going well. You should come and see when you're ready. And Henry's got all sorts of ideas for opening up the house and bringing people into the village. I think he'd like to show you. Oh and he's got the best idea for the last night of the festival.'

'You called him Henry.' Ava felt a pang of jealousy at the familiarity.

'Well, I couldn't carry on calling him Lord Whateverington when we're talking business and I'm seeing him most days, could I? Besides, he's all right, you know. I think he genuinely wants to help the village and the charity.'

Ava knew Henry's intentions were genuine. He was a good person. A person who she still very much had feelings for. But how could she disrespect her parents' wishes and follow her heart, knowing what she knew now? Her dad had died driving her away from the estate. And her mum had told her many times to stay away from the grounds and the Bramlingtons. If only she'd listened, her life would be less complicated. Whenever she let herself think about the prospect of being with Henry she remembered the accident. Previously buried in her subconscious, it now haunted her.

'Gino said he'll be over once the rush dies down and sent

these.' Flo took her seat, put the three drinks down on the table and sipped hers. 'Ooo that's good!'

'What are they?' Ava looked at the pink blush liquid, complete with ice and a lime wedge on the rim of the glass.

'Pamela I think he said. Three parts grapefruit soda and one part tequila. Funny name for a drink, but ever so refreshing.'

Ava took a sip. 'Blimey, that is good.'

When the mariachi band began to play, she jumped. Goodness knows where Gino had found them, but they were very good, encouraging people to join in and even have a dance. While Mary proved to have a natural ability for it, Ava found, despite her best efforts, her own dancing was less impressive.

By the time Gino joined them they were taking a break, rosy-cheeked and on their third round of drinks. Ava shuffled her seat along to ensure the only place he could add a chair was next to Mary.

'So ladies, how is your night? Did you enjoy the food?'

'Mary said it was a triumph.' Ava grinned.

Gino's cheeks flushed. 'Thank you. I'll give your compliments to Chef.'

'Didn't you create this menu?' Ava asked, knowing that he had but wanting to make the point to Mary.

'You know I did. I was working on it when I came to see my girl, Luna.'

'Oh, yes. Sorry, I forgot.'

'What colour collar does Luna have?' Flo pulled up a picture of Myrtle's puppies on her phone.

'Yellow.'

'Well, she was a pickle today and kept trying to eat the plants. She's got so much energy, that one. It's good the pups are allowed in the garden for exercise and toilet-training but it'll be better when they're allowed to actually go for walks.'

'Gino knows what she's like, but he loves her.' Ava sighed. 'Headstrong and independent.'

'You'll soon train her. A bit of positive reinforcement and she'll be putty in your hands before you know it.' Mary looked at Gino.

Ava tried not to giggle. Being subtle was clearly going over Mary's head but it made for entertaining conversation when she inadvertently responded.

'Perhaps you could help me when I get her? My parents had a dog, but I've never owned one myself before.'

'Of course I will.' Mary smiled.

Ava almost spat her drink out. *Oh my goodness, that's it. The puppy will bring them together!* It was like a Disney film playing out in her mind.

'Don't you think, Ava?'

Hearing her name, Ava returned her focus to the conversation. 'Sorry I was miles away. What were you saying?' She looked at Gino, sure that the expression on his face was more than a little pleased with himself.

'The costumes look great, don't they? Do you recognise many from the charity shop? I haven't checked the till yet to see if many brought in vouchers.'

'The odd picnic blanket.' Ava looked at Flo and laughed.

'This is what's the word now? Upcycling! There was a TV show about it. Bloody nonsense – it was called common sense to reuse, mend and make do in my day.'

Mary looked at Flo, quizzically. 'I'm not sure cutting a hole in a perfectly good picnic blanket can be classed as upcycling. It's more like vandalism.'

'I'll have you know I have measured the appropriate size, blanket stitched all around the hole, added pockets and made a belt to go with this little number. Look, this side is waterproof. It'll be just the job in the rain.'

Mary burst out a giggle. 'Only you, Flo.'

Gino looked around the room, his expression crestfallen. 'I'm sorry people aren't buying as much from the charity shop as we thought they would.'

'Not everyone has Flo's vision.' Mary laughed.

Ava went to kick her under the table but couldn't with Gino sitting between them. 'Honestly, it's fine. It was always a long shot. But I'm pleased it's been a success for you. I recognise so many people from the village in here now and not just on themed nights but at other times too. It's like you've reminded them their local is still here.'

'Yes, we've had a few people say how they'd forgotten about us, how much they enjoy the atmosphere, and how good it is to have the opportunity to come to these nights and try something new.'

'Well, Pamela is Flo's new best friend,' Mary declared.

'That's nice.' Gino looked at Flo, who raised her glass. He pushed his dark fringe back from his eyes. 'Who is Pamela?'

'The drink, the drinks you served us.'

'Paloma!' Gino laughed.

'Pamela, Paloma, Palamino, whatever the name it tastes blooming great!' Flo declared before draining her glass.

Ava giggled. She loved her friends; they always had a way of making her smile. She knew she had lots to be grateful for. The puppies were fit and healthy and almost eight weeks old. In two weeks they would, with the exception of Blossom – the smallest of the litter, that she'd decided to keep – all be going to good homes within Dapplebury. The charity was doing well, despite the fact the silly season was well and truly upon them, and on top of their general wildlife casualties they had eleven gulls, three crows and two jackdaws to look after. And, while she couldn't currently involve herself with the move in the way she had hoped to, she did feel it was a new beginning for the charity. In the face of everything positive, a broken heart was a small matter. Wasn't it? Ava wondered what she could possibly throw herself into after the festival was over. She had been planning it like a woman possessed; maximum effort meant minimal time to think, and she liked it that way.

'Let's dance.'

Mary pulled Ava onto the makeshift dance floor. As she stood, she did a double take, sure that she had seen Henry standing at the bar. Her heart leapt, but as she looked back, he'd gone. *And now you're going bloody crazy! Focus, Ava. It's what you promised yourself you would do.*

Chapter Thirty-Four

Henry ended the call after thanking Dermot Dixon for his co-operation. In the two months that had passed since he spoke to Ava, he felt he was making a difference, turning the fortunes of the estate and Dapplebury House around. He had plans underway for opening the house, the legalities and insurance were complicated but not insurmountable, and he had set to on the other practicalities involved. While all of these things took time and money, he was beginning to see how his plans could come to fruition. Mrs Jenkins had been an asset. The woman who once walked the corridors of Dapplebury House and lurked like a ghost, now had a purpose and was putting her organisational skills to great use.

Henry looked at Critters' Cottage, trying to summon the courage to leave the car and knock on the door. A week ago he'd slipped discreetly into the pub with the hope of bumping into Ava. But having seen her looking so happy, Gino next to her, he had decided to leave. But no matter what he did, he couldn't get her out of his mind.

Every step he made towards realising his vision for the village and Dapplebury House, he wanted to share with her. And it wasn't just the big things either; every time he ran in the grounds and spotted evidence of a new creature or plant in the woods he wanted to tell her. He wanted to tell her that he was having the lake dredged, he wanted to tell her how much Granger missed her, and ... Who was he kidding? He wanted to tell her how much he missed her.

He had taken time to decide if sharing his feelings and daring to hope she might feel the same was fair. His family had impacted on her life in ways he could never undo. While his mother's revelations hadn't proven she was directly responsible for Connor Flynn's death, she had been instrumental in the events of that night. He wasn't sure how or if he and Ava could come back from that. Ava hadn't returned to Dapplebury House or, as far as he knew, the grounds since the day she had visited him there. She hadn't even been to see the progress of the move. Despite Mary explaining that Ava's haemophobia tended to keep her away, he found himself hoping she'd come each day.

Now he was sitting outside her cottage, he wasn't sure what he was going to say, or how he intended to say it. Except he knew he had to speak to her. He had to find out if she had feelings for Gino because he knew they weren't an item when he'd first returned to Dapplebury, and yet he'd heard her say she loved him. In light of all that had passed between them, that was confusing.

Henry was good at reading people, and he'd been sure Ava's reaction towards him, and the feelings she expressed were genuine. For him, being intimate with Ava felt unlike being with any other woman he had known. *Surely that wasn't one-sided.* More than anything, he had to know if there was any chance of Ava considering a future with him.

He was here for answers. Bolstered by his thoughts, Henry left the car. As he rang the bell, he heard a chorus of yaps and barks and smiled, despite the slight quake of nerves he could feel growing inside. He knew the puppies must be nine weeks old and would be going to new homes soon. Seeing them would be good.

'Hello.' Mary smiled.

Henry looked at her as she opened the door, disappointment twisting in his stomach. Not that he hadn't come to like her; he did. Since they'd been working together on the charity relocation, he had come to appreciate her no-nonsense, say-it-as-it-is approach to life. But he had hoped to see Ava alone, and whenever he tried that at her cottage, Mary somehow thwarted it.

'Is Ava home?'

'No, she's at the shop today. I'm here on puppy duty. Do you want to come in? I've put the kettle on.'

Henry's initial instinct was to head to the charity shop while his confidence allowed, but realising this might be his last chance to see the puppies he decided to take Mary up on her offer.

'Thanks, that would be good.' He ducked to enter, wiped his feet and followed Mary through to the kitchen, remembering the all-too-brief but thoroughly lovely times he had spent in the cottage with Ava.

'Wow! Look at you all.' Henry took in the sight of a very excited Myrtle and her five energetic puppies. While he'd watched many litters grow, the stark contrast between seeing these pups being born to the bundles of energy that were before him now was staggering. It was a reminder of how much time had passed. And how much had changed as the weeks had gone by.

Their shiny coats were chocolate, the colour of Granger, while they had Myrtle's ears and build. Their markings were varied, from white socks to flashes on their chest and exuberant tails. All had big paws and, he was sure, mischief on their minds. As he stepped over the baby gate erected at the kitchen door, he became an instant source of fascination with the puppies who snuffled around his feet and chewed his laces. Bending down, he attempted to distract them with their array of toys; squeaky balls, teddies, knotted ropes – none seemed to interest them as much as his trainers.

'Ava will be sorry she missed you.'

'Really? Do you think so?'

Having just taken the milk from the fridge, Mary paused. 'Honestly. I don't know. I mean, I know she wants to see you. I'm just not sure if she thinks it's the best idea.'

'For who?' Henry realised his voice sounded curt. He and Mary were getting along, and he didn't want to spoil that by allowing his frustration and confusion over the situation with

Ava to make him appear abrupt. He attempted to rephrase the question. 'Do you know what makes her think it's not the best thing?' He had to be careful; he wasn't sure how much Mary knew. Their conversations until now had focused mainly on the charity and the facilities at Dapplebury House. If, and when, Ava decided to share the details of her – *their* – mothers' pasts was up to her.

Mary turned to look at him. She screwed up her nose and offered him a small smile. 'We're best friends and friends talk. I know ... everything.' She poured milk into two mugs before putting it back in the fridge.

'OK.' Henry nodded. Being careful to avoid the puppies, he pulled a chair out. As it scraped against the flagstone floor, one attempted to bark at the noise. Henry laughed.

'Are you quacking at me?'

The puppy, with a yellow collar and white markings that made it look like it was wearing socks, tried again. Henry ruffled the fur around its too-big ears and sat down before letting out a long breath. 'When you say everything ...'

Mary removed the teabags from their mugs and lifted the sugar bowl.

Henry shook his head. 'No, thank you.'

'You two as children and teenagers, your parents as friends and ... lovers.'

Henry nodded. 'So literally everything.' He said it with a smile; there was no other way to respond. He'd never wanted to imagine anything intimate between his parents. Hearing of his mother's affair had given him a whole lot more to try to put to the back of his mind.

Mary took the two mugs of tea from the side and walked towards the table, a task that was akin to running the gauntlet as she avoided the puppies. Joining Henry, she sat down.

'So did you come to see the puppies, or did you have something you wanted to say to Ava?'

'If I told you I was here just to see the puppies, would you believe me?'

'No.'

'Ha, well, I think you have your answer.'

Mary smiled. She rubbed her thumb around the rim of her mug before making eye contact. 'Henry, look. The past between your parents, it's complicated. Really complicated. But I'll tell you what I've tried to tell Ava – don't let the past stop you from having the future you want. You and Ava are both lovely people. Lovely people who are hanging on to promises and responsibilities to parents who lived their lives in the way they chose to. This is your time now – don't let the past stand in your way.'

Henry was a little taken aback. He took a moment to absorb Mary's words and stroked Myrtle who had decided it was her turn for a fuss. 'But Ava—'

'Loves you.' Mary bit her lip. 'Sorry, I don't know if I was supposed to say that. Actually, I'm pretty sure I wasn't supposed to say that but—'

'The night the puppies were born I heard her say she loves Gino. You were here. She said it to you.'

'Of course she loves Gino. She loves him as she loves me. He's her friend; he has been since he took over The Brown Dog. He's a good listener and helped her when her mum passed. He's not her best friend, obviously, that's me, but—'

'So she's not *in love* with Gino.' Henry felt a little dizzy.

'No, she never has been. Gino can be a right pain but he has a lot of good qualities too. Yes, he's very good-looking, but he's also kind, caring, a good listener—'

'OK, I get the picture.'

Mary's cheeks flushed. 'Anyway, I tried to get them together but it was never going to happen. They hit it off as friends and they've stayed that way ever since.'

'And you think she loves me.' Henry felt an uncontainable grin tugging at his lips.

'If you can't see that you're blind. I can see it every time she speaks about you.'

'But with what happened, how can she be with me when—' Henry bent to pick up the puppy that was tugging and growling at his shoelace. She had a white front like Myrtle's and adorable Malteser eyes; he held her in his arms. 'When being with me will remind her of why she grew up without a father.'

'She always knew about her father's accident, even if she blocked the details out. You two shouldn't be punished for the actions of your parents. If Lily had told her the truth it wouldn't be something she's coping with now, without her mum here to answer questions. Don't get me wrong, I loved Lily. She was an amazing woman. But this, it isn't fair. Perhaps knowing more, understanding the things she'd blocked out, might have helped Ava with her fear of blood. Lily must have known that but still she chose not to tell her. Parents, they have a lot to answer for.'

'I guess.' Henry thought about his own parents and remembered his mum saying she'd been twenty-one when she and his father had taken over Dapplebury House and the estate. 'But how old were they when the accident happened?'

'Probably similar to our ages now.' Mary shrugged.

'And do you feel you've got a handle on life or all of the answers? Because I don't.'

Mary looked thoughtful. 'Bugger me! Don't get philosophical on me. I have a long list of things I hold my parents personally responsible for and I am not sure I'm ready to change my world view on that.'

Henry laughed, and the pink-collared puppy licked his face.

'Well, Myrtle and Blossom are fans. Now all you have to do is convince Ava to give you a chance.'

'Blossom?'

'Ava's keeping that pup. She was the weakest and needed the most care and now she says she can't let her go.'

Henry looked at Blossom, then down at Myrtle still snuggled up close to him. If only Ava's affections were as easy to gain as that of her dogs.

Mary took a sip of her tea. 'That's the thing about Ava. She has a big heart and she's loyal. Once she loves you, you know she'll love you forever.'

Henry hung on to the words. He knew she loved him once; she hadn't denied their teenage affection for each other when his mother mentioned it, any more than he had. 'I hope you're right. I'm just not sure Ava will think being together is the right thing in light of …' He let his words trail off.

'Then you'll have to convince her, won't you. And I think your plans for the end of the festival will be just the time to do it.'

Chapter Thirty-Five

'And then there were two!' Ava walked into the kitchen that felt far too empty now that three of the puppies had gone to their new owners. She knew they would all have happy lives. She'd made sure they were going to good homes to people she knew within the village, but for ten weeks they'd been her babies. She had been on call to them day and night, watched them grow and begin to develop their characters, only taking her shifts at the charity shop as she needed to and an evening out to the Mexican night at The Brown Dog as a break. Gino, who was holding Luna, put his arm around Ava's shoulders.

'You know you're still going to see them all, don't you? And you'll never get rid of Luna and me. Adopting this one means I am now officially part of your family.'

Ava smiled. 'You already feel like family to me!'

Gino leaned in to kiss Ava's cheek and Luna tugged on Ava's ponytail.

'Ouch! There are some things I won't miss. These pickles have become cheeky these past weeks.' Ava extricated her hair from Luna's mouth and offered her a toy instead. 'Puppy classes here we come.' She sat on the edge of the sofa, watching Blossom as she investigated the newly puppy-proofed living room.

'It will be a family reunion. I think we're all booked in at the village hall for as soon as their jabs are done and they're allowed to go out and socialise. A pub dog has to have manners, Luna, ha?' Gino knelt on the floor and held his puppy out to look into her face. She squirmed, wriggling in his hands as if swimming in the air and he put her down. 'I have confidence,' he said with the cheeky smile that Ava never tired of.

'You're confident and optimistic about all things, except one.'

'I think training my Luna will be easier than getting Mary to see how I feel about her.' Gino moved Luna out from behind the television.

'You've been a bit subtle about the whole thing. I think maybe Mary needs something a little more … *oomphy*.' Ava thought for a moment. 'I'm not sure that's a word, but you know what I mean. Subtle isn't really her style, is it?'

Gino nodded wistfully. 'Maybe at the festival when …'

'When?'

'When the timing is right – *l'amore trova un modo*. But this is a busy time. There's plenty of other things to concentrate on with the festival only two weeks away.' He brushed the subject of Mary aside.

L'amore trova un modo. Love will find a way. Ava had heard Gino say this before and wondered if it were true. And if it was, what might that mean for her and Henry. She pushed the thought aside. She couldn't think about that now either. Besides, whoever came up with the saying obviously hadn't fallen for the son of their mum's lesbian lover! Ava shook her head. She'd had ten weeks to get used to the idea and yet it still seemed surreal. With the puppies leaving and the festival looming, she'd enough to think about without allowing her mind to slip into thoughts of family secrets and what might have been.

She decided to stick to a safer subject. 'So three gourmets down. Chinese night this Friday, and what are you planning for the festival weekend? You mentioned a barbecue when we last spoke, but I know you better than that, you're not talking charred sausages in a bun are you?'

'Ha, no! I'm talking a Texan street barbecue with ribs, corn, brisket, spicy sausages and more. Slow-cooked over a wood-fired barbecue. And there'll be potato salad, beans and bread. Plenty to make everyone thirsty. We're going big and bold with this one. I've got hay bales coming to sit on, and some flags to put up. Make the most of the festival feel. You'll dress up won't you? I've ordered chaps and a Stetson. Oh and Ted's offered to play the fiddle.'

'He's what?'

'Offered to play the fiddle.'

'I didn't know he could play.' Ava thought about the fact Ted had known about her parents' connection to the Bramlingtons. She hadn't known that either. Another person she'd thought she knew was turning out to be somebody else entirely.

'Ava? So, what do you think? You looked miles away there. Don't you like the idea?' Gino held onto a rope while Blossom and Luna tugged at each end. Myrtle jumped up onto the sofa next to Ava, seemingly grateful to have someone else entertaining her puppies.

Ava moved to accommodate the dog and smiled while her mind caught up with Gino's words. 'A Texan barbecue. I think it's great. I'll sort a rail of suitable clothes for the shop this weekend. Lucky for us we always have plenty of checked shirts and denim and that should appeal. That's if you're offering the dessert deal.'

'Of course. Sopapilla cheesecake and a vegan pecan pie.'

'OK, then I'll definitely put the rail out.'

'And I think you should put out some fancy dresses – formal types of long dresses.' Gino gesticulated with his hands to make his point.

'Really? Why?'

'Isn't it prom season? You should know that. Don't you want to grab people before they go and buy from the high street?'

Ava looked at Gino, surprised by his sudden interest in what she put out on the shop floor. Of course she knew they were entering prom season, but she was planning to hold off with a formal gown rail until after the festival. The shop was small and she was hoping for greater footfall over the festival period.

'My sister told me. The weather is good, people are happier to buy when the sun is shining, and it isn't that far off. I'll tell Mamma to bring Sofia down to look. You'll definitely put the dresses out?'

'Yes, though I don't see why it can't wait until after the festival weekend. I'm hoping the shop will be busy and the space would be—'

'There, I've texted my Mamma to tell her. You wouldn't want to let her down would you?'

Ava shook her head as she looked at the sent text displayed on Gino's phone as he held it up. She realised he probably wanted to feel like he was helping the shop, especially after the Around the World in Eight Gourmets evenings had been a greater success for him than her. She smiled.

'Of course. I've got the dresses stored here. I'll take them into the shop and put some out tomorrow.' She really could have done without the bother but she didn't want to let Gino's mum and sister down, or to thwart him when he was trying to help.

The inaugural, Dapplebury festival weekend had been weeks in the planning. She had live music in the village square, and stalls to line the streets – on loan from the farmer's market. Each restaurant, shop and antique dealership had been encouraged to have a stall outside their premises, thus ensuring they were open and active when it came to the event. Then she'd organised a range of acts, including the local school choir, a demonstration from the Jive to Thrive group, art exhibitions, a street magician, face painting and a learn to knit hub manned by Flo's Knit and Natter group. She hoped it would be a success for the whole village as well as bringing in extra revenue for the charity, who were not only having a book and cake sale outside the shop but were also responsible for the dog show in her mum's honour.

'Did I tell you I've got the local press on board?' Ava stroked Myrtle while Gino continued to play with Luna and Blossom.

'That's great. And your website?'

'Is good to go, with all of mum's old paper clippings archived and lots about our current work too, including a blog that we can use to keep people up to date with our rescues. It will be good. Sometimes people bring animals to us, or phone about them and then don't like to trouble us to ask how they're doing. We appreciate it. It's good to keep the phone lines clear but this way we can keep people informed. Mary's starting us off with a post about drunken gulls.'

'Drunken gulls?' Gino looked at Ava.

'Well, gulls in general really but it's a headline. The charity had almost four hundred calls about gulls last year, more than half of those we, Mary and her team, put on rooftops near to where they'd been found. Gull parents rarely abandon their young. They'll keep feeding and defending them even if down a chimney or stuck on the ground.'

'So drunken gulls, because?'

'Because when the flying ants come, the birds gorge on them. The formic acid overdose makes them behave a little drunk. They'll be on the ground, wandering in roads and generally not moving so well. They recover but people need to be aware – so drunken gulls!'

'Of course, it all makes sense now.' Gino laughed. 'I'm sure it will get people's attention. And the move, how is that going?'

Ava took a breath. 'Obviously it's early days, but the office buildings are in situ and Mary has plans for a phased move for the animals. We are mid our busiest season at the moment, so making use of the extra space will be great. I can make the official announcement at the festival. Hen—' Ava swallowed. 'Mary says Lord Bramlington is booked and intending to come along and talk about it with me.' Ava hadn't yet considered how she was going to deal with that. But remaining in denial about having to have a normal conversation when so much had been said, and so much remained unsaid, was her way of coping. 'We've got coverage from the local paper and radio, and who knows – with his involvement we might make a small column in the nationals if it's a slow news day.' Ava laughed but it sounded too shrill even to her.

'A very slow news day,' Gino teased. 'And what about the skydive. Have you hired your hedgehog costume and booked the jump?'

'Ha bloody ha!' Ava picked up a squeaky ball and threw it at Gino, causing both puppies and Myrtle to leap towards him.

'I wish I'd seen your face.' Gino threw the ball into the hallway, and the dogs all scampered after it.

'It was a rotten tease. I'd had a little too much whisky, my ankle was throbbing, and the last thing I could imagine myself doing was jumping out of an aeroplane.'

'But now you've not been drinking whisky, and your ankle is all better, so …'

'No, absolutely not! I'm not jumping out of an aeroplane, no matter how much it might raise. But if you would like to, you know, all in a good cause – please do.' Ava laughed.

Gino pondered. 'Do I have to dress as a hedgehog?'

'Oh no, Gino, don't I was only joking. Please don't feel you have to jump out of an aeroplane for us because the gourmets' plan went a bit tits-up.' Ava saw the wounded expression on Gino's face and instantly regretted the words.

'I'm sorry that hasn't worked out for you. But honestly, I think good things are coming your way.'

'Thanks, Gino. It does feel like it. I've learnt a lot over these past weeks, raising the puppies, finding out more about my parents. I always imagined they had this perfect life, the perfect relationship. In some ways knowing they were fallible is reassuring. Like it's OK that I haven't got everything sorted. Do you think that makes me sound like a bad person, that I'm pleased to know my parents stuffed up too?'

'No, not when you've spent so long trying to live up to their ideals.'

'Isn't it funny how you can put people on a pedestal, or damn them for their behaviour without really knowing the truth.' Ava thought about her long-held misconceptions about Lady Bramlington's behaviour towards her.

'That's why you should worry about what is right for you and not what others do, or think.' Gino looked at her knowingly.

'Bugger me! When did you get so wise.'

'I am a landlord. I listen. I know things.' He laughed.

'Well, oh wise landlord you. You were right about one thing – this does feel like my time. There's a new start for the charity and it feels like a new beginning for me.'

'And will you seize new opportunities?'

'So long as you don't mean jumping out of an aeroplane then yes, *abso-bloomin-lutely!*' Ava giggled, feeling buoyed by the conviction of her words.

'That's great. It really is.'

Gino took the ball from a triumphant Myrtle as she walked back in the room, Blossom following. Standing to see what was keeping Luna, he dashed out the door. 'Outside, outside, Luna. Sorry, Ava! Mind that puddle.'

Ava looked at Blossom. 'Uh oh, come on. You'd better go out too or there'll be double puddles.'

Chapter Thirty-Six

Ava looked around the shop. It was ready. She had put out the last of the Texan inspired outfits she could muster and replenished the formal gown rail – it's popularity taking her by surprise as it seemed almost the whole village had "fallen in love with" or "simply must have" one of the dresses or another. The takings leading up to the festival had set new records for the shop. It was a welcome bonus as those hidden costs for the move, and Mary's ambition for a larger, better-equipped rescue centre had started to have an impact. Ava knew she needed to thank Gino. He'd been right about the timing, and not just because his mum and sister had visited and spent a considerable sum on outfits.

Realising the time, Ava opened the door and switched the sign as Flo and a chilly breeze blustered in. 'Well that's not what the weather forecast promised is it?'

Ava shut the door. 'No! All week my weather app has been saying sunshine for today. I woke this morning and it had changed to cloud with a forty per cent chance of rain. I could cry.'

'Nonsense! Let's have none of that. The day will be a success, you mark my words.'

Ava welcomed Flo's optimism, but with grey clouds in the sky and a chilly wind blowing, she wondered if people would take a punt and come out and support the festival.

Flo unbuttoned her coat and placed a laden carrier bag on the shop counter, before pulling out a large tin and popping the lid off. 'Here's my tomato soup cake.'

'Your what?' Ava screwed up her nose and walked to the counter.

'Yes, I know it sounds an odd 'un but rest assured it tastes every bit as good as it looks.'

Ava was surprised to see an appealing looking cake,

encased in cream cheese frosting. The unexpected sweet smell made her mouth water. 'Maybe we shouldn't say what's in it.'

'Nonsense. We have to what with allergies and what not – besides folks'll be intrigued. You'll see. It was a big hit at my cousin's funeral.'

'Oh.' Ava didn't want to associate the festival weekend with a wake and tried to focus on the positive as she put the lid back on the tin. 'Let's hope you're right. I'm sure it will be a first for many. I'll pop it out the back with the cakes the other volunteers have dropped off. Once things start picking up, I'll put them out. I tried to put the books out the front earlier but the wind was flapping the covers. I'd turn them but then they'd be upside down to passers-by.'

'I'm sure the wind will pass, and with a bit of luck it will take the cloud with it.'

Ava hoped Flo was right. 'And you're sure you're happy to stay and man the till this morning?'

'Of course, it's blowing a hooley out there.'

'Flo!'

'I'm teasing, you daft beggar. It's going to pass. And don't you worry the rota is all sorted: Thursday Sue is coming in shortly and we'll be as right as r—*whoops* let's not risk saying the r word.' Flo smiled before continuing. 'Monday Chris is covering this afternoon and Friday Pat is coming in to help her. Though you know how Friday Pat is. She loves to stand and chat – I'll have a word with Chris, make sure she keeps her on task.'

Ava smiled. She knew the shop was in safe hands and how lucky she was to have so many wonderful volunteers, even if they did insist on referring to each other by the day they worked as well as their name.

'I've got Knit and Natter in the village hall from one o'clock, so I'll have a nosey around the stalls before I go and set up.' Flo slipped on her name badge and glasses, readying herself at the till. 'All you need to focus on is checking that everyone's where they should be and that everything's sorted for the dog show.'

'The dog show! Flo, I've forgotten to buy the runner-up prizes. I knew there was something. I've got the rosettes for first place in each category and the best in show trophy but nothing for the runners-up. What shall I do?' Ava looked around the shop, seeing if there was anything suitable.

Flo raised her hand halting Ava mid-panic. 'Leave it to me! I've got just the thing at home. Perfect prizes for an animal show. The dogs will love 'em.'

'Really?' Ava thought about the tomato soup cake and wondered if Flo's idea of perfect matched her own.

'Trust me.'

'Maybe I'll get some dog treats and sweets or something. It will be mostly children who enter I'm sure and—'

'Nonsense. I told you I've got just the thing. I'll pop home before Knit and Natter and will drop them down to the arena on the green. You've no need to worry. Oh, and there now, here's our first customer.'

The shop door rattled open and the bell rang.

'Hello.' Ava smiled at Mrs Dent who had owned the Post Office for as long as she could remember.

'Hello, Ava dear. My joints say rain is brewing and I remembered you sold brollies.'

Ava tried to maintain her smile. 'Yes, we do. I'm sure Flo will be able to help you find one.' Clutching the tomato soup cake and taking Flo's coat, Ava rolled her eyes and headed for the back of the shop.

Looking at her watch, she realised she'd just enough time to make Flo a cup of tea before heading out to the square to meet Dave, the grandson of her old school headmistress. With some persuasion from his gran, a regular visitor to the charity shop, he'd donated a sound system and his compère skills for the weekend. Waiting for the kettle to boil, Ava looked at the flier she'd had printed, listing all the events, sponsors and participating shops and cafes over the next two days. She felt proud at the achievement of bringing it all together – and sick as she registered the countless opportunities for it all to go wrong. *It's going to be OK.*

'Right I'm here. What do you need?'

Ava jumped and turned; she had never been happier to see Mary.

'Oh, and here's my offering. Ultimate, vegan, chocolate fudge cake.'

Ava looked at the large chocolate cake Mary proffered on a plate.

'That looks amazing! Did you bake it?'

'Of course, didn't you know baking is one of my many talents?'

'No!' Ava took the cake, the sight and smell making her mouth water. 'Why did I not know this about you before now?'

'Because I'm lying! Of course I didn't bake it, you dozy mare. I got the café to knock it up for me.'

'Really? I didn't know they did that. It looks and smells delicious! And it puts my lemon drizzle from a packet to shame.'

'I'm sure it's great. What else have you got?' Mary looked at the tins spread over the sorting table.

'Two Victoria sponges, a carrot cake, a fruit cake, a coffee and walnut, and Flo's tomato soup cake. Don't ask, apparently it's a hit at funerals.'

'Of course!'

They both giggled.

While Ava made tea, Mary sliced the cakes into doorstop wedges and put them under glass cloches with a cake slice. No matter what she tried in terms of additional fundraising in the shop, nothing beat a cake stall when it came to achieving the optimum ratio of time, effort and profit.

After delivering Flo's tea, Ava looked at Mary who was

scraping the chocolate frosting from the knife she'd used to cut up the cake she'd donated.

'I've got to see a man about the music and check everyone is sorted. Can you help?'

'Sure, do you want me to deal with Mr Music?'

'No, thank you. But maybe you could start at The Brown Dog and work your way up that side of the street, just checking everyone is in place and all sorted, while I take this side?' Ava was sure Gino would be dressed in his cowboy outfit, a fact that might help him register on Mary's radar. 'And then it should be time for you to set up the dog show on the green. Are you still OK to do that?'

'Of course, and while I remember, Henry said he'd see you at twelve o'clock in the square unless there are any changes, in which case let him know.'

Ava felt heat flush in her cheeks as her stomach did a nervous flip. She had avoided Henry and the grounds of Dapplebury House, and successfully managed to coordinate everything related to the move via Mary, so far, but today she was going to have to face him. She'd known she'd have to at some point, especially with the lodge moving to Dapplebury House. It was only now that she realised putting it off meant she would be facing him, for the first time since the revelations about their parents, in public. Would that make it harder or easier? She didn't know but a glance at her watch told her she'd find out in a few short hours.

Having checked in with Dave the DJ and ensured that everyone was ready on her side of the street, Ava realised it was almost time to declare the festival officially open. Dave had assured her he'd be all set for her to give a brief speech before he launched into his summer tunes set. Deciding, while she waited, to switch her phone to aeroplane mode for fear of it ringing or giving feedback Ava saw a message from Mary. Taking in the sight of the photograph she had sent of Gino, with Luna in his arms, Ava smiled. *Who can resist the charms of a muscled Italian man, dressed as a cowboy, holding a Springador puppy?* Ava really hoped, not Mary. Looking at the mischievous dog, Ava was pleased she'd arranged a pet sitter for Myrtle and Blossom. Knowing they were sorted and happy meant one less thing to worry about.

When at last Dave had sorted the sound system, Ava made her way to the microphone. She'd attempted to prepare a speech, but it seemed silly saying too much when the only people currently listening were Dave and a few stallholders who'd managed to set up because the breeze didn't hamper their wares. Instead of going on too much, she thanked everyone for their amazing efforts, said some things about making this a festival to remember and, for some reason known only to her brain, shouted, 'Let the games begin.' At which point a somewhat confused Dave read the event sheet, reminding people of all that was on offer to see and do. Something she should have done.

Feeling a fool, Ava walked towards The Brown Dog. Looking up to the sky she could see the sun struggling to come out from behind the clouds. In the distance, over the top of Dapplebury House, there was even a hint of blue sky. The sight lifted her spirits. Though looking in that direction meant she couldn't help but think of Henry and the fact she would be face to face with him soon. Her pulse quickened at the prospect, as her pace hastened towards the pub in search of a fortifying drink to settle her nerves.

Walking around the central block of shops, Ava was taken aback. Outside the pub was an array of colour with bright bunting, hay bales and a few customers dressed appropriately as cowboys, including Gino, looking every bit as handsome as his picture in his jeans, red checked shirt, Stetson and chaps. Mary came out of the pub holding Luna in her arms and laughing as the puppy attempted to lick her face.

'You're still here!' Ava felt a sense of panic as she wondered if she should have gone to check the other stalls herself.

'Don't worry, I've been up and down this side of the street. I even took Luna with me. Everyone is all sorted. I just had to come back here to return this one to Magic Mike there.'

Ava burst out giggling. 'He does look a little bit—'

'Who looks what?' Gino walked towards them, and Luna wriggled with excitement.

'You have to admit you look a bit Magic Mike.'

'A bit what? You don't think I look like a cowboy?' Gino looked crestfallen.

'Oh no, you look every bit a cowboy. Just a certain sort.' Mary passed Luna over with a wry smile and offered to get a round of drinks in.

As Mary walked into the pub, Gino looked at Ava. 'I hoped she'd notice me like this, but she thinks I am some magician or something.'

'Believe me, she's noticed you.' Ava smiled as she pictured the male strippers in Magic Mike, a film both she and Mary had enjoyed at the cinema together. 'And what she said – I'd take it as a compliment.'

Gino looked buoyed by Ava's words. 'Come and see Chef. He's had the barbecue going since early.'

Ava followed Gino. The smell of the barbecue was making her hungry and the sight of the food caused her stomach to rumble. 'Those ribs look wonderful.'

'Do you want to try some? The secret is in cooking low and slow, no white heat. And to mop every hour with marinade,' Chef enthused.

He was obviously very proud of his efforts, and Ava felt it would be rude to say no. She took a paper plate from the stack and held it up while Chef served her.

Gino smiled. 'Ted is going to play soon. You've worked so hard, you should sit awhile enjoy your ribs and the music.'

Ava took her place on a hay bale that offered more authenticity than comfort but welcomed the time to soak up the atmosphere. She could hear the music from the square drifting in and out on the breeze that was more ambient than it had been first thing. She looked along the street at the stalls and was pleased to see some families browsing. While she could recognise the locals, many of whom were regular visitors to her shop, she could also see that people had come from further afield. For the first time since she had woken up, she dared to hope the day would be a success.

Carrying the drinks out, Mary sat next to her, placing their iced teas behind the hay bales to stop an over-exuberant Luna from knocking them over.

'They've got bourbon on the Texan drinks board, but I've seen what whisky does to you.'

'Haha!' Ava bit into the juicy, tender ribs, feeling the sticky sauce cover her mouth before she wiped it away.

'These are bloody good! I know you don't eat meat, but seriously, if I were vegan these would convert me.'

Mary laughed. 'I'll be having some of the corn later. I'm sure that'll be just as good.'

As Ted came out from the pub, he caught Ava's eye; with a knowing look he walked towards her.

'Ava, I wanted to speak to you.' He placed his fiddle at his side and gestured to ask if he could sit down.

'I think Luna and I should check out that corn – it might be ready.' Mary lifted the dog over the hay bale and headed towards Gino.

Ava looked at Ted. The man who was generally scruffily dressed, rooting around the grounds of Dapplebury House, was wearing jeans and a granddad style shirt, his hair streaked back under a Stetson. She'd known him her whole life, but as she looked at him now, his brow furrowed, she realised that perhaps she hadn't known him at all.

'I never told you about knowing your parents, and about … the night of the accident because—'

'It's OK. I get it. Everyone kept the secret from me. It

protected Mum's reputation and the Bramlingtons' too. You didn't have a choice. You had your job to think about and—'

Ted turned to look at her more directly. His hazel eyes focused on her. 'No. It wasn't like that. I wasn't protecting myself, or them. I was protecting you. The woods and the grounds, being with Henry, it seemed like your sanctuary from everything. I didn't want to tarnish that. I'm sorry. Maybe I should have said.' He sighed, removed his hat and wiped his brow. 'My late Eadie, God rest her soul, and I weren't blessed with children, looking out for you two—'

'Ted, really, it's fine. I'm grateful you didn't tell me. It wasn't your place, and … you're right. Being with Henry, being in the grounds of Dapplebury House, it always made me feel like me. It still does.' Ava heard her voice crack as she admitted it as much to herself as to the older man.

Ted smiled, his leathery skin wrinkling around his eyes. 'I'm glad you know that. He's a good boy, Henry. He's different to the rest. You were each other's sanctuary while your parents lived up to being the people everyone wanted them to be. Don't judge them for that. Things were different then, and your generation you're the lucky ones. You get to be who you want to be.'

Ava swallowed. As Ted stood and began to walk away, she called after him, 'Who told you that I know … about my parents and everything?'

'The lad. He's been waiting for you to come back. We both have.'

Ava nodded and looked down at her plate; it was going to be hard to swallow past the tightness in her throat.

Chapter Thirty-Seven

Henry walked towards the village. The sun was warm against his back, and he was pleased the clouds of earlier in the day had lifted. He felt a ball of nerves in the pit of his stomach, not about the radio interview, or making his announcement about Dapplebury House, but about seeing Ava. He wished they'd had the opportunity to speak before, but he wanted to give her time and space. He wanted to leave it to her to make the first move. But she hadn't. Perhaps he should accept that as a testament to her feelings, but his conversation with Mary had given him hope. He wasn't going to give up without fighting for her. He'd done that before and he wasn't going to do it again. If he had fought harder as a teenager, perhaps the secrets would have come out sooner and Ava could have spoken to her mum, instead of finding hidden pictures and discovering the past the way she did. How different might things be now if he had?

Henry welcomed Granger's company; the dog's once chocolate brown coat auburn from the sun, and his muzzle showing flecks of grey as he trotted along next to him.

'You might see some of your pups here. Rumour has it there's a dog show. Shall we enter?'

Passing the station at the edge of the village, Henry was surprised to see the number of people getting off the train. Mary had said Ava was advertising the event far and wide and it seemed her efforts had paid off. He followed the throng towards the village centre and was taken aback as he took in the sight of colourful bunting, the cobbled streets lined with stalls, music playing, and people – families, some local, but plenty of them not – all having a good time. Some of it he'd seen in the distance, and expected, but the stark contrast to the atmosphere compared to his visit to the village the day he'd taken his donation to the charity shop was palpable.

Chatting to some familiar faces as he went, Henry remained resolute in his promise to himself not to be drawn into talking about estate affairs. The festival was to be a celebration of the village, and he wanted to respect that. Granger stayed by his side, pausing only to sniff the various food stands. Listening to the music coming from the square, Henry made out the words "Everything means nothing if I can't have you". He looked at All Critters Great and Small and shook his head. 'How apt, eh Granger.'

Hearing his name, the dog looked up and Henry smiled.

'Let's go and find Ted.' Henry knew his old friend was performing at the pub and wanted to offer his support.

With half an hour until he was due to speak with Ava, Henry walked around the central shops to The Brown Dog. Seeing the older man in his element brought a smile to Henry's face. Ted's elbow was moving more nimbly than Henry imagined possible as he played – his note changes fast-paced and his folk rhythm, lively.

Gino had made an effort, and not just in his outfit; Henry couldn't help but be impressed as he took in the sight of the honky-tonk style hangout he'd created outside the pub. Seeing the Italian standing, with a Springador puppy, Henry made his way over to say hello. Granger followed.

'One of Myrtle's? I hope you don't mind. I thought Granger might like to say hello.' Henry wondered why he hadn't just said he wanted to see the puppy himself. In truth, he wanted to see the puppy and he wanted to speak to Gino, properly. Since his return to Dapplebury, he'd made assumptions about the man, and other than his first night in the bar hadn't actually spoken to him. It was time to put that right.

'Of course, this is Luna. She is into everything today, and soon she is going inside for a sleep.' Gino smiled proudly as he showed the puppy off.

'She's beautiful.' Henry stroked Luna, who tried to nibble his hand with her small sharp teeth.

'And we have to thank you, I believe. Weren't you with Ava when they were born?'

Henry held Granger's collar while he said hello. He was an old dog but still liked to play if the opportunity arose. Sniffing and tail wagging tended to lead to play bowing and barking. Henry didn't want him being too boisterous for Luna.

'Yes, but it was a privilege.' Henry pushed away an image of Ava watching the puppies, fascinated by the new arrivals; she'd been fixated by them while he couldn't take his eyes off her.

Gino scooped Luna into his arms. 'Well, thank you anyway. And for what it's worth, I hope everything goes well for you and Ava. Mary told me what you have planned for tomorrow. In fact, she got me to get Ava to sort the shop rails, said it would be less obvious coming from me.'

'Really? Thank you.' Henry realised he'd wasted too long thinking Gino was a threat to his relationship with Ava, especially when it seemed he might just have turned out to be an ally. 'Mary never said.'

'Well don't worry. *Il tuo segreto è al sicuro con me.*' Gino tapped the side of his nose reassuring Henry that his secret was safe with him.

'Thank you. Knowing what this place is like, I'm surprised the secret hasn't got out yet.'

'Well Lily Flynn is legendary around here and, as she has stepped into her shoes keeping the charity going, people love Ava. Who else do you think could have pulled all this off?' Gino gestured to their surroundings.

Henry looked up the street. It was true; there was a time when he would never have imagined Dapplebury putting on a festival. Now the place had come alive, with everybody working together, thanks to Ava.

'Even Pauline has managed to keep quiet.' Gino laughed and looked round to check she wasn't within earshot, before looking at his watch. 'Sorry I have to be somewhere.'

Henry put out his hand before Gino could go. 'Thank you. I don't deserve your help, but I do appreciate it.'

Realising shaking hands was a little tricky with Gino holding Luna, Henry laughed. But Gino wiggled the puppy over to one arm and took Henry's hand.

'Well, Mary says you're right for Ava, and you're going to be good for the village.'

'She does? That's good to know. Thank you.' Having both of Ava's friends on side bolstered Henry's confidence.

'And Mary's not easy to impress, believe me, I know.'

As Gino walked towards the pub, Henry stood and listened to Ted a little longer. Clapping as the older man finished his song, Henry congratulated him on his set.

Thanking him, Ted hesitated before speaking. 'Ava was here. You've not long missed her.'

Henry looked at his watch. 'I'm going to meet her now.'

'Good. I'm glad to hear it.'

Ted smiled, and Henry didn't have the heart to tell him it was for a radio and newspaper interview, arranged by Ava for publicity.

With Granger in tow, Henry headed towards the main square. Spotting Ava, he faltered. The length of her skater dress and the cowgirl boots she wore accentuated the shape of her legs. Her hair was mostly loose with small plaits brought round from the front being tied at the back. She looked naturally beautiful. Taking a breath, he approached. As she looked at him, he saw the hint of a smile in her expression. It was only as he got nearer that Henry noticed Mrs Jenkins standing by her side. There was something different about his PA's appearance, and Henry took a moment to register that she was without her formal jacket and handbag.

'Mrs Jenkins, do you need me?'

'No. I'm here for the festival, but as your interview was in the diary, I thought I'd come for moral support.'

'Right, OK ... thank you.' Henry didn't know if he found

casual Mrs Jenkins more unnerving than formal Mrs Jenkins. He was thrown by her appearance, as much as he was thrown by the realisation he wouldn't be able to speak to Ava alone, not even for a moment, before the interview.

Gathering his faculties, he looked at Ava. 'It's good to see you.' He moved closer, wondering if he should shake her hand or kiss her cheek. She put out her hand and he felt a swell of disappointment in his chest at the sight. But as she took his hand in hers, he noticed she held on to it a little longer than was necessary. He met her eyes and smiled. *It's there, the spark. She feels it too.* Granger broke the moment by pushing his way between them and greeting Ava like an old friend. She knelt to stroke him and the dog lapped up the attention as she took a biscuit from her pocket and gave it to him.

'As if I'd forget a second time.'

Henry couldn't help but smile. With all Ava must have on her mind, she had thought about Granger. *Or maybe the twenty other dogs here, today.* He pushed the negative voice from his mind.

As Ava stood, she looked at Henry. 'It turns out Mrs Jenkins fosters cats. Mary knew her straight away when she saw her at Dapplebury House. She's looked after cats and kittens brought into the charity – Mary's dropped strays off to her cottage many times. Being a wildlife rescue, we can't keep them, but people like Glinda kindly take them in for local charities who can – offering them a safe place to stay until they can be rehomed. It's much less stressful than spending time in a cattery.'

'Really?' Henry looked at Mrs Jenkins and congratulated himself on not saying he could imagine her with a clowder of black cats.

'Did I never mention?' Glinda asked, pushing her glasses up her nose.

Henry thought for a moment. Had she ever mentioned? Perhaps she had, but he couldn't be sure, not when he'd convinced himself she lurked in Dapplebury House, appearing as an apparition at the start of each day. 'I don't think so. I'm sure I would have remembered.'

'I'm really sorry we've got to go.' Ava directed Henry towards the centre stage, moving him away from Mrs Jenkins.

'The woman is a mystery. She's quite like a cat come to think of it. Aloof when she wants to be, creeping up on me silently.'

'Stop it! She'll hear you.' Ava laughed.

'I bet you feel more relaxed about this interview now though, don't you?' Henry smiled.

'I do, thank you.'

As she turned towards him, Henry looked at her smile and knew he must tell her. 'Ava.' He reached up, but she got the wrong idea and stopped his hand, holding it in hers.

'Henry, not now. I can't do this now,' she whispered.

'But—'

Ignoring Henry's protestations, Ava turned to the presenter from the radio who'd readied herself to do their live interview. She made the introductions, and Henry wondered how he could tell her what he wanted to say without embarrassing her.

The bubbly presenter in her mid-forties wore too much lipstick but had a bright smile and a jolly demeanour. She put out her hand.

'You must be Lord Bramlington. It is a pleasure to meet you.' Henry smiled and shook her hand.

'And Ava you—'

As Ava offered the woman a broad smile, the presenter stopped. 'Good grief. I know it's radio but as there'll be press pictures too, you might want to remove whatever that is from your teeth.'

Ava's cheeks burned red, and Henry wished he'd been able to tell her.

She put her hand over her mouth and ran around behind

the DJ, who was waiting for DJ Jazzy Jeff and The Fresh Prince's "Summertime" to finish so that he could make way for the radio interview. When she reappeared, she could barely make eye contact with Henry. He hoped her moment of awkwardness wouldn't stop her from focusing on the interview. While he'd his own announcement to make about opening up Dapplebury House, he wanted the main focus to be Ava and the future of the charity.

Chapter Thirty-Eight

Ava felt heat blaze in her cheeks. She had managed so well to keep a cool, calm façade when Henry had approached. Having Mrs Jenkins and Granger there had enabled her to take time to calm her pulse. She couldn't believe how well it had been going until she had mortified herself by grinning with a lump of rib meat stuck in her teeth. *What a fool!* Now her mind was flustered and her cheeks were burning. As the presenter began speaking, Ava realised that was what Henry had tried to tell her when she thought he was going to say something more personal. *Not now, Henry. I can't.* Her words echoed through her mind. She ventured a look at him. His sympathetic smile made her feel worse.

The presenter spoke about Dapplebury's first festival and the significant changes afoot for the village. A small audience had gathered as passers-by stopped to listen, and the school choir who were up next had begun to assemble. It was clear the woman was a little taken with Henry as she flicked her hair and flashed her smile at every opportunity. Ava blew out a breath. She had to focus. She had points she wanted to make and she had learnt from radio interviews she'd done before about the charity, the time always went too quickly and left you playing a reel through your mind of all the things you wished you had said.

As the woman praised the family-friendly, fun atmosphere, it was Henry who directed her to speak to Ava.

'And for that we have to thank Ava Flynn, the head of All Critters Great and Small, a locally based charity that has served the community and the surrounding area for many years.'

Ava swallowed, her mouth felt dry; she wished she'd brought a drink over from the pub. The sun moved from behind a cloud, making her feel hot and exposed on the cobbles of the village square. Her body trembled and she attempted to breathe her nerves away as she felt all eyes upon her.

There was a moment of silence and then ... and then she heard herself doing it. She was speaking like the head of the charity. There was authority in her tone and knowledge in her words. She spoke about the fantastic work her mum had done, and the launch of their new website that included newspaper archives of previous rescues. She remembered to read the web address slowly and clearly and to reiterate there would be a blog that would appeal to children and adults alike who were interested in wildlife care and conservation. She was on fire and not in her cheeks this time. She fed off the ripples of approval from the crowd and made all the points she wanted to make. Finally she announced the big news that Critters' Lodge, the long-term home of the charity's rescue centre, would be moving to Dapplebury House, enabling easier access, and with the support of Lord Bramlington and all those who donated money and time to the charity, future expansion. The crowd clapped, and Ava smiled. She had no idea how, but she had delivered every word she had wanted to say.

The presenter, who had made appropriate comments as Ava spoke, turned to Henry.

'And I believe this is just one of the big changes we can expect at Dapplebury House?'

Henry looked at Ava, his smile genuine as he acknowledged with a single look how good her speech had been.

'Yes, Dapplebury House has long been set apart from the village and the rest of the estate. My father and those who came before him were well-respected figureheads of the Bramlington Estate. But times have changed. As I settle into my role I don't want to be a figurehead for the community, but a part of it.'

Ava wondered who had swooned more as Henry spoke, the presenter or Glinda Jenkins. While they fixated on his title,

Ava couldn't help but focus on his intent. *He means it; he's going to stay!*

Ava looked at him. Dressed in tapered denim jeans, leather trainers, a fitted white T-shirt and cropped navy jacket; he was pulling off smart casual every bit as well as Ryan Gosling; a man Mary had once described as the king of smart casual. Gone was the dark suit and family crest cufflinks. He had the hint of stubble across his chin, and his hair was slightly ruffled. He looked relaxed and happy as he spoke – comfortable as he mentioned his title and, with Granger by his side, at home in his surroundings.

'The west wing of Dapplebury House will be opening to the public. It's my intention that all should be able to enjoy the history and beauty of what has been the ancestral home of the Bramlingtons for over three centuries. In addition to the public area, which will, of course, be kept apart from All Critters Great and Small – the animals need peace to recuperate, and that remains a priority—'

Henry met Ava's gaze, and she smiled.

'In addition to these changes, I intend to open a wellbeing and hypnotherapy centre at Dapplebury House. Plans remain at an early stage, but I hope to provide a sanctuary for those who need time to reset and …'

Henry kept talking, but Ava's mind slipped to Ted's words of earlier; the grounds of Dapplebury House had been a sanctuary for her and Henry. Was it wrong for her to feel jealous that others would be encroaching on what had always been their space? She put her hand to her chest, trying to rid herself of the ache she could feel growing there. She needed to smile. This was a good thing; a positive thing for Henry. He was making his life his own, pursuing his interests, taking the hand he'd been dealt and turning it to his advantage. She should be pleased for him; a part of her knew she should admire him for that. It was something she hadn't achieved with her mum's charity. Ava was pulled back to the moment as the presenter laughed.

'Goodness changes afoot indeed. When you're up and running, you'll have to invite me along to show me what those healing hands are capable of.'

Ava couldn't help herself and interjected, 'Thank you. I'll have our animal rescue officer contact you. I'm sure she'd love to show you the wonderful work she carries out too.' As she glanced at Henry, Ava became aware of her cheeks turning pink. She'd no right to interfere if this woman wanted to flirt with him, but instinct had kicked in.

With the interview drawing to a close, photographs were taken for the local paper. The radio presenter called Henry to one side, insisting on giving him her number. Ava's eyes boggled at the woman's cheek. She stroked Granger, pretending to be nonchalant while straining to hear what was being said. Hearing Henry thank her, and direct her to his PA, Mrs Jenkins, made Ava want to jump up and put her arms around him. Instead, she gave Granger an extra rub around the ears and a kiss on the head. When she stood, her gaze met Henry's deep green eyes.

Ava tried to contain her smile. 'Thank you for joining me for the interview, and for all you're doing for the village. We really do appreciate it.' She wished her voice was less tight and she could form a sentence that made her sound less like a public service announcement.

Henry took hold of her arm and moved her to one side as the school choir took their place, centre stage in the square. Dave, the DJ announced them, adjusted their microphones and stood back while their teacher attempted to get them focused and ready.

'I'd love for you to come and see the changes at Dapplebury House.'

Ava tried not to think how it felt to have his hand on her arm and his breath brush her cheek as he spoke. 'I know I should. I've promised Mary I'll do it soon.'

'That's not what I meant, though of course you should

come and see how the move is going too. But I meant the changes I've made in preparation for the opening and the wellbeing centre.'

As the choir began their enthusiastic rendition of OneRepublic's "Counting Stars", Ava welcomed the opportunity to change the subject. She knew she'd have to be careful regarding what she said about the changes Henry was making. It all made complete sense for him. But for her it felt like the end of an era – when the grounds were theirs and theirs alone.

'Wow! We used to squeak our way through hymns when I was at school. This is much more upbeat, isn't it?' Ava looked at the children all singing their hearts out, most looking as though their parents had cleaned their uniform and preened their hair for the occasion, others making up with enthusiasm what they lacked in fitting uniform.

Henry smiled and nodded. She could see the disappointment in his eyes at her not responding but she wasn't sure how without pouring out much more than was appropriate in the middle of the festival. Instead, she looked at her watch. 'I'm really sorry. I've got to go. I promised Flo I'd look in on Knit and Natter in the village hall, and the dog show starts soon. It's in honour of my mum. It's a big deal.'

'Perhaps I should come, maybe enter Granger?'

'I think it's probably more of a children's thing.' Ava felt bad the minute the words left her mouth. The competition was open to all, and Henry was trying to be supportive.

'OK, well we'll get going then—'

'Why don't you come and give out prizes? If you want to.' Ava looked at Henry and felt as well as saw his smile, before remembering that she'd no idea what prizes Flo was providing.

Chapter Thirty-Nine

Discovering that Flo, the ladies and one gentleman of Knit and Natter were knitting blankets for the rescue centre was heart-warming. Ava thanked them all for their kindness, relieved the festival hadn't coincided with their previous charity knit, titled nudi-knits for breast cancer awareness. Their table at the festival would have required an eighteen rating if their guffawing descriptions were anything to go by. Listening to Flo and her friend Doris discussing the problems they'd had getting their nipples straight, Ava was grateful she had agreed to meet Henry at the arena on the village green.

Stopping by the charity shop to check all was going well and that the cake table had been replenished, Ava was amazed to see many of the rails looking half empty.

'Wow! You must be having a great day. I'll fill up before I go.'

'No, don't you worry. Pat was about to do it, weren't you love?'

Chris, the regular Monday volunteer, looked pointedly at her colleague who was stood by her, hands on hips, at the till.

'Yes, of course. I'll start with the fancy frocks, and then work my way around.'

'Thank you. I appreciate it. The dog show is due to start shortly.'

'You're lucky the weather has held. I thought it was going to rain—' Pat began.

'La la la!' Ava put her hands over her ears; they had been lucky so far. The weather had to hold for just a few more hours and then it could do what it liked overnight until the festival continued the next day. 'I'm not listening. This is strictly a good weather zone.'

As Ava left the shop, she glanced at the table of cakes; the tomato soup cake had proved popular. She shook her head. *Really?*

Approaching the village green Ava was grateful to Mary. It looked wonderful. Fencing had been erected to make a small arena, bunting made it look bright and colourful, the music from the village square could be heard on the breeze, but there was also a small sound system to call and commentate on each category. People of all ages had turned up with their pooches and made themselves comfortable with deckchairs and picnics around the arena. The sun was still shining, and the breeze of earlier in the day had long gone.

Ava felt Henry's presence before he spoke.

'I'm not late, am I?'

She turned to see him smiling.

'No, Mary's about to call the first category.' She took a flier from her pocket and unfolded it. 'Obedience.'

Henry leaned in closer to read the schedule. Now free from the nerves of the interview, his proximity and clean, fresh scent, played with her mind as he read:

'Then best rescue, young handler, fancy dress—'

'Mary hated that idea but Flo thought it would be fun,' Ava interrupted.

'I'm sure it will be interesting.' Henry smiled a cheeky grin and looked around the crowd, taking in the sight of the boxer and elderly gentleman sitting nearby. 'There's no most like their owner category, is there?'

Ava giggled and nudged him, pleased that despite the awkwardness that could be between them, they couldn't help but share a natural banter. 'As I said, fancy dress, followed by cutest puppy, waggiest tail, golden oldie and best in show.'

'And you're not entering Myrtle or Blossom?'

Ava looked at him. 'How do you know about Blossom?'

Henry hesitated for a moment. 'This is Dapplebury. Everyone knows everything, you know that.'

'Or so we thought.' Ava regretted the words as soon as she'd said them. Just when she felt more relaxed in Henry's company, she'd alluded to their parents' past.

'Fair point,' Henry conceded.

As Mary called the first category, Ava was grateful for the distraction.

'And we're off. Where would you like me?'

Back in my kitchen, the night the puppies were born. Ava attempted to push the thought away before her cheeks blushed, and looked around. 'I guess that's the judges' table. Why don't you and Granger go and join Mary? She's judging along with that lady there.' Ava pointed across the arena to a tall blonde lady, cradling a clipboard, who wouldn't have looked out of place at Crufts. 'She runs the obedience classes in the village hall – as Granger and Myrtle have brought her an increase in business she's doing us a favour here today.'

'Won't you be joining us?' Henry looked a little disappointed, and Ava felt her stomach flip.

'I think I should stay impartial. I'll go and fetch you all a drink.' Ava gestured towards the refreshment van parked on the edge of the green. 'Then I'll mingle with the crowd a bit and check out the stalls.'

Henry took his seat while Ava joined the tea queue. As she glanced towards the arena, she could see the dogs being put through their obedience paces. She felt for the embarrassed owner who dropped all of her treats, causing not only her West Highland Terrier to go into a frenzy but the Labrador next to it too. Meanwhile, a nearby Cockapoo dribbled but held its sit and stay, much to the pleasure of its rather smug looking owner. Catching sight of Granger behind Henry, carrying out each command he heard called, Ava smiled. *Bless him.* Seeing the dog's enthusiasm, she felt mean for not letting him enter and decided to tell Henry to add him to the golden oldies category.

When Ava returned precariously holding a laden drinks carrier, the dogs had carried out each of their commands and two runner-ups were being selected, along with the winner.

Ava put the tea on the table. 'Oh heck, the prizes. Did Flo deliver them?' She looked at Mary.

'Oh, yes! They're over there. Take a look.'

Ava went to the box Mary had pointed at and opened the lid.

'Wow! These are great. Did she make them?' Ava had to admit Flo was a marvel with a sewing machine.

'Yes.'

Mary seemed to be holding back a giggle, but Ava had no idea why. Inside the box was a range of toy turtles in a variety of colours. They had stitched eyes and cute smiles. It was almost a shame to give them to the dogs.

'Henry, would you mind doing the honours?'

'Of course not.' Henry stood, and Ava passed him a winner's rosette, and a colourful toy turtle for each of the two runner-ups.

Ava stood behind Mary. Those called to the centre of the arena posed for photographs. Ava tilted her head. There was something familiar about the turtles, but she wasn't sure what it was; something about their bright colours. She was sure she'd seen them before. Realisation dawning, she rushed back to the box. There inside, she looked more closely at the patterns on the turtle's backs. Amidst the array of bright colours were various animal prints including zebra.

Mary laughed. 'And she's got it.'

'Oh my goodness, Mary. These are ... they're—'

'Yep! Made from that donated bag of bras. It's genius really. You even get two for the price of one.' Mary leaned over, took out two turtles and held them up to her chest.

Ava snatched them back and closed the lid. 'But we've just given them to Henry to hand out in the middle of an arena of local people who might have seen them in their original, you know'—Ava motioned to her chest—'state.'

'Oh, don't worry. You actually wore one and it took long enough for the penny to drop. The lingerie shop wasn't that popular. Otherwise, it wouldn't have closed. Besides, I think he quite likes them.'

Ava looked towards the arena, her eyes going wide as she saw Henry squeezing one to see if it would squeak.

'I think it's a shame they don't make a honking sound, don't you?' Mary burst out another giggle.

Ava couldn't help but join in. 'I suppose it could have been worse.'

'At least they're not sex toys.'

'What aren't?'

Hearing Henry's voice as he returned to the judge's table, Ava jumped. 'Nothing. Just Mary's idea of a joke when she should be calling the next category.' Ava kicked Mary and wished the heat in her cheeks didn't make it seem as if she'd been talking about something more explicit.

She picked up her tea from the carrier and stood as if ready to drink the molten liquid from the takeaway cup. A gesture she hoped Henry would read as her being unable to discuss the subject any further.

Henry raised his eyebrow at her, offering a cheeky but very lovely grin before taking his seat.

Watching the rescue dogs make their way to the arena made Ava's heart swell. They came in all shapes and sizes and were as scruffy as they were gorgeous, parading around with a variety of unusual gaits. Being the category Mary had requested, she was judging and took time to speak to each of the owners individually. As their stories echoed through the microphone, Ava was touched to learn each entrant had a sad history and had found love in a new life. Ava was grateful she wasn't judging and went to mingle with the crowd and to take a look at the few stalls on the green.

Finding a variety of homemade preserves, sweets, and "delectable dog treats" on offer she realised she could have purchased runner-up prizes from them. But as she thought about Flo's turtles, she knew they were perfect. Ava stood chatting to those she recognised from around the village, including Mrs Dent, whose enthusiasm about having not used her umbrella seemed more about the hope of a refund, than her joy at the festival not being a washout. As she went, Ava welcomed everyone's kind feedback about the festival. While she wouldn't truly relax until the end, she was allowing herself to feel a sense of achievement.

Hearing a kafuffle from the arena, Ava turned. Seeing an irate parent in the centre of the arena fronting up to Mary while Henry attempted to calm the situation, Ava wondered what had happened. Trying to take in the scene and what might have caused the issue, she hurried in.

'Stop! Whatever's the matter?'

Everyone went to speak at once, but Ava held up her hands. 'Stop! Please, one at a time. What's happened?'

The parent, a portly middle-aged man who had his arm around his crying child, spoke first. 'You cannot let a child win the young handler competition with a stuffed toy!' he protested.

'What?' Ava looked around at the entrants. There, sure enough, was a young boy she recognised as one of those with an ill-fitting uniform from the school choir, holding a life-sized toy Labrador protectively to his chest. She looked at Mary, hoping there was a good explanation. Before Mary could speak, the parent was shouting again.

'Excuse me, sir, I must be able to speak with the judges.' Ava motioned for them to step away while Henry moved to speak to the man.

Ava led Mary and their obedience professional to one side, her eyes wide. 'What the—'

The professional interjected, 'I said it wasn't fair but—'

'It's my fault. He wasn't the winner, but he was who I announced.' Mary looked at Ava, her eyes imploring. 'He said his mum couldn't afford a dog, but he's always wanted one, and that he'd learnt everything he had to do ready for today.'

Ava felt as if the air had left her. 'Oh, really?' She looked at the boy and the other children in the arena. 'But they've all actually done the same, but with a real dog. That has to be harder.' She thought about her cheeky puppy at home. 'I know why you've chosen him. I get it, I do, but it isn't fair, is it?'

Mary folded her arms. 'But if we say he's not the winner now, that will make him feel terrible and that bully will have won.'

Ava let out a long breath.

'I'm sorry for shouting.'

The three women turned to see the parent, his stature seeming smaller as he spoke.

Henry stood at his side.

'I'm just upset for my girl and Fred. They've worked hard for this, and it just didn't seem fair.'

Ava looked at the man and then at Henry, hoping he hadn't hypnotised him.

'Thank you for apologising.' She caught Mary's eye and determined that for her friend's sake, she couldn't let the man win. 'And you're right. Everyone has worked so hard, all of the children and their dogs did so well.' She hoped he hadn't noticed that she'd not watched this round of the show. 'That's why I'm giving everyone a runner-up prize for their dogs and a sweet of their choosing from the stall over there.' The children all cheered, and as Ava gave them each a turtle, they began making their way to the sweet stall. When the boy with the toy dog approached her, he screwed up his nose.

'Thank you. I'm sorry for causing trouble.'

Ava took the winner's rosette from the judge's table and handed it to him with a smile. 'You didn't.'

As he went to walk away, Ava called him back. 'I've got a puppy. If you're as good as Mary says I could do with some help training her. If your mum agrees. Get her to stop by All Critters Great and Small, and we can arrange it.'

The boy beamed. 'Really?'

'Of course.'

Mary hugged Ava and kissed her on the cheek. 'That was a nice thing you did.'

Ava returned the hug. Knowing her friend had lived in poverty for much of her childhood, her stepdad a bully, made Ava hold her a little tighter. While her mum's habit of wanting to rescue and rehabilitate those who were injured often frustrated Ava, it had also brought Mary into their lives, and she was grateful for that. As she looked at the boy skipping away with his rosette, Ava couldn't help but think it might even have rubbed off on her just a little bit. With tears in their eyes, they released each other.

'Whatever you do, though, that Andrex dog can't win the Lily Flynn best in show trophy, even if Mum would approve!' Ava laughed.

'Oh bugger!' Mary smiled, and they prepared themselves for the fancy dress round.

As they retook their places standing by the judges' table, Ava looked at Henry and shook her head.

'In all the time we've spent together, did you ever imagine we'd end up here, watching a pug dressed as Elvis parade around the village green?'

Henry laughed, a deep sound that Ava felt resonate within. As she welcomed the glint the laughter caused in his eyes, he leaned towards her, holding her gaze. 'In all the time we've spent together, I've imagined many things, but not this.' Ava looked at him. He was so temptingly close. It would be so easy to kiss his soft lips as they formed the hint of a mischievous smile. But she knew she couldn't. They had things they needed to discuss; their parents' history, of course, but she also wanted him to know she and the charity didn't need a knight in shining armour, *or a thoroughly lovely looking Lord*, to rescue them. After all, she'd only conceded to moving the charity to Dapplebury House because it was sound business sense. What was best for the charity, always came first. Her mum had instilled that in her. *Cheaper rent, room for expansion* ... Ava was losing her train of thought and was leaning towards him. Knowing she shouldn't, while not being able to resist.

'Look!'

Ava and Henry jumped back, both looking to the sky, where Mary had pointed. Tilting her head, Ava took in the sight of the aeroplane cutting through the blue sky, trailing a banner. Squinting against the sun, they all tried to make out what it said.

'Mary? Does that say Mary?' Mary put her hand up to shield her eyes.

Ava read the words and beamed as she waited for Mary to work them out.

'Mary, we're ... we're meant to be together, love Gino! What does that? Why has he—?'

Mary looked at Ava, confusion in her expression.

Ava smiled. 'Sometimes the people we're meant to be with are right in front of us.' She ventured the briefest glance at Henry, every nerve in her body still enlivened from the thought of kissing him.

'Did you know about this?' Mary asked.

'The aeroplane, no. How he feels ... yes.'

Mary paled as she tried to take it in. 'Why hasn't he said? Why get a plane and ...'

'Maybe because ...' Seeing Gino, looking every bit an Italian cowboy on a mission, walking towards Mary, Ava stopped and smiled. Her heart was leaping with joy for her friends.

As Mary turned, Gino stood before her.

'I'm telling you now! Mary, we're meant to be together. Please, take a chance on me.'

Ava put her hand to her mouth, touched by the moment. The seconds stretched out while they all waited for Mary to answer. Everybody around the arena stilled; even the dogs seemed to sense the occasion – momentarily stunned into silence. Mary looked at Gino, tears welling in her eyes. 'Gino, I ... yes, I will.'

A broad smile on his face, Gino pulled Mary into his arms and kissed her.

Ava felt a happy sob escape her. It was beautiful. The perfect moment. She smiled up at Henry. If only everything wasn't so complicated for them, then it might be the two of them kissing. Henry offered her a smile, and she went to speak—

'He's not going to win the fancy dress round is he?'

All eyes turned to see the irate parent from earlier pointing at Gino. Red faced, the man's daughter stood by his side, her dog dressed as Elsa from Frozen. 'If Sheriff Woody there wins, I'll ...'

Henry shook his head and directed the man back to the arena, offering him reassurance that Gino wasn't a contender for the prize, while Gino looked to Mary for an explanation.

Ava watched Henry move away, a mix of emotions making her want to laugh and cry at the same time. *Thwarted again*. Giving her friends a hug, and telling them it was about time they got their acts together, she made her excuses and went to check on the rest of the festival.

Chapter Forty

'What was I thinking?' Having arrived at Ava's door at breakfast time, Mary sat awkwardly on the kitchen chair, her knees tucked underneath her, and her arms wrapped around her legs, while Blossom and Myrtle slept under the table.

'That you might be happy with Gino? That the two of you are meant for each other?'

Mary looked at her, incredulous. 'Meant for each other? How can we be? He's from a huge family, and I'm from, well I'm not sure you can even call it a family. He's just taken on a puppy, and he's so …'

'Lovely?' Ava smiled. She'd expected Mary to panic at some point; she just hadn't expected it to be the morning after Gino's declaration.

'Seriously, I don't know why I came here. I'd hoped for—'

'Someone who'd convince you you're right to give up on this relationship before it's even started? Well, I'm sorry, you've come to the wrong place. Being with someone who will care for you is what I've always wanted for you and, despite what you think, it's what you deserve.'

'Blimey, Ava, you make me sound like one of the animals I look after. I'm not injured. I'm tough. I'm a player and so is Gino. You know he's a terrible flirt at the bar and we've both seen him the morning after all those late nights, doing goodness knows what.'

Ava put her toast down. 'Hmm, we were wrong there. Not about him being a flirt, it's part of his job'—Ava shrugged—'or the late nights. He does have late nights. But the reason … the reason is …' Ava wondered if it was OK to spill all of Gino's secrets now the biggest was out.

'What? What's the reason?'

'He's into astronomy.'

Mary put her feet on the floor and took a moment to absorb Ava's words. 'Astronomy? Gino?'

'Yes. Gino told me about it after the French night.'

Mary looked at her, discombobulated. 'The moon and stars and stuff?'

Ava nodded.

'Really? And that's why he has all of those late nights?'

'Yes. It's fascinating really, you should—'

'And you think he's genuinely got feelings for me?'

Ava giggled. 'He literally told you he wants to be with you on a banner attached to an aeroplane above the village. It seemed pretty genuine to me.'

'I don't know if that scares me more or less.' Mary leaned across and took a piece of toast from Ava's plate and bit into it. 'Astronomy!' She swallowed. 'There's obviously a lot I don't know about him.'

'But there's plenty you do know. Like what a good friend he is, and how much he cares about those he loves. Maybe that's what you're finding a bit scary.'

'Maybe I just can't do this.'

Ava leaned across the table and held Mary's hand. 'You're only worried because you know Gino's special. If he weren't, you'd already be planning your exit. But you're not. You're questioning if and how you can make this work.' Releasing Mary's hand, Ava smiled.

'I'm questioning how I won't stuff this up.'

'It's the same thing. Normally you stuff things up on purpose. This time I think you're scared you might do it out of habit when you don't want to. But Mary you can't worry about past habits or the future. Now is what's important. And the two of you, you'll find your way. I know you will.'

Mary looked at Ava, with tears in her eyes. 'Bugger me, Ava Flynn, when did you get so wise?'

'Ha, I'm not sure I'm that wise. Look how things have turned out for Henry and me.'

'Henry! Oh, my goodness!' Mary stood up, causing both dogs to go on full alert. She checked her phone and when she saw the screen, grimaced. 'I've got to go. Thank you for the chat and the toast.' Mary made towards the door.

'What is it? Where have you got to go?'

'There are things … things I was meant to do for today and I haven't.' Wiggling her feet into her boots, Mary hurriedly tied the laces, despite Blossom's best efforts to stop her.

'Things for what? Is it the festival? Is there something I've missed? I checked everything last night. It's Sunday so things are starting a little later—'

'For the festival, yes. But nothing for you to worry about. I can't explain now but will you meet me in the charity shop at six?'

'At the shop? Why? I thought we'd be celebrating the end of the festival and heading to the pub by then.' Ava didn't want to hang around the shop unnecessarily. After the lead-up to the festival, the nerves of it getting underway, and the constant sense of fear that something might go wrong since it started, she was longing for a relaxing evening with her friends.

'We will celebrate, I promise, but I have to meet you at the shop first.'

'OK. But I'll see you about, today, won't I?'

'I'm on duty for a bit this afternoon, so if I miss you, make sure you meet me at six.'

Ava went to speak, but Mary was already heading out the back door. She looked at the dogs and lifted her hands. Both Myrtle and Blossom seemed as surprised by Mary's swift exit as Ava.

Chapter Forty-One

Moving back the cotton sheet, Henry slipped on his lounge pants, stood and stretched, wondering if he'd time for a run. Pleased he had rejected Mrs Jenkins' appeals for him to stay at the festival into the evening and learn how to jive (*who knew she had it in her?*) he'd woken early with a clear head. Checking his watch, he swallowed. Less than twelve hours to go until the big event.

The first day of the festival had been a success. Dapplebury had come alive with a family-friendly atmosphere he hoped would entice visitors to return for the second day and beyond. Seeing the transformation gave him hope for the future of the village and his plans for the estate. Of course, he was also pleased for Ava; she'd put so much into it and managed to get everyone on board in a way he doubted he, or anyone else, ever could. Even the weather had held, the sunshine eventually putting in an appearance and adding to the festival spirit.

Hearing a noise at the door, Henry turned to see Granger pushing it open with his nose and wandering in with his zebra print turtle nestled in his soft jowls. While he hadn't won the golden oldies category at the dog show, Granger had taken the defeat in his stride and seemed more than happy with his runner-up prize. And while one of his puppies had won its category and the Lily Flynn Cup, as best in show, Granger had barely noticed, too busy sniffing around the food stands. As Granger padded across the room, his tail wagging, Henry greeted him with a smile and a rub behind the ears.

Looking out of the window, Henry could see an array of vans already pulling up outside. Tables, chairs, floral displays and more were being unloaded in readiness for the evening's festivities. Hosting a charity shop ball at Dapplebury House had seemed like a good idea, but the nearer it drew, the more he wished he'd told Ava. Despite what Mary had advised, it didn't seem right that the guest of honour was the only one in the village who didn't know.

Thinking of Mary, Henry smiled at the memory of Gino's declaration. He felt genuinely pleased for them both and not because it allayed any fears he had of Gino having feelings for Ava or vice versa. Mary had already set him straight on that matter. It was, honestly good to see two people looking so happy.

Feeling nerves building in the pit of his stomach as he watched the events outside, he hoped Mary had done as she said and organised Ava's outfit for the ball. While he had a nagging fear Gino's declaration may have distracted her, he reminded himself she wouldn't have left it until the last minute. She had, after all, known about the plan for the ball from its inception, and been the one to suggest that surprising Ava was a good idea. In theory, it seemed like a way to replace memories linked to Dapplebury House from the past with new, positive ones. Henry wondered if, in reality, it would turn out to be a mistake. Ava had determined not to go anywhere near the place – not even in the grounds, since hearing about their parents. Getting her there, in front of the village, was going to be a task. *A task made even harder if she has nothing to wear.* Henry smiled at the thought and then shook his head. He really did need to get out for a run and to concentrate on ensuring everything was ready.

The grounds looked beautiful in the early morning light. Henry could already feel the warmth of the day building and welcomed the dappled shade from the leafy canopy of the trees. Long sunny days, mixed with occasional rain, had transformed the woods into a lush landscape. While the bluebells had died off, new plants were growing in abundance, their lime green, shiny shoots heralding their arrival. The smells were rich, from the damp earthy tones of the undergrowth to the heady scent of the honeysuckle and foxgloves. Henry was pleased to see the insects were prospering, albeit that he was sure he'd swallowed more than one fly. Bees and butterflies danced between flowers, while black armoured beetles burrowed into rotten wood. A brief stop to see the progress at the pond revealed evidence of toadlets. He hadn't spotted any deer; they would no doubt be sticking to the long grasses with their young, but there was evidence of the herd. A fox, brazen enough to be out after dawn, stood momentarily in his path, staring at Granger, before flitting into the cover of the undergrowth. Henry wanted to share it all with Ava and longed to be in the woods with her, the two of them as it had always been.

By the time he and Granger returned to Dapplebury House, the caterers had arrived. Both the entrance and the marbled, grand hall were being transformed in readiness for the evening. While Mrs Jenkins stood at the front of the house directing people where to go, his mother was fussing over floral displays. He couldn't remember seeing her so animated and wondered when the last time she'd been able to play host for a large event at Dapplebury House had been. She seemed to have come alive; the sight of her smile warmed him. She'd even forgone the black outfits she'd worn since his father's death and had a red scarf tied in her hair.

After answering the many questions everyone seemed to have been waiting to ask him and confirming plans with his mother and Mrs Jenkins, Henry ran up the grand staircase to change, Granger following. He needed to get changed and, on his run, had decided to go and seek out Mary. She was in charge of getting the guest of honour to the ball and he had to know she was focused on her mission. He felt as if he were operating on adrenalin, too alert as he obsessed over every detail of the coming evening in his mind. He wanted it to be perfect. Ava had organised an entire festival which ran mainly without a hitch; he couldn't get his single contribution wrong, especially when it was in her honour.

Henry pushed the hot water from the shower through his hair, and shampoo suds ran down his back and chest. His pulse felt as if it were racing. He was usually good at controlling his feelings, but this was for Ava; he wanted to get it right. Wrapping a fresh white towel around his hips, he stepped into his bedroom. Remembering seeing Ava there as he came out of the shower on the day they had learned about their parents' connection did nothing to settle his nerves.

He was going to tell her how he felt. He knew they had obstacles in their way, history between their families, but he had to do it. Seeing Gino declare his feelings for Mary had given him hope; a happy ever after happened sometimes. Maybe it could happen for them too. *Of course, happy ever afters don't usually involve a love triangle between your parents.* Henry dismissed the thought. He and Ava deserved their own lives and to find their happiness. He only hoped she would see that too.

Once dressed, Henry went to the old stable block in search of Mary. She had been there most days since the move. He looked at the sign they'd hung above the door and hoped Ava would like it. It was typical that now he needed Mary, he couldn't find her. The volunteers staffing the office told him she was on emergency calls only and said he might want to try The Brown Dog. Henry rolled his eyes. As much as he was happy for Mary and Gino, he needed her focused. Taking out his phone, he dialled her number. It went to voice mail. He looked at Granger.

'Fancy a trip into the village then?'

Leaving Dapplebury House in the capable hands of his mother and Mrs Jenkins – who he knew would carry out every detail of his plans with precision – he strode into the village, heading straight for The Brown Dog; Gino met him with a smile.

'Dress-down cowboy today?' Henry asked.

'It's hot already, isn't it. The chaps and Stetson have had

to go. I've moved the barbecue into the shade. But still, it's hot.'

'There should be some cloud later, that might help.' Henry wondered why he'd entered into small talk when really he wanted to know where Mary was and if she was on task. Gino continued to talk about the day ahead. Henry rubbed his hand round his jaw in frustration. When at last Gino came up for air, Henry jumped in.

'Sorry Gino, but is Mary with you? I need to speak to her about tonight.'

'No, I haven't seen her since last night. Anything I can help you with?'

Henry smiled at the gesture, grateful for Gino's kindness and feeling a tad guilty for his impatience. 'Not unless you're going to find an outfit for Ava and get her to the ball tonight.'

'Ah! Not sure that's my area of expertise. Mary's on duty this afternoon so you might need to catch her soon.'

Henry thanked Gino and decided to go to the charity shop. While he risked seeing Ava and then having to lie about why he was there, it might be his only chance of catching up with Mary.

Chapter Forty-Two

By eleven o'clock, Ava had walked Myrtle, had a shower and settled the dogs with the pet sitter. As she rode her bike into the village, she smiled. If the festival became the annual event she hoped it would, then she would be bringing both dogs along with her next year. It was unusual for her not to have Myrtle in tow on a sunny Sunday, but with the blue sky and the gentle breeze against her face, she felt happy and ready to embrace the day ahead.

Drawing near the village, the bunting looked bright and colourful and if she wasn't mistaken, DJ Dave had already got the day off to a good start with a track from the Beach Boys. She was impressed by the effort he'd put in, and hoped he would be getting lots of future bookings from it. With the day's schedule consisting of more of the fun had on the previous day and a few extras, such as face-painting, pavement art, and a display from a street magician, Ava had a good feeling.

Some families were already out and about, saying good morning or waving to her as she cycled by. For the first time in a very long time, she didn't feel like she was hiding away at the back of the charity shop, trying to live up to her mum's memory. Coping with the loss of her mum, and the pressure she felt to carry on for the charity's sake often felt too much. But she finally felt like she was taking control of her life. She had orchestrated the festival. It was her idea – albeit in an accidental, drunken moment of madness – but so far it had been a success. Ava crossed her fingers, not wanting to celebrate too early. There was still a packed programme of events lined up for the day, and she knew plenty could go wrong. But, for now, she was willing to own the fact she felt happy.

Before heading to the shop to check all was well, and to set up the cake stall with the bakes put aside on the previous day, she circled the central block of shops and stopped outside The

Brown Dog. Luna seemed to recognise her as her tail went into a frenzy. Gino walked the excited puppy over.

'Howdy cowboy!' Ava smiled.

'Ciao!' Gino kissed her cheek.

'That's not a very Texan greeting, is it?' Ava laughed.

'Mary and I are at last together, my puppy slept through the night, it is hot – but at least the sun is shining. I'm happy.'

'And that brings out the Italian in you?' Ava smiled.

'*Sempre!*' *Always.*

'Well I'm just stopping by to say I'm so pleased for you and Mary. I couldn't believe it when I saw that plane. You finally did it. And you did it in style.'

Gino lifted Luna off the hay bale she'd climbed and looked at Ava from under his dark fringe. 'I have a confession to make. I was meant to jump from the aeroplane.'

'What? When? But you were on the ground.'

'Well, not that plane exactly. I was going to surprise you and do a skydive. I thought it would be good for getting Mary's attention, and to raise money for the charity, of course. But then I saw an advert for plane banners and I thought—'

'That would get Mary's attention without having to jump?' Ava laughed.

'Yes, something like that. I'm sorry about the charity, but with the … the other things you have going on during the festival, I think you're going to have a successful weekend.'

'Thanks, Gino, me too. And honestly, I'm glad you didn't do the jump. I wouldn't want anything to happen to you. Besides as much as I love that puppy, she's your responsibility now.' Ava pointed to Luna, who had walked along the hay bales and was chewing on some bunting. 'If you break a leg who will chase after her?' Ava giggled, knowing full well she would step in should anything so drastic happen, but she enjoyed teasing Gino, especially as there was no doubt Luna was the most mischievous of the litter.

Having secured her bike, Ava unlocked the back door of

the charity shop. Flo had been in to open up and had, once again, organised the volunteers to cover the day, freeing Ava to watch over the festival and troubleshoot where needed. Hearing Mary, Ava paused. She was muttering to herself and Ava couldn't quite make out her words. Thinking that if she were still fretting over her new relationship with Gino she would jolt her out of it, Ava decided to make her jump. Leaping in through the door she shouted, 'Surprise!'

Startled, Mary screamed and turned to Ava, shock on her face and chocolate cake down the ice blue, off-the-shoulder satin gown she was randomly wearing.

'What the hell! Ava, look at me!' Mary ran to the sink and began rubbing the chocolate with a wet paper towel.

'I'm sorry, I had no idea … And now I have so many questions.' She scanned the back of the shop and the array of gowns Mary had scattered across the sorting table and floor. 'What are you doing?'

'What am I doing? What are you doing more like?'

'What are you both doing?' Ava and Mary turned to see Flo, Henry and Granger staring at them. 'We could hear the commotion from the front of the shop. I thought we had burglars or something'—Flo put her hand to her chest as if fending off a heart attack—'but here you are playing dress-ups, again, the pair of you.'

'I'm not playing anything. I've just got here,' Ava protested, her cheeks going red at being told off in front of Henry in her own shop.

'And I was just trying to eat the piece of my own cake you made me buy.'

Flo looked at Mary and giggled. 'Miss your mouth?'

'Only when Ava burst in like a wild woman. You were supposed to be keeping a lookout while I tried this on.' Mary fixed Henry with an admonishing glare.

'And I was. At the front of the shop,' he replied.

'She must have ridden past the window.'

'I might have looked away for a moment.'

'And I was on the till, so you can't blame me,' Flo put in.

Ava tried to make sense of what they were saying, but couldn't. She lifted her hands in the air. 'Will somebody, please, tell me what's going on?'

Silence fell and stretched between them for a few moments until Flo coughed.

'I'll pop back out front. There'll be customers waiting.' Moving past Henry, she headed back to the shop floor.

Ava looked between Mary and Henry. 'So, what's going on?'

'Honestly, I just wanted to try this dress on, that's all.' Mary pushed Granger away; he'd taken a keen interest in the cake down her front.

Henry folded his arms and Ava directed her attention to Mary.

'So why did you need a lookout? You know I wouldn't have minded you trying the dress on. It looks bloody great on you by the way – perfect with your fair complexion and blonde hair! Sorry about making you jump and the …' Grabbing a paper towel, Ava ran it under the tap and joined in wiping the chocolate cake from the dress before realisation dawned. 'Oh, wait! You're going somewhere you don't want me to know about, aren't you? That's why you needed a lookout.' Ava looked at Henry's guilty face and knew he was hiding something.

Throwing the paper towel in the bin – causing a momentary distraction for Granger as he pulled it back out again – Ava felt an ache in her chest. 'Are you two going somewhere? Is something going on? What about Gino?'

'Mary, we have to come clean. It's stupid to try to keep the whole thing a secret, now.'

Ava felt as if the room was closing in. The piles of clothes and other donated stock jeering at her as a swell of pain grew in her chest.

Mary held Ava's gaze. 'It's not what you think. We're not doing anything behind your back or going anywhere in secret. Well, we are, but not in the way you think. I was going to tell you. That's why I'm meeting you here at six. It was going to be a surprise.'

'Well, I'm here. So why don't you tell me now.' Ava congratulated herself on keeping her voice even.

'Ava, I didn't want you to find out like this,' Henry began.

'Sorry,' Mary whispered, looking uncharacteristically apologetic.

Ava put her hands on her hips, hoping bravado would see her through whatever Henry had to say. She tried not to look into his imploring and very hard to resist eyes.

'I'm hosting a charity shop ball, tonight, at Dapplebury House.'

Ava swallowed. They were right; it wasn't what she thought, but still the revelation hurt. 'And I'm not invited?' She knew she sounded like a fool. Why should she be invited after all that had passed between her family and the Bramlingtons? But as she stood staring at Henry and Mary she couldn't help but feel as dejected as Cinderella – the last to hear the news, invitation-less and, judging by the number of dresses sold in the previous weeks, the only person in Dapplebury not going to the ball.

Henry moved forward and, despite her sadness, Ava felt her body responding to his proximity.

'Of course, you're invited. You're the guest of honour. All proceeds are going to All Critters Great and Small, and the stipulation was that every dress must be a charity shop purchase. Mary has sorted your outfit.'

Henry gave Mary a pointed look, as if for confirmation.

'Of course I have. It's mine I forgot. Yours is hidden out the back. I hope you like it.'

'Mary said you wouldn't mind.'

Ava saw Henry's eyes searching her face as he waited for her response. She glanced towards the back office, feeling a little light-headed. She was sure she would like anything Mary chose; she trusted her taste implicitly, but this was a lot to take in. 'Of course.'

'It was meant to be a way to thank you for all your hard work on the festival and to mark the new beginning. Having All Critters Great and Small based at Dapplebury House, it's important we can all get on.'

All get on. In a single phrase, Henry turned the wonderful thought of a ball held in her honour into what sounded like a business transaction – something to ease the transition. Ava tried to balance her thoughts. The charity was bound to do well from it, and it was a kind gesture. She smiled. 'Thank you. Both of you. You've obviously put a lot of planning into this. I promise to do my best to come along, especially as Mary's gone to the trouble of sorting me a dress.' Ava smiled at Mary who was staying unusually quiet.

'It's for you, Ava. It's all for you. Please come.' Henry pushed his hand through his hair.

'Of course. There's no need to meet you here now, I guess?' Ava looked at Mary. She needed to get out of the confines of the shop to contemplate how she felt. 'So at the end of the festival, I'll take my dress home and meet you at Dapplebury House.'

Ava saw a look pass between Mary and Henry, but she couldn't promise any more at the moment; it felt too much.

'I'm still happy to take you. We can go together.'

'Don't be silly. You should go with Gino. I guess he's in on this too. His interest in prom-style dresses suddenly makes sense.'

'Yes but—'

'Then you should definitely concentrate your efforts on him. He can't go to the ball dressed as a cowboy, can he?' Ava smiled.

Henry spoke, his voice unsure. 'I'm happy to come and collect you. The only reason I—'

'You will not. You'll have more than enough to do at Dapplebury House. You should probably be there now, shouldn't you?'

'Mrs Jenkins and my—'

'Then you should go and help them, really.'

Henry seemed hesitant, and again Ava noticed a look pass between him and Mary. 'OK, I'll go. But Ava, please, don't—'

'I'll be there.' She attempted to smile, but she could feel the tension in her lips. 'Right now I have a festival to organise.'

Henry called Granger to his side, and the dog reluctantly left the paper towel he was shredding.

As the two of them left, Mary turned to Ava, eyes wide. 'Ava Flynn if you don't turn up tonight I will personally come and find you. And remember I have access to tranquillisers and a very particular set of tracking skills, skills I have acquired over a long career, skills that mean I will find you and I will drag you there if I have to.'

Ava giggled, releasing the tension she'd been holding inside. 'All right Liam Neeson, don't get your frock in a twist. I said I'd go.'

'You bloody should go. It's a very lovely thing he's doing for you.'

'For the charity, he's helping the charity. After all we've discovered about our parents, and then the sale of the land from under Critters' Lodge, it's a very kind, probably guilt-motivated gesture. But I do appreciate it.'

'Guilt? You think that's his motivation?' Mary wiped some chocolate frosting off her dress and licked it from her finger. 'You're probably right. I'm dressed like a fairy godmother and all, but what do I actually know of matters of the heart?'

'Clearly nothing. It took a thirty-foot plus high banner pulled by an aeroplane for you to get the hint. That's a pretty grand gesture.'

'True, and it's not like a ball, at a manor, where you're the guest of honour, in front of the whole village, is a grand gesture, is it?'

Ava put her hands over her ears. 'I'm not listening. If everything's sorted here, I have a festival to attend to. I am off to check out the face-painting, and you really need to find a dress that doesn't have chocolate down the front!'

Chapter Forty-Three

After a soak in the bath, Ava looked in the mirror. The festival was over and she was both buzzing from the success and a little sad that after her weeks of planning and the two wonderful days, it was over. She was already determined to make it happen again the following year, maybe for longer and this time with a proper committee behind her to organise it. Everybody who had spoken to her congratulated her and thanked her for her efforts. None had mentioned the ball, not even Pauline, who Ava was amazed didn't crack when she spoke to her for a full five minutes on her plans for a relaxing evening. *Why the surprise? You've already learnt the people of Dapplebury can keep a secret?* She tried to push the negative thought away. Her mind had been whirring since arriving home.

Looking at the suntan she'd inadvertently got over the last two days, she hoped no visible tan lines would show in her dress – if she wore her dress. And if she actually went to the ball. Even as she was going through the motions of getting ready, she still hadn't fully committed to the idea. Screwing up her nose, she looked at her freckles; they were back in abundance, and she quite liked them. They reminded her of her old self.

Walking into the bedroom, Ava looked at the dress hanging in front of her wardrobe. Mary had picked very well, and had selected accessories to match too. She hoped Mary had managed to salvage her own dress from the chocolate cake disaster or found another to fit. Ava wondered if she should have stayed longer in the charity shop to help her, especially as she'd gone to so much trouble on her behalf.

Ava flicked her eyes to her bedside clock. It was gone six. Mary had told her, guests would be arriving at the ball from seven. Sitting on the edge of her bed – no longer adorned in an animal print duvet cover since taking Henry's lead and modernising her room – she stroked Myrtle. The dog was dozing with Blossom snuggled up, curled into her front paws. Myrtle lifted her heavy eyelids, and Ava smiled.

'So, Myrtle, shall I go or shall I stay? You, me and Blossom, a quiet night in celebrating the end of the festival. How does that sound?'

Myrtle sat up and barked. Blossom rolled across the bed and Ava wondered if it was a sign but as the doorbell rang, she realised the cause of the sudden reaction. Swapping her towel for a robe, she walked down the stairs. Sure that Mary and Gino had come for her to make sure she didn't back out, she opened the door.

'Bog off, you two. Oh, bugger me!'

'Is that an automatic reaction each time a door opens near you?'

'Lady Bramlington! You're here! Shouldn't you be there? At the ball, I mean. Shouldn't you be at the ball?'

'Shouldn't you?'

Looking feistier than the last time Ava had seen her, Lady Bramlington cocked an eyebrow and gestured as if to ask if she was going to be invited in. Ava stood speechless, trying to imagine this woman, dressed in a sleek black gown with what looked like diamond accessories, in her living room. She had altered the place, to make it feel more like her own home, but still, it remained rustic.

As if reading her mind, Lady Bramlington looked at Ava apologetically. 'I've been here before and I won't keep you long. But I do need to speak to you.'

Ava nodded and glanced at Myrtle and Blossom who were scampering around behind the door, eager to see who the highly perfumed visitor was.

'I'll put the dogs in the kitchen.' With that, Ava shut the door and ushered the dogs through the hall. *You've just shut the door on Lady Bramlington.* Ava blushed at the thought, despite the fact her teenage self was celebrating inside. Glancing around the living room, she adjusted a couple of cushions and moved the dog blanket from the sofa.

Realising she was in a robe, she ran upstairs and slipped on some underwear, jeans and an All Critters Great and Small sweatshirt. Running back downstairs, she stood for a beat behind the door before reopening it.

'Please, come in.'

Lady Bramlington stepped inside.

Remembering she said she had been before, Ava gestured for her to go through to the lounge. As they both sat, Ava wondered if she should offer her a drink but hoped she wouldn't be stopping that long.

Perched on the edge of the sofa, Lady Bramlington's eyes flicked around the room. Ava wondered what memories she had of being inside the cottage. Deciding she might not want to know, she held the question back.

'So, did Henry send you?'

'No! Definitely not. He doesn't know I am here. I slipped out and can't stay long.'

Phew! Ava tried to hide the relief she felt at this being a brief visit, before wondering what Lady Bramlington had to say that she couldn't tell Henry. *She's going to warn you off. Tell you to stay away.* With that thought, Ava knew she couldn't; she wouldn't agree. The idea of not seeing Henry now that he'd returned to her life was too much.

'I won't not see him.'

'I wouldn't try to stop you.'

'Oh. Then why are you here?'

'Because I know how it feels to love someone and not be with them. I know the hurt. And I don't want what I told you to stop you from following your heart.'

Ava looked at the woman before her, registering the sad expression in her eyes and the sincerity in her tone.

'Henry loves you. He always has. I should never have come between the two of you. I put my feelings for Lily and my concerns for her, over my own son's happiness. I have to live with that, but it's not too late for both of you.'

Ava's pulse quickened. Thoughts rushed through her mind: her mum's determination that she stay away from the Bramlingtons, her dad driving too fast; her fear in that moment as she clung to Raspberry rabbit, crying, screaming for him to stop. *But he wouldn't, he just drove on faster, more erratic.*

'Lily, Connor, my husband and I, we lived our lives. We made our mistakes and we have no right to stand in your way.'

'But—'

'He's here to stay, Ava. He had the chance to sell the estate and not return.'

'What?'

'Like his father, he thinks I don't know, but of course I do. My husband was a proud man but a financial fool. He made bad investments, squandered and borrowed money from the wrong people. He wouldn't accept help, from me or anyone else, even though he was running the estate into financial ruin; typically of his generation, he was too proud to admit any of it to his wife. I wanted to give Henry the chance to walk away from the obligation of his title and his father's debts. I love Dapplebury House, but I love my son more.

'The man, Dermot Dixon.'

Ava nodded, acknowledging she knew the name. 'I had him contact Henry in Los Angeles, offering him a deal to sell – Dapplebury House, the grounds, the estate. I even got him to apply pressure once he was back. But by then, it was too late ...'

'Too late, why?'

'Henry had rediscovered the things he loved and left behind. The grounds were so much a part of him when he was growing up. You know how passionate he was, and still is about the land. But that's not the reason he's staying. His deal with Mr Dixon, moving the charity, the ball tonight, it's all about you, Ava. You're the reason he's staying. If you feel for him, as he does for you, don't let anything stand in your way.'

Ava felt a swell of emotion, unsure whether to cry or embrace Lady Bramlington.

'Thank you. Thank you for telling me. I know all of this can't have been easy for you.' Ava stood, suddenly not knowing what to do first. She had to get dressed. She had an idea, something she wanted to do, and her plan meant she needed to go to the charity shop before going to the ball.

Lady Bramlington stood. 'I'll leave you, but I hope to see you later.'

'Of course. Wait.' Ava hugged her, unsure if that was something she should do.

Lady Bramlington stood back, looking as if that might be the first hug she'd received in years and was unsure what to do in response. When she smiled, Ava felt relieved.

'You're so much like your parents.'

Ava wasn't sure if that was intended as a compliment but as Lady Bramlington was still smiling, she decided to take it as one. They walked to the door, Ava's heart pounding even faster than when she had let her in.

'Wait! Before you go. Do you know Mary? Is she at Dapplebury House?'

'Yes, I know Mary.'

Ava had no idea what was implied in Lady Bramlington's tone but was sure her friend had made an impact.

'Please, can you give her something for me?'

Ava ran back to the living room and scribbled a note, folding it before handing it over.

Lady Bramlington cocked her head. 'Of course.'

Ava shut the door and exhaled. *And now you've got Lady Bramlington delivering notes!* She shook her head; she really needed to read up on etiquette.

Letting the dogs out of the kitchen, Ava squealed and jumped up and down with them before running upstairs. The excited dogs followed. It was almost seven o'clock and she still had so much to do.

Chapter Forty-Four

Henry twisted his cuff links, before checking his watch, again. Most of the village seemed to have assembled outside Dapplebury House as canapés and drinks were served on the front lawn overlooking the pleasure grounds. It was mid-summer and the evening air was warm. The bright blue sky provided the perfect backdrop for the stunning view. He chatted with as many people as possible. All but a few complimented him on his plans for the future of Dapplebury House. Of course there were a few dissenters, those who weren't keen on encouraging tourists into the village, but Henry had expected that.

As the time to move through to the marbled grand hall approached, Henry began to lose hope that Ava would come. Searching the crowd for what felt like the hundredth time, he saw his mother talking to Mary and Gino – a sight he neither expected nor trusted. Walking over to them, he couldn't help but notice a change in their stance as they spotted him. He smiled in greeting.

'I trust everything is OK?'

'Yes, thank you.' Mary beamed but as he watched her, Henry noticed she slipped a piece of paper into Gino's jacket pocket.

Gino's automatic reaction to place his hand over it convinced Henry it had something to do with either himself or Ava. They were hiding something.

'Are you sure? Is Ava OK? Have you heard from her?'

'No.' All three faces turned to him, but only Mary held his gaze.

The fact she touched her throat as she spoke and didn't blink the whole time she held eye contact, added to his suspicions.

Lady Bramlington coughed and changed the subject. 'We'll have to go in soon. The caterers will be ready to serve.'

Mary seemed to ponder for a moment. 'Actually, Gino and I have to go somewhere but we'll be back before anybody notices we've gone.'

Henry pushed his hand through his hair. 'Really?'

'Yes.'

'Oh, I don't think you need to go anywhere, do you?' Lady Bramlington looked at them with a puzzled expression.

'Yes, I think we really do,' Mary insisted.

Gino shrugged and apologised before Mary led him away.

Henry turned to his mother. 'Does this have anything to do with you?'

'Don't be ridiculous. I have more than enough going on here. Besides, you know Mary, she's always got animals to check or emergencies to go to.'

Henry did know Mary. He just hadn't been aware, until now, that his mother knew her too. He looked at her, incredulous.

'You can take that look off your face. You didn't expect me not to introduce myself to the people who run the charity when you've moved them onto the grounds, did you?'

'No, I just ...' *Never imagined you would.*

'Thought I was some old relic, like all those antiques inside? They can always use an extra pair of hands you know. All those animals won't feed themselves.'

As his mother began moving forward and motioning for guests to enter the house, Henry stared in her wake. She cut an elegant figure in her black gown – not a charity shop purchase, but one she insisted should have been donated years ago, and so must surely count. Henry was pleased to see her looking so well and full of life. She seemed different since revealing her secret; less guarded, more approachable. There was time for them to build a new relationship and he was pleased about that.

Inside the grand hall, large round tables were spaced around the room and laid with white table cloths, crockery and cutlery, that contrasted with deep berry, velvet chairs. The magnificent venue had come into its own. Marble columns, walls lined with gilt-framed historic masterpieces, and elaborately designed ceilings were made to be shown off. It looked lavish in a way that belied the budget Henry had mustered to pull it all together. The curtains had been lifted to reveal optimum views of the grounds and light poured in through the windows. Albeit that Henry had to seek professional advice on whether this was advisable, to appease his mother. Foliage, from the grounds, and artfully placed floral displays added to the grandeur. The chandeliers were lit but would show their true beauty as the evening drew in.

Once everyone was seated according to the seating plan Pauline from The Brown Dog had helped with after it occurred to Henry she would know all the villagers, and where they would be best placed, Henry said a few words. He thanked them for coming to support the charity – at which point Flo whooped and cheers went up from around the room where various volunteers were seated. He assured the guests that Ava, and Mary, as the chief animal rescue officer, were on their way. A fact he could only hope was true. Before taking his seat, he reminded everyone that the tombola tree in the entrance hall was stocked with golden leaves, each promising a prize donated by the generosity of local businesses. Finally, he thanked his mother and Mrs Jenkins for their work in organising the ball, and the students of the local college who were contributing to the night in so many ways, including: doing the floral displays, providing the orchestra, and acting as servers; while the catering was all being done by final year students under the watchful gaze of Chef and his team from The Brown Dog.

It was a whole village effort and, for that, Henry was grateful. As he looked at those who sat before him, the women dressed in elegant gowns Ava would surely recognise, and ruddy-faced men in tuxedos, Henry felt proud to be a part of the community. The ball, held in Ava's honour, and for the benefit of the charity, was also an inspired way to bring everyone together. Barriers between them were lost as they sat in readiness to dine together on a smoked salmon medley, rack of Bramlington lamb with new potatoes and asparagus, and summer fruit pavlova, in the house that was a part of their history as well as his own.

As the first dishes were brought in, delicious smells filled the air and the sound of cutlery on crockery resounded around the room. Henry looked at the seats intended for Ava, Mary and Gino. Seeing them empty caused an ache in his chest. As the college orchestra began to play, Henry wondered if the guest of honour would make it for any of the meal, or even the dancing. The room, filled with people for the first time in decades, felt empty without her.

Chapter Forty-Five

'What the hell are you doing here? You almost gave me a heart attack!' Ava stared at Mary and Gino, her eyes wide and her heart thumping as they burst through the door of the charity shop.

'We could ask you the same thing.'

'But I literally just asked you!' Ava looked at Mary.

'I thought something terrible had happened. I got your note.' Mary held the piece of paper Lady Bramlington had given her up so Ava could see it.

'The note that says'—Ava took it from her and read aloud—'I am so bloody happy! I am going to the charity shop but will be with you as soon as possible.'

'Yes.'

'What part of that made you think I was in trouble?'

'I thought it was a coded message. The allusion to happiness, the mention of blood, the fact you were coming here when you should be there.'

'I told you nobody, and I mean *nobody* does that! Didn't Lady Bramlington tell you she'd spoken to me when she gave it to you?'

'Briefly, yes. But she said not to tell Henry and then when he came over she started acting all cagey and I thought maybe you'd sent the note as a cry for help.'

Ava looked at Mary in disbelief and then at Gino who was usually the voice of reason.

'Hey, I didn't read it. I just followed Mary's lead and then drove straight here.'

'You are both as crazy and as lovely as each other.' Ava smiled. 'What must Henry think?'

'He's probably thinking where the hell is the guest of honour?' Mary stated, putting her hands on her hips.

'Oh, God! We have to get there. I'm so late.'

'We know!' Mary and Gino chimed in unison.

'Henry loves me.' Ava couldn't help saying it.

'We know!' they chimed again.

'I love—'

'We know!'

'But if you don't hurry up you're going to miss the ball and this beautiful opportunity to tell him,' Mary said, her exasperation evident in her tone.

'Well, now you're here you can help me. Here, take this.' Ava passed them the package she was tying string round when they'd burst through the door.

'What's in it?'

'It's a surprise but hopefully a good one.' Ava smiled at them both for a moment, before remembering herself. 'Quick, now let's go.'

'Wait!'

Ava and Mary halted and turned to look at Gino as he spoke.

'You look beautiful, by the way. *Molto bella!*' He smiled a very lovely smile.

Mary pulled Ava into a hug. 'He's right. You look bloody gorgeous.'

Ava beamed. 'Thank you. I have an excellent wardrobe lady. And you both look pretty amazing yourselves. I'm so pleased the cake came out. Now let's get to that ball.'

'Talking of cake, I'm starving. Do you think we'll make it back for the food?' Gino rubbed his stomach, and turned out the lights of the shop. 'I know what's being served, and Mary, there's a vegan menu for you.'

Mary kissed Gino's cheek. 'I'm a lucky girl!'

Finding her key, Ava giggled. 'For somebody so sworn against it, you're turning into quite the romantic, Mary Clarke.'

The words earned her a playful punch but there was no time to feign injury. Gino had the car doors open and they were ready to go. Grateful she wouldn't have to ride her bike back up the hill out of the village, something she was sure wouldn't be as easy as freewheeling down in her gown had been, Ava slid into the back seat, her gift for Henry safely at her side and her heart pounding.

Chapter Forty-Six

Henry picked at his lamb, trying to show willing. The catering team had done a great job and he didn't want them to think he hadn't enjoyed it. Henry thought about Granger, lying across the foot of the double bed up in his room, where he left him as he had dressed and come down. Having him by his side now might have helped him out; he was a Labrador after all with a pit for a stomach.

Mrs Jenkins, or Glinda as he now called her, drew Henry's attention.

'She'll come, you know.'

'Pardon?'

'Ava, she'll come.'

'Is it that obvious?' Henry smiled.

'Yes, but don't worry. I don't think anybody else has noticed. They look like they're having a wonderful time.' She motioned to the room, and it was true. Everyone was smiling, eating, drinking and chatting. There was no ostentatious drunkenness, but everyone looked on the right side of merry. Henry was pleased to see Ted talking to Flo who laughed raucously at whatever he'd said.

'You did a brilliant job helping me with the organisation. Really, thank you. The orchestra is much more fitting than Dave the DJ's offer of a disco. Contacting the college was inspired. I'm not sure we could have carried this whole thing off otherwise.'

'You're most welcome, and I've enjoyed it. It was hard, watching your father. He wouldn't let me help enough. I sometimes felt I was walking on eggshells around him.' Glinda looked at Henry with a look that made him wonder how much she knew.

'The tumour caused mood swings – my mother has said the same.' Henry didn't think that was what Glinda meant but wasn't going to be drawn into talking about the estate's affairs.

She smiled and nodded. 'I'm sorry I seemed stiff when you first took over everything.'

Henry looked at her, deciding it was safer not to comment.

'I worked for your father for a long time, and I love this house. The family and the estate mean a lot to me. My family have worked here for generations. Forgive me, but I thought … I thought you might give up on it and sell. Some people would have.'

Henry looked at her. He had no idea if it was the alcohol making her speak this way but he welcomed the honesty.

He smiled. 'I'm here to stay and, Glinda, I misjudged you too. I'm sorry for that.'

'Really, what did you think of me?'

Henry pushed away all images of apparitions and broomsticks. 'Why don't we just start over?' He lifted his glass. 'To new beginnings.'

Glinda smiled and repeated his toast as her glass met his.

'I think I'll join that toast.' Lady Bramlington stretched across the table, her glass meeting theirs. 'To new beginnings.'

Henry wondered if he saw a lingering look between the two women, and decided not to question it. Instead, he drained his glass.

As he placed it, empty, back on the table, he saw Mary and Gino slipping into their seats. His pulse raced as his eyes searched the room. And then he saw her. Ava was standing in the doorway. When he looked in her direction she smiled.

Excusing himself, Henry stood and walked towards her, both pleased and nervous at her arrival.

'You came, and you look incredible.' His voice was a deep whisper as he took in the sight of her. Emerald green satin caressed her body, pooling at her feet – contrasting with her flame-red hair, pale skin tone and the smattering of freckles across her nose and cheeks. Her blue eyes glinted as she offered him a smile that he felt as well as saw.

'Thank you. You look stunning yourself.'

Henry felt his cheeks blush as Ava's flirtatious eyes met his.

'I should announce you're here. Most of the village has turned out to support the charity – but I wish we were alone.'

Ava leaned up and kissed his cheek. The sensation of her hair touching his face, her scent, and the brush of silk against his arm, was intoxicating. He released an appreciative sigh.

'Me too,' she whispered, slipping her hand in his.

He looked down, and then back to her smile, wondering how he was going to contain the things he wanted to say and do with her until it was polite to slip away.

When at last the dancing was well underway, and most people were occupied being taught a choreographed waltz by one of the dance students who had agreed to help for the evening, Henry seized his moment. Taking Ava by the hand, he led her outside into the privacy of a walled courtyard.

'Are you cold?'

'No.' She smiled.

The sun had all but set, its final flourish creating streaks of red and purple in the late evening sky.

'I wanted to take you to the lake, but perhaps another time.' Henry motioned to her dress.

'No, I want to go. Please.' Ava leaned against him and slipped off the high-heeled satin shoes Mary chose for her. 'To be honest, these were killing me.' She laughed.

'OK, but you have to wear this. The warmth from inside won't last all the way.' Henry slipped off his jacket and placed it around her shoulders before opening a gate that looked like it should take them to a secret garden.

Walking hand in hand, they made their way towards the lake. The sound of music and laughter floated on the breeze until being replaced by the evening bird song as they drew near the woods.

'Thank you for tonight. I really do appreciate it.' Ava smiled.

'I was concerned you wouldn't come.'

'I wasn't sure I was going to. I was worried.'

'Why?'

'Worried about our families, the past and if I'd be able to move on from that and—'

'Can you move on from that?'

'I have to. I can't stop my feelings for you and, if I'm honest, I don't want to.'

Henry tried not to respond so she could go on talking, but couldn't help the slight increase on his grip of her hand as he gave it an affectionate squeeze.

Ava continued, 'You're not responsible for your mum's actions, and I can't live to please my parents. I've tried and it doesn't work.'

Henry couldn't help the smile that played with his lips but knew he had to control his feelings until he'd heard her out. 'There was something else. I thought you were going to say something else before I interrupted you.'

'It's silly, I know it is, but part of me was worried you thought I needed help with the charity. Moving the charity here, and throwing a ball is a big deal ... like a fairytale. But I'm not looking for fairytales. I don't need rescuing, and neither does the charity. I almost let that stop me.'

'But it didn't.'

'No, because ... I realised it was a nice thing you were doing and that's OK. '

Henry stopped and she turned to face him. A hint of colour had crept across her cheeks from the evening air.

'If you hadn't have come, I would have come to find you.'

'I'm pleased to hear it.' She smiled before they continued to make their way to the lake.

As they drew near, the sound of the fountain could be heard. Ava turned to Henry, the look in her eyes making the effort worth it.

'It's working again, isn't it?' Lifting her dress with one hand and holding on to Henry's jacket with the other, she ran the rest of the way, Henry following.

'It's beautiful.'

'It's a work in progress, but I wanted you to see it.'

Henry watched as she moved her hand over the stone edge before she touched the water – the reflection of the last of the sunset rippled across the surface in response.

'It must be cold.'

She flicked a little water at him. 'It is.'

As he leaned around her to splash her back, she squealed. Henry pulled her to him, stopping her with a kiss that she returned.

When they paused for breath, Henry looked into Ava's eyes. 'I love you, Ava Flynn. I've always loved you. And I have never thought you needed rescuing. If anything, now, and when I was younger, it is you who has rescued me. And in case you ever wonder if I mind that, I don't. I really don't.' Henry laughed, the sound deep in the still evening air. 'In fact, I would like you to keep rescuing me for the rest of our lives.'

Ava smiled a broad, happy smile. 'Really?'

'Yes.'

'Good. Because I love you too and that sounds perfect.'

Henry slipped one hand into her hair and moved her closer as they kissed once more, his other arm slipping inside the jacket he had draped over her. He felt the silk of her dress, the only barrier to her smooth, soft skin he could feel beneath the fabric.

'Wait!' Ava moved back, just inches from his face, her rapid breathing evident in the rise and fall of her chest still pressed against him. 'I have something for you.'

Henry smiled.

'Probably not what you're thinking, but something up at the house. It's a gift.'

'Really?' Henry was intrigued. What more could she give him when he already had everything he wanted enwrapped in his arms?

'Come on.' Ava began making her way back to the house. Henry followed, catching her hand in his as he drew level with her – their silhouettes in contrast to the lights and sound of the house they moved towards.

Henry felt Ava's hand in his; her words still echoing in his mind. *I love you too.* They walked in contented silence until Ava spoke.

'Henry, I don't mind being rescued sometimes.'

Henry laughed. 'Good, then I can do this.' He swooped her off her feet and lifted her into his arms. 'Now I get to hold you close and you don't have to walk through the damp grass.'

With Gino standing by her side, Mary sat on the steps at the back of Dapplebury House, stroking Granger. As they drew near to them, Henry saw a massive grin spread across her face before she spoke. 'Oh my goodness, you've finally sorted yourselves out.'

Henry placed Ava's feet back on the ground and smiled. Granger trotted to them, his innocent eyes belying his escape from Henry's room.

'I really must fix that door.' Henry shook his head and greeted the dog with a rub behind the ears.

Gino looked at the three of them. 'So you're together now? Only, I didn't see a plane or anything as impressive,' he teased.

'Ha, no but there was a lake and you know'—Ava gestured to the house where the music continued to play—'an orchestra.'

'I did my best.' Henry shrugged.

Ava passed Henry back his jacket, put her shoes on and attempted to straighten out her dress.

'Looking a bit ruffled there, Miss Flynn.' Mary laughed.

'Honestly, who chose silk? It's very unforgiving.' Ava smiled before turning to Henry. 'Now, wait here.' She slipped inside the house.

Henry looked at Mary and Gino.

'We don't know what it is either. We only know she had a waiter stash it away,' Mary confessed.

As Ava walked back out, she held a package, wrapped in brown paper and tied with string.

'I hope you like it.'

She looked nervous and Henry could see the quiver in her hands as she passed the gift over.

'Thank you.' He looked at Mary and Gino and then back at Ava.

'I'd tell them to go but I think there's a slim to no chance of that happening.'

'She's right.' Mary nodded, and Gino sat next to her on the steps as if to make the point.

Henry untied the string and slipped his hand into the brown paper wrapping, feeling a frame inside, wondering what the picture might be.

Ava wrung her hands. 'You don't have to keep the frame. It's all I had at the shop.'

Henry paused to listen but as he went to resume unwrapping the gift, Ava spoke again.

'And if you don't like it, that's fine. Please don't feel you have to keep it. Well, you should keep it. Not keeping it would be rude. But you don't have to display it or—'

'Ava! Will you let the man open his present,' Mary interjected.

'Yes, sorry, go on.'

Henry pulled the paper off the parcel, his eyes transfixed by what he saw.

'I remember this day.' His eyes welled with emotion at the picture, sketched by Ava on a hot summer's day, too long ago.

'I thought you should have a portrait of you, the real you,

when you were younger.' Ava's voice betrayed her nerves and Henry felt his chest swell.

'You're amazing, thank you.' He walked to Ava, kissing her in thanks, the frame held carefully in his hand.

'Ah hum, can we see?' Mary asked.

Henry turned the picture. It was a sketch of him in the woods, he must have been around fifteen, his hair and clothes messy. He and Ava had been foraging for blackberries, staining their skin and clothes before they decided to wash it all off by skinny-dipping in the lake.

'Wow! Ava, that's great. It really is.'

'You're very talented.' Gino echoed Mary's sentiment.

Ava blushed, the colour of her hair.

Chapter Forty-Seven

Five Months Later

Ava sat outside the back of Dapplebury House, sketching the view. Granger, Myrtle and Blossom played in the distance. It was November, and the air had a bite to it, but Ava didn't care. She wanted to do a series of landscapes that reflected the grounds in each season. Dapplebury House wasn't her official home, but it was safe to say she spent most of her time there, and it was beginning to feel like home. A very big, very old, beautifully situated home and while by Christmas some of it would be opened up to the public, she knew Henry intended to keep some of the grounds private – a sanctuary and personal space for them.

'Are you ready?'

Ava turned and smiled as Henry stepped outside.

'Dermot's expecting us shortly.'

'Yes. Sorry. I'm putting this away now.'

'What about the dogs? Shall I put them in?'

'Your mum is taking them for a walk.' Ava smiled. Lady Bramlington had become a friend. She could still be feisty, but generally as a result of her being passionate in her beliefs, much like Mary. Ava could see why she and her parents had been friends.

Walking round to the old stables, now aptly dedicated to the memory of Lily Flynn, with an All Critters Great and Small sign hanging proudly above the door, Ava and Henry waited for Mary to appear.

'Sorry I'm ready. There was an incident with—'

'Is that blood on your top?' Ava looked at the red stains on Mary's sweatshirt.

'No, it's jam. There was an incident with a doughnut.'

'What was the incident?' Henry asked.

'It missed my mouth.'

Laughing, they made their way to the car. Ava looked at Mary.

'Just so you know, if it had been blood I would have been OK with it thanks to my very handsome boyfriend and his powers of hypnosis.'

'Really? Ava, that's great. I'm so proud of you. You know what this means? I'll be able to put you on the rota at the centre and—'

'I'm not sure I'm ready for that just yet, but Henry says knowing the first incident that caused my phobia makes it easier to alter the association in my mind.'

Mary hugged Ava. 'That's great. I hope it works out for you.'

'Me too.'

When they pulled up outside the land that once housed Critters' Lodge, Ava was amazed by the change. She thought she would be sad to see houses built on it. But the development was considered, and with the first phase complete, and show homes opening, Dermot was keen to show them how things were progressing. He strode over to meet them.

'Don't worry. I am unarmed, not a hose in sight.' The rotund man, beamed.

Mary stepped out and closed her car door, walking over with her hand outstretched. 'Sorry, that was down to me.'

'Don't be silly. I'm teasing you.' Dermot laughed as he shook her hand.

Henry closed Ava's door as she stepped out of the car.

Noticing the road name, she put her hand to her mouth. 'Lily Lane, is that ... named after my mum?' She looked between Dermot and Henry.

'Take a look at the site map.' Dermot directed their attention to the large sign erected at the front of the development.

On it, Connor Crescent, Critters Way and Flynn Road all featured. Ava felt a swell of emotion. 'That's a lovely dedication. They'll be a permanent fixture of Dapplebury.' She wiped a tear from the corner of her eye and smiled.

'Lady Bramlington's family have connections to mine from way back. I wouldn't have dared not follow her wishes,' Dermot explained. 'And she's been strict with her ideas for the houses and gardens too. Dapplebury is a precious place and she, like Henry here, wants to see it kept that way.'

Ava took Henry's hand and gave it a squeeze as they all set off to take a tour of the development.

After they had listened to Dermot speak passionately about the ecological and economic considerations in the houses, they moved on to the gardens. Bat boxes and hedgehog homes had been erected, and natural areas had been left or created with a mix of trees and pollinating plants to encourage insects and preserve nesting sites – something Mary had been promoting on their blog and Ava expounded in a recent visit to the local school.

When they said their goodbyes and got back in the car, Ava placed her hand on Henry's leg. 'It's wonderful.'

'As the land sale was necessary, I'm pleased it went to Dermot. I had no idea about his connections to my mother, but she has certainly managed to work her influence on him.'

Ava bit her lip. She knew Henry still had financial burdens to carry. He had spoken to her about the bank loan he'd managed to secure which would need repaying, the sum raised from the sale of the land and plans he had in place to help secure the future of Dapplebury House and the Bramlington estate. But he never mentioned how it had come to be in financial difficulty; out of respect for the late Lord Bramlington, neither had she.

Mary looked at her watch. 'Well, I'd say I'm ready for a tasty Italian. How about you?'

Ava laughed. 'Did you say "a" tasty Italian or "some" tasty Italian?'

'I was planning on having both but the rest of you will have to settle for the fine cuisine.'

Having succeeded in putting on eight gourmet nights from around the world, including a popular tapas night and a hard to source Australian night, Gino had settled for Friday night being Italian night at The Brown Dog. For him, there really had been one standout gourmet.

'I'm up for that.' Henry smiled. 'Is Flo joining us?'

'Once she shuts the shop. She's taking her new role as co-manager very seriously. She's enjoying it, and says she's happy to come out of retirement in more ways than one but I didn't like to ask her to explain – especially as I know she's been visiting Ted.'

Mary giggled. 'I hope I'm as full of life as Flo when I'm her age.'

The Brown Dog was warm and cosy with a fire in the hearth. Luna greeted them with a wagging tail. Gino came over from behind the bar, kissed Mary and greeted everyone, before encouraging them to take the table near the fire.

'How is Luna doing?' Henry asked.

'She can sit and stay for a full minute.'

'That's great. I taught Blossom to roll over this week.' Henry spoke the words, his expression full of pride.

As the two women slipped off their coats and took their seats, Ava looked at Mary. 'What are they like?' She knew Blossom was the star of her training class, but it was no wonder when she also had extra help courtesy of the boy from the pet show.

Gino shook his head. 'Well, Luna is more of a thinker. She likes to—'

'Is that a bar towel?' Henry looked around him and laughed as Luna trotted out from behind the bar, a bar towel hanging from her mouth.

'Ah Luna, what have I told you? That is not your blankie.'

They all laughed at the sight of the cheeky puppy.

'Can you imagine them once they become dads?' Ava whispered.

'Woah! One step at a time. I'm just getting used to the man and the puppy in my life,' Mary said, calling Luna to her and picking her up, complete with her prize possession still in her mouth.

'And how is that going?' Ava asked, watching Mary as she made a fuss of the dog.

'It's all a bit lovely really, but don't tell anyone I said that.'

'Your secret's safe with me.' Ava giggled.

Gino joined Mary in making a fuss of Luna. Ava looked at her friends and knew she couldn't feel happier for them. As Henry took his seat next to her, she couldn't resist leaning up and kissing him. He looked at her, a cheeky grin on his face that she knew she'd never tire of looking at.

'What was that for?'

'Because I can.' Ava smiled. Life really was all a bit lovely, and Gino was right, love had found a way.

Thank You

Dear Reader,

Thank you so much for reading A Summer of Second Chances. If you enjoyed it, please tell your friends, and take a moment to leave a review on the site where you purchased it. Reviews, no matter what their length, help authors and their work get noticed. They really do mean an awful lot.

If you would like to discover more about my writing, you can find details at the end of my author profile on the next page. I enjoy getting my social media followers involved, with competitions and occasionally asking for research help, so why not give me a follow, say hello, and join in? I'd love to hear from you.

Best wishes,
Carol xx

About the Author

Carol Thomas lives on the south coast of England with her husband, four children and lively Labrador. A volunteer at Cancer Research UK, she has been a primary school teacher for over twenty years and has a passion for reading, writing and people watching. When she is not in school, chasing after her own children or stopping her dog from eating things he shouldn't, she can be found loitering in cafes drinking too much tea and working on her next book.

Find out more about Carol Thomas here:
www.carol-thomas.co.uk
www.facebook.com/carolthomasauthor
www.twitter.com/carol_thomas2
www.instagram.com/carol_thomas2/

More Ruby Fiction

From Carol Thomas

The Purrfect Pet Sitter

Book 1 in the Lisa Blake series

**Introducing Lisa Blake,
the purrfect pet sitter!**

When Lisa Blake's life in London falls apart, she returns to her hometown rebranding herself as 'the purrfect petsitter' – which may or may not be false advertising as she has a rather unfortunate habit of (temporarily) losing dogs!

But being back where she grew up, Lisa can't escape her past. There's her estranged best friend Flick who she bumps into in an embarrassing encounter in a local supermarket. And her first love, Nathan Baker, who, considering their history, is sure to be even more surprised by her drunken Facebook friend request than Lisa is.

As she becomes involved in the lives of her old friends Lisa must confront the hurt she has caused, discover the truth about her mysterious leather-clad admirer, and learn how to move forward when the things she wants most are affected by the decisions of her past.

Visit www.rubyfiction.com for details.

Maybe Baby

Book 2 in the Lisa Blake series

Just when you thought you had it all worked out …

Best friends Lisa and Felicity think – maybe, just maybe – they finally have everything sorted out in their lives.

Lisa is in a happy relationship with her old flame, and busy mum Felicity has managed to reignite the passion with her husband, Pete, after a romantic getaway.

But when Lisa walks in on a half-naked woman in her boyfriend's flat and Felicity is left reeling from a shocking discovery, it becomes clear that life is nothing but full of surprises …

Visit www.rubyfiction.com for details.

Introducing Choc Lit